THE WEAPON AND THE FRUIT:

ANY BODY CAN MURDER

ISBN (paperback) 978-1-0685738-2-8

ISBN (e-book) 978-1-0685738-3-5

Cover by Lisa Brewster

First published 2025 by

Aneurysm Cupcake,

Cambridge, United Kingdom

L. E. Bendon

THE WEAPON AND THE FRUIT: ANY BODY CAN MURDER

Dedicated to my dear friend Yashwanth, whose home in Hyderabad became a de facto writing retreat when I came to visit him and he didn't turn up until a week later.

"Interesting characters, quite funny and intelligent dialogue." ~ Maria Ljungdahl, Sweden.

"Ciara Gallen was by far my favourite character. She is brash, confident, and unapologetically ambitious in her career." ~ Kayleigh Suggett, Canada.

"The dramatic conclusion took me by surprise. I quite enjoyed it." ~ Mike Berrow, U.S.A.

"I loved the writing in this book. It was simple, to the point, hilarious, and clever." ~ Marwah (The Booklore Fairy), U.A.E.

"Highly enjoyable. The humour, coupled with the distinctive writing style, constitute its primary strengths." ~ Razeena, U.K.

"With themes of acceptance, loads of humor, and a quirky cast, this book still lingers in my mind, rent free!" ~ Jordan Prewitt, U.S.A.

"I know I would read another mystery with Lance at the helm." ~ Chana, U.S.A.

"Fun and intriguing. I could definitely reread." ~ Jayla Booker, U.S.A.

"I was holding on throughout it, wondering how these pieces were connected together" ~ Zoë Partyka, U.S.A.

"A fun read that reminded me how engaging a whodunnit can be." ~ Jan Miklaszewicz, Indonesia.

"There is plenty of action to pull you through the book and you'll find yourself invested in each person's life." ~ Cydney Adger, U.S.A.

"Charmingly odd characters that continue to interest and amuse throughout." ~ Charlotte (The Pen Not The Sword), U.K.

Contents:

Chapter 1:

Little sparks of self-doubt and second-guessing were gnawing away at Private Detective Lance Pomegranate's concentration. Would he regret letting one of these last few bouts of semi-decent weather in London for the year pass him by? It wouldn't be long before he'd begin feeling nostalgic for room temperature outdoors while adjusting once again to the feel of freezing pavements beneath his feet, but here he was, sitting at his desk, looking at his emails. He reassured himself that it would all be fine. Future Lance of two hours' time would be doing the next run on the Couch to 5k programme while the sun gracefully disappeared behind the Shepherd's Bush skyline. For now, he would instead make do with the unceremonious deletion of nonsense from his spam folder.

It seemed he'd been selected for a miracle treatment of every known medical condition under the sun, from erectile dysfunction to tinnitus. Every financial institution he'd heard of, including a fair few he was convinced didn't spell their names quite like that, was warning him he was about to lose his account with them. His website was apparently in dire need of search engine optimisation, and would he like to host some adverts for an online casino while he was at it? And then there was a generous-sounding invitation to do business with a certain Malcolm Dombattu.

Dear Mr or Mrs Lancepome,

My name is Malcolm Dombattu, a lawyer representing a diseassed businessman who recently passed out in Kano, leaving behind an estate agent in access of $50 Bajillion (USD) Dollars, at least a quarter of which was liquidised. In his will this business man expressed his wishes to dedicate much of his funds to God, and particularly the Catholic Church of which Mr Bajillion was very fond and a good Christian man with a pension to help the needy. Without an heir to lay claim to the funds or bare the responsibility of exiting the will, the duty falls up on me, his legal representatative, who lawyered him throughbought his long and hounourable leif.

I would like to put my trust in you, noble Mr or Mrs, to ensure that a portion of the funds are delivered to your local Catholic Christian Parish, in whichever part of the United Kingdom of Greater London and the Northern Line you live. If you are willing to help, you will receive a sum of money equivalent to $4 Million (USD) Dollars in a bank account of your choice, to then transfer to the glory of God. As a token of my appreciation, you may retain 50% of these funds for yourself to use as you see feet, for example to provide for your future baby Lancepomes.

Be rest assured that your information will be safe and secure and that everything is honest and legal.

With deep trust,

Malcolm Dombattu MLyer pHD

This looked fun. Lance didn't get many 419 advance-fee scams these days. They'd rather gone out of fashion as far as he could tell. Either that or there was so much automated junk email now that even the copy-and-paste-happy human scammers just couldn't compete with the volume and rarely got noticed. *Well, Mr Dombattu*, Lance thought to himself, *it's your lucky day. You're getting some human interaction.* And with any luck a vulnerable victim would get to keep some hard-earned money while Lance wasted this scammer's time. The sunshine could wait.

Lance hit the reply button, but before continuing he flipped open the dropdown menu in the *From* field to send from his alter ego – the account he kept exclusively for scambaiting, under the name of Robert Prawn. He then scrolled down to the inclusion of the email he was replying to, and edited the header information so it appeared to have been addressed to his alternative address to begin with: nuclearbutler@gmail.com. Lastly, he replaced every instance of the name Lancepom with the name Robert. He had considered going with nuclearbut, or even nuclearbutt, but decided against it. It wasn't too important, Lance felt. Dombattu, or whatever he was really called, must surely have sent out thousands of these. There's no way he would notice that he'd never emailed a Robert Prawn. He began to type his response.

Dear Mr Dombattu,

Thank you ever so much for your generous offer and the trust you have placed in me. I would be delighted to assist with the transfer of the $50 billion dollars to my local Catholic Church, St Baby Eating Bishop of Dunny-on-the-Wold who are in desperate need of funding to cover the hush money for many distressed parents within the parish, who grow in number year upon year.

It is certainly very reassuring to hear that everything is honest and legal. Especially before I even expressed any doubt that it would be. I appreciate your care and courtesy. It's very thoughtful of you in fact, and thus I am ready to provide all of the information that one would not normally give to a stranger on the internet ever. Please specify exactly which details of mine are required.

Robert Prawn Grade 2 Piano

And send.

Back to the junk mail folder. With his shift key, his left mouse button and delete key, he worked his way through the list, dozens of emails at a time – many duplicated by the dozen, in fact. It was as if there were a constant cycling in and out of fads that lasted three to four days at a time, in which all of the spam producers participated together. In the opening week of the previous month for example, he apparently was in dire need of a treatment for nail fungus. By the double-digit days, however, he must have been miraculously cured, though his healthy fingers and toes must have come at the cost of blurry vision. But only for a few more days it seemed. Then his main need was for a magical purple powder proven to reduce heart risk. And so on, and so on, and so on until a noise and an icon told him that his inbox had an email that was one hundred times more likely to be worth reading than all of these combined.

Malcolm Dombattu had replied.

Dear Mr Lance,

I am delighted to hear back from you. It's so touching that the good Christians in your local community want to donate money in secret to help struggling parents in their time of need. Now I know I was right to select you for this important task. Please provide me with your good full name, home address and Great British Baking details.

4

Extinguished sentiments and worn rear guards,

Malcolm Dombattu MLyer pHD Cycling Proficiency

Odd, Lance immediately thought. Why address him as Lance? Not Robert, and not even Lancepom. And this time the writing mistakes were as creative and calculated as his own. This was no scammer, at least not of the ordinary kind, and that email clearly had not been spammed out to all and sundry. He decided to reply once more, still as Robert Prawn, and see if he could discover Malcolm's agenda and endgame.

Dear Mr Malcolm,

Gladly I will provide all of the information you requested. My full name, which I agree is a good one and I'm so pleased you like it too, is Robert Invergordon Prawn. My home address is 17 Cherry Tree Lane, Peckham, SE3 1YA. My Baking details are as follows: Middle shelf, Gas mark 4 for 2 hours. Stick a fork in me to see if I'm done. I am very excited to facilitate the important redistribution of obscene wealth. I trust there will be some sort of advance fee to unlock the funds. Please let me know the amount and preferred payment method.

Kisses and warm unguarded rears,

Robert Prawn BAGA5

Lance took a sip of his tea and went back to the spam folder. He'd only hit the delete button once or twice when he heard the notification sound. Another reply from Malcolm Dombattu.

All right, let's stop fucking about, Lance Pomegranate. Have you forgotten your Google ID pic? I'd recognise those dirty feet anywhere. As you will no doubt have already guessed, being the genius that you are, there is no advance fee, no prepaid ATM card and no dead Nigerian billionaire. And by that I mean there is no scam at all. I'm not going to pay you anything, obviously, and you're not going to pay me anything either. This is not about money. It's just going to be you, me and a few unfortunate deaths. Does the name Alexander Bonaparte Cust ring any bells? That's right. We're doing that.

***

Detective Inspector Esi Owusu signed in at the reception desk of Ladbroke Upper School, graciously accepted the lanyard with her visitor's badge and hung it around her neck, before taking a seat and waiting for her diminutive escort to arrive and lead her to her meeting. She looked up and down at the school publicity material and work samples that adorned every wall, somewhat upstaged by a ten-minute video loop shown on a large television screen. The loop began with action shots from the school's sports fixtures, fading into staged photos of children pretending to conduct experiments in the science labs. This was followed by genuine photos of children attempting to perform plays by Oscar Wilde, John Godber and Willy Russell in the school theatre. The concluding burst of photographs showed the same children previously seen performing the lead roles in those plays affecting wide-eyed smiles of delight towards the camera, pencils in hand, with their maths books open in front of them. The small girl who admirably waded past her with an enormous cello case on her back, like a tortoise on a mission, didn't seem to have made the cut for some reason.

"Excuse me," came a quiet, polite and barely supported voice, which brought Owusu's attention away from the screen and back into the room. "Are you Adrian's mother? I've been sent to show you to the head's office."

6

"Yes, that's right. Thank you. What's your name?"

"I'm Antonia and I'm in year 8."

"Wonderful. OK, lead the way please."

The corridors, right-angled turns and wide staircases – all with light glossy walls, reflecting the bright sunlight coming in through the large windows – were unusually easy to negotiate at this time, with most of the school's complement already on its way home. Owusu was relieved not to be going against a sturdy torrent of oncoming and not-especially-disciplined traffic as she followed the bouncing blonde pigtails in front of her.

"Here we are," her guide proudly declared, as they crossed the border from squeaky grey lino to scratchy brown carpet. "They told me to tell you that you can knock on the door. I'm going home now. Bye."

"Bye, Antonia. Thank you."

Owusu knocked three times.

"Come," came the expected male voice from the other side.

She opened the door and stepped in.

"Please have a seat, Detective Inspector," said the headmaster, a thin man with short brown hair and a greying beard. He was also tall according to both of Owusu's sons, though she only had their word for that at present, as he was seated behind his desk. The presumably tall man was wearing a dark suit, pristine white shirt and a plain burgundy tie. It was like walking into the office of a Mirror Universe's counterpart to her own boss, D.C.I. Kieran Murphy. Everything so different, and yet oddly familiar. The headmaster sat behind a name plaque: Dr D. Call. Head teacher. That explained her sons' nickname for him of 'Doofa'. To the right of the empty seat in front of Dr Call's desk, sat her younger son Adrian's chemistry teacher, Mr Phil Pike.

After she was evidently comfortably seated, the headmaster said, "Thank you for coming. Have you been informed of what this is about?"

"Yes, thank you. I was fairly certain of it beforehand, even. My son does talk to me, after all. Both of them do."

"Good. I'll be clear anyway. Adrian, though he's doing fine on the academic front, including in chemistry, is getting into far too many physical fights. We've had to place him in detention on two Fridays already this term, and it's still only September."

"Yes, I'm aware of that. Are you aware of what the fights are about?"

"We know he's being verbally taunted. We know he's frustrated. He's written two long essays during his detentions describing what he sees as injustices and failings on the part of the school. One was rather unkind towards Mr Pike here, which is why he's joining us this afternoon."

"That's correct," added the chemistry teacher. "It was hard to read, because when it comes to chemistry, Adrian gets on really well. He clearly loves the subject and responds intelligently to everything I throw at him."

"The intelligent response would be to duck every time," quipped Owusu.

"Very good, Inspector." Mr Pike feigned a polite laugh. "But this is serious. There's no question against his academic work or progress. But when I see him giving nosebleeds to two boys while winding a third, there's no good pretending nothing's wrong."

"Obviously something's wrong, and you know what it is."

"That he can't control his temper? Of course. And I do sympathise. It's not nice being teased . . ."

"Not nice being teased. Really? Is that how you're spinning this?" Owusu was hungry. Why had they not offered her tea and biscuits yet? Murder suspects often invited her into their homes and offered her tea and biscuits, and not even a hint of strychnine. Why couldn't Tim Nice-But-Dim and Dimmer do the same?

"Sorry, I don't mean to be dismissive," the chemistry teacher continued. "I mean to say that I do sympathise, but I can't condone young Adrian's response."

"But you are condoning it," said Owusu coldly.

"Excuse me?" said Dr Call.

"You're condoning it. You're taking the exact action that forces him to keep doing it again and again. Oh, you think a punishment like a detention will discourage him and teach him that he's not making the right choice, but look at what's happening. He's using the detentions as an opportunity to articulate the problem, and you're still not listening. So the bullying continues. He just wants to go about his day without boys approaching him and calling him names and continuing on and on until they provoke him. So he stops them in the only

9

way he can, because those of you responsible for the wellbeing and safety of every child in the school are choosing to let it continue." In her mind, she continued, *Probably just as well you haven't offered me coffee or tea, as I'd still have low blood sugar and the only thing to show for it would be stained shirts and first-degree burns on two morons.*

"I'm sorry you feel that way, Detective Inspector. We really do want to help Adrian, and every one of our pupils."

"Do you? Because he's getting bullied, and ignored by you both orally and in writing, and while his essay writing skills will no doubt benefit, it's unjustly costing him a good chunk of his free time. Meanwhile the bullies are not learning to improve their behaviour, and they're suffering minor physical injuries as well. So whom are you actually helping here?"

"There's only so much we can do. If we observe misbehaviour, breach of school rules, something which most certainly includes violent outbursts, we have to punish it. But we cannot punish others based on hearsay of name-calling. We can only punish actions for which we have evidence. Surely as a police officer you understand that. Is your role very different from ours in that regard?"

There was no hiding Owusu's 'how-dare-you' face now. "It's not my job to punish at all. My job is to gather evidence and provide it to those whose job it is to dispense justice. May I ask how many tokens collected from packets of crisps you had to send off to get your PhD, Dr Call?"

Dr Call hesitated with the occasional splutter. Mr Pike was eerily still, and seemed to be hoping that the scorned mother with experience in dealing with vicious criminals would keep her attention away from him, if he could just keep his mouth shut for the rest of the meeting.

Owusu continued, "If there isn't enough evidence, you gather the evidence. Do I make myself clear?"

"Quite clear, Detective Inspector Owusu."

"Good, I think we're finished. Interview terminated at 1634. Have a pleasant evening, gentlemen. I am free to go. Oh, and next time, offer me a cup of tea, for heaven's sake!"

***

Alexander Bonaparte Cust. A.B.C. The first Poirot story Lance had ever read, though that had to be coincidence, was *The ABC Murders. So that's what this is,* he thought to himself. *A psychopath fancies himself as a genius and I'm the yardstick with which he intends to prove it?* He hit the reply button.

We're 'doing', as you put it, The ABC Murders? Mate, I should warn you that technology's come a long way since then. Give me a name and a place all beginning with A and I promise you the police will be all over you before you get within earshot of the person. You wouldn't stand a chance. I'd give up now if I were you. I don't know who you are. I've no wish to find out. You can drop it with no harm done, and get back to trolling people on the internet. You have a talent for it – I'm serious. Applause. G'day.

Lance went back to his spam folder, right-clicked and emptied the rest at once. He wasn't in the mood to check for anything else. If he missed something important, so be it. They could always call him, or even visit his office. He waited in there for the lion's share of office hours for that entire purpose after all, even when the weather was decent. It was almost five o'clock. He closed his laptop and decided that was enough for today. He got changed into his running clothes. It didn't take much. He replaced his smart polo shirt with a high-vis sleeveless shirt, and his chinos with matching shorts. His running footwear being the same as his work footwear, i.e. none, made this a task that took all of thirty seconds.

He tidied away his work things and folded his clothes. They could wait for him to return in the morning. He put in his headphones, opened up a playlist of jazzy Brazilian hip-hop, pressed play, then loaded his Couch to 5k app. Lance was ready for the dulcet tones of Sanjeev Kohli to guide him through the next instalment of light jogging. His route was already planned in his head. It would take him back towards Hammersmith tube station, along the smooth, warm, and hopefully not too densely populated paving slabs of King Street, and into Ravenscourt Park, covering as much of its perimeter as he could, before Sanjeev would tell him he could stop.

When his close friend Sahana, a fit and healthy - seemingly effortlessly so - jazz musician, had nudged him to give the programme a try, he had never believed he'd get very far into it. That was several weeks ago, and now he was taking pride in proving himself wrong. He was just about to hit start on the running app, when he saw an email notification at the top of his screen. Before he could apply any better judgement, he had already opened it. Dombattu had replied again.

Chapter 2:

Lance paused the music and read.

No, not at all Mr Pomegranate. Don't take me for a derivative pastiche monkey. We'll certainly be switching things up a bit, don't you worry. Also, we'll be skipping the letter A. Jane Alder can be A, if you like; if you have a compulsion for completeness perhaps. I'm going to murder someone beginning with B. And just to get you off to a gentle start, it's going to be someone you're quite familiar with. The time and date are still to be decided, but I promise you it will be soon! You get one clue as well. B is for Bin day.

The mention of Jane Alder unsettled him. That case was solved and closed. Her murderer had been convicted and there were no remaining loose ends. It shouldn't be relevant to anyone at all two and a half years later. Perhaps Dombattu simply wanted Lance to know how closely he was studying him. Lance went to his contacts and called his friend Detective Sergeant Pawel Krol.

"Hi, Pav, mate, yeah, fine thanks. I've got something to report. I don't know what you can do about it at this stage, but you have to know at least. It's a weird one."

13

. . .

"Sure. Best if I just forward you the emails for you to show everyone. Cheers, mate. Have a good evening. Speak soon!"

Lance ended the call, resumed the music and began his run. That is to say, he began the five-minute brisk walk that was part of the run. Never skimp on the stretches, or the brisk walks that bookend the hard part. That was what was reinforced every time, and who was he to argue? But as soon as he did get to the point where it was time to pick up the pace, everything around him changed. Not so much the feeling in his chest, or his calves or quads, but it was the looks on the faces of those he passed. Gone were the looks of puzzlement, shock or disapproval, to which he'd grown accustomed ever since moving halfway around the world from Melbourne to settle in London, and instead there was only awe, admiration and respect. Sincere thumbs-up gestures were proffered towards him as he lightly skipped along the pavement. It seemed that walking barefoot on a street was insane, uncouth, dangerous, anti-social or even perverted; but running barefoot, now that was completely different. It showed bravery, commitment, a respect for humans' evolutionary history and a hardy attitude towards physical discomfort.

Lance could only laugh at the illogic of it all. Although he knew what the logic really was. If you run barefoot, people assume you'll be putting your shoes back on when you've finished. You're perfectly normal really. You're just into 'natural' running, whatever that's supposed to mean. It's not like walking barefoot, which implies that you're in your natural state and that you will also continue to do the things you intend to do, at the place you're walking towards, in your bare feet. That's just plain weird and not right at all. His music was interrupted by the ringing of the halfway bell, and then a few seconds later by Sanjeev announcing that he'll be hearing the halfway bell very soon. That always made him chuckle. Perhaps that was why they chose not to fix the little error. Amusement is good for morale after all.

***

Ciara Gallen sat at her desk, staring at a blank screen. She had a deadline to meet and very little to comment on that she hadn't already done to death. She'd already drained the well of boats on the channel, of people not believing enough in Brexit, and of how Liz Truss had been so criminally understood. Such careful scrutiny had only made life needlessly difficult for the Prime Minister. Truss of course had yet to be in charge for a whole month. It was far too early to judge her. Surely six months down the line, no-one would be talking about a few teething problems.

Ciara reminded herself of her golden rule of writing: Put any old nonsense onto the page, and make it better later. Just seeing what rubbish you've written can inspire you to write something better. Looking at a blank page inspires nothing. She began to type.

Why we won't have to wait much longer for a Brexit benefit.

It's only been thirty-two months since we stuck two fingers up at Brussels and waved goodbye, never to have our rules made for us again, by them or anyone else, and already, despite the pandemic and the war in Ukraine, our sovereignty is shining a light ahead of us, showing the way to the sunlit uplands.

She stopped and stared at her opening sentence-cum-paragraph. Looking for changes to make, she decided to add

15

the word *global* before pandemic and was satisfied that without improving anything she'd already brought herself one step closer to her word count goal. Now to think of something truly provocative. Something that would get people coming back to the comments section again and again, and keep the ad impression revenue flowing.

I have previously suggested that it was a lack of belief in Brexit that had chiefly held us back. But in today's column, I'm going to do something that I almost never do. I am going to admit that I made a mistake. Yes, that's right. I was wrong. You see, it occurred to me recently that a lack of belief in Brexit, while significant, has not been the biggest factor. The biggest factor is that Liz Truss, Britain's third female prime minister, and hence an irrefutable demonstration that she represents the most forward-thinking political party this country has ever seen, let alone elected into government, is being undermined by greedy, insecure, selfish old men.

That's right. I, Ciara Gallen, proud career woman and mother, though I have always been, am stepping into new territory. As of today, I do declare that I am, to the maximum extent of the word, a feminist. Not your blue-haired nose-ringed tattooed and obese man-hating lesbian. I am a woman's woman, who wants to lift other women, real women, up.

She looked at her writing. *No, that's too far*, she thought. She deleted the last sentence, removing any hint of the variety of feminism that approached radical transphobia from her piece. Ciara Gallen could deal with being called racist. Being known as a heartless bitch was just fine by her. She was one, and proud of it as far as she was concerned. No problem with being called elitist either. To other people elitism was just what she recognised as meritocracy.

Transphobia though? She wasn't ready for that. Ciara didn't believe in it at all. Not that she cared about it. She had

16

no inclination to engage with those unfortunate people who had to mutilate their bodies just to come close to living the life their brains should have been born into. It freaked her out to look at them because all she could see was the pain she would have felt at having such invasive procedures on her own body.

And in a very real sense she was scared. Not of what they might do to her in a public loo. She knew that if a man wanted to assault a woman, whether in a nominally exclusive female space or not, he would just waltz in and do it, without going through the hassle of disguising himself first. But she did always have a fear of talking to them. It was too easy to say the wrong thing, upset them or make them angry, and she simply did not have the facts necessary to talk about their existence in a productive way. So, she felt it best to leave them alone to live as they saw fit. They hadn't caused her any harm yet. They weren't the ones coming over and stealing everyone's jobs after all.

She went back to her text and sought another angle from which to approach her controversial personal revelation. Then she thought about writing an anti-TERF diatribe instead. It would definitely be controversial for the *Daily Mail*, but unfortunately the wrong kind of rage bait. She resigned herself to reverting to the blank page from which she had begun. What a pity. Perhaps this was something worth saving though. Something for the Graun under a pseudonym?

So, back to square one then. She scoured the online news for stories related to local crime. A grooming gang had just been convicted. No, that wouldn't work for her column. The named members all sounded white and British. What else? Multiple arrests made on suspicion of burglary going back several years, among them a certain young man named Jordan Forbes. That she could talk about. A case she remembered very well thanks to personal involvement. She still had his aunt's phone number. Print-ready pithy sentences were already forming in her mind as her fingers navigated her contact list on autopilot.

***

The following Wednesday evening, D.I. Esi Owusu and D.S. Pawel Krol were in a rare situation. They were socialising together off duty, on what one might crudely approximate to be a double date with their spouses. They were seated around a large table far enough away from the bar to be able to hear each other speak without having to shout. It wouldn't be long before the football fans arrived for whichever Champions League game the pub chose to show. Likely either Man City at home to Copenhagen, or what Pawel described as a Mickey Mouse outfit from down the road, playing right down the road from where he currently sat, there and then against Milan. So, this wasn't a date as such. Just a rare opportunity to unwind and socialise over a few beers, before they went home for an early night. A few skinheads in shirts of two different shades of blue were hovering by the bar. At the table next to them sat a young woman, hood over her head, headphones in, slowly sipping a pint while scrolling on her phone.

"Hope she isn't intending to keep that table to herself when it starts filling up," said Peter Owusu.

"Good luck if she does," added Lena Krol, chuckling. "I'm not sorry that we won't be here to see what happens. Anyway, glad you could make it out with us tonight, Esi. Both of you really. It hasn't happened very often."

"A bit more often now, we hope," said D.I. Owusu. "Now Simon and Adrian are old enough not to need a babysitter."

"So you two don't need to feel so smug about your freedom any more," added Peter.

Lena looked crestfallen.

"Sorry, Peter, you weren't to know," said Pawel in between sips of his drink. "But Lena's wanted a baby for some time. We've been trying for the last five months. It hasn't happened, and it really should have by now, shouldn't it?"

"Five months isn't an unusually long time, as it happens," said the inspector. "No need to stress just yet."

"Maybe," said Lena. "But I do have a reason to worry. I blame those thugs. Pawel got into that stupid fight with them. That's why it's not happening, isn't it."

"Lena, with all the love in the world," Esi prefaced gently, "your husband did not get into a stupid fight. He did his job, saved a man's life and helped us all catch a killer. You told me yourself how proud you were of him."

"That was three and a half years ago, and this is the result. If I could have five minutes with that burglar, Jason what's-his-name. I have a few things to say to him when he comes out of prison."

"That's bad timing. I wish you hadn't said that, my lovely." Pawel reached over and gently squeezed his wife's hand. "We've just found out today, that Jason Bampton's been released."

"He's out? I can go and talk to him? I'll break his things and see how he likes it."

"Oh no. You're not going anywhere near him. For one thing, he's not allowed within shouting distance of you or me, isn't that right, Inspector?"

"Call me Esi, please. We're off duty."

"Sorry, Sir. Er, Esi."

First-name terms with the inspector still felt strange. Nearly all of the time they spent together was on duty. But he'd grown perfectly comfortable calling her 'Sir', as she preferred, instead of 'Ma'am'. This adjustment too would just be a matter of time.

"But you are correct," said Esi. "He'd been in HM Feltham for over three years, but was released after he had his sentence shortened in exchange for giving us some other names and enough information to put them away."

Peter burst out laughing. "Literally no honour among thieves!" Only then did he read the room. "Sorry. Sorry."

"His release is conditional of course. We have to know his whereabouts at all times. It seems he likes to spend most evenings drinking in the Cock Tavern, most Tuesdays and Thursdays."

"In West Brompton?"

"Correct. So we've got officers covering the area often, on the off-chance that they overhear something worth acting on. And he has to report in regularly. Anyway, I'm sorry to have thrown two awkward topics at you so suddenly. Let me get the next round. Peter, hand me your card."

**

Owusu looked across the interview table at the two young women shrouded in warm blankets, which the police had provided to do the work that the clothes they were wearing simply could not. Their faces were an impressionist watercolour of tears and makeup. "Interview commenced on Thursday the 6th of October, at 11:15 pm. Officers present are myself, Detective Inspector Esi Owusu, and Detective Sergeant Pawel Krol. Statements being taken from . . ."

Owusu hesitated, and then gently said to the two women, "I do apologise, but we need your legal names, rather than your professional sobriquets."

"Sorry, our what?" said the girl on the left with a bob of hair dyed a bright colour reminiscent of a clown's nose, in her direct clipped Essex tone, who then resumed taking sips from her cup of tea.

"She means your model name, Blossom," replied her bleach-blonde companion in a gentle Spanish accent. "We have to give our real names to the police."

"Oh. It's going to be kept confidential, right?"

"Of course," replied Owusu.

"OK. Jade Butcher."

"Thank you, Ms Butcher. And you?" Owusu said, turning towards her Iberian companion.

"Soledad Corvillo Panadero."

"Where's the candlestick maker?" quipped D.S. Krol, before adding "Never mind," through a sheepish expression.

"Statements being taken from Jade Butcher and Soledad Corvillo Panadero, also known as Blossom Bounty and Charming Carmen respectively, presenting their grievance with the conduct of –" she looked down at her notes – "Mrs Erma Sumun, manager of the Fulham strip club known as Tasteful Treats."

She looked across to the two young women, no longer shivering thanks to their blankets and tea. "Is that correct?"

They both nodded firmly, until Owusu pointed at the microphone in the room. "Yes," they said together, just as firmly.

"That's right," added Blossom. "She's always been difficult to work with, but in this past few weeks it's got unbearable, innit, Carm?"

"Correct," said Carmen. "She never had anything positive to say to any of us, would rush us to finish our sessions to make way for big client bookings well before the changeover time."

"Changeover?" asked D.S. Krol.

"We work at the venue for an early evening ticketed event run by a third party. Some of the girls also do the strip club afterwards each time, but Blossom and I usually leave at the end of the earlier party. The club's own event begins immediately afterwards and they often have VIP clients attending there with bigger budgets than those who come to our parties, so the manager, Mrs Sumun, tends to see us as an obstacle to her preparation for that."

"I think I follow you so far," said Owusu. "Please continue."

"But our own boss, the party organiser, pays fairly to book the premises and our clients who attend are the sweetest, gentlest guys. I really hate the way she bosses us and them around. But that's not why we're here.

"I said we usually don't stay for the main strip club event, but that wasn't the case tonight. They needed some more girls to fill in a vacancy and I'm saving up for a holiday so I decided to take on the extra work. We both did."

Blossom took over. "Tonight she had no security on the door."

"Inadequate security," Carmen clarified.

"Well, same fing innit, Carm," Blossom asserted. "The usual bloke was sick, I heard, and she'd brought in a spotty sixth-former at the last minute who was worse than useless. I didn't feel safe. Did you, Carm?"

"No, I didn't," her companion replied, before placing her empty teacup down on the table.

Blossom continued. "But that manager told us she'd bar us from the club and dox us too if we didn't stay for the whole night. She had another rule as well that we weren't allowed to say no to anyone. And that's normally fine with the foot party. Those guys are great, mainly because they're incredibly grateful, but still. And we have our own security man as well so it's never an issue. But this was different. You're a lot more vulnerable, and it's much harder to predict what might happen, especially as I'd only done this kind of thing on camera before."

"Just to clarify," said Owusu. "The foot party as you call it, is your usual event?"

The girls nodded together, before Blossom picked up where she had left off.

"And then there was this one guy, and well, he didn't actually touch me in the end, but the way he was talking, I was fearing the worst. He might have just been role-playing but I couldn't know that until it was over. I went to security, who was probably more concerned about his A-level geography coursework than anyone's safety, and then I went to the manager, and she just said, *'Don't be a whiny little bitch. If you sleep with your clients, don't be surprised by the reputation that gets you.'* She said that out loud in the middle of the club for everyone to hear. You heard it too, didn't you, Carm?"

"Yes, I did. That's why I'm here to reinforce Blossom's statement."

"And then what happened?" asked Owusu.

"I couldn't work any more after that. Everyone staring at me, looking at me like I was some sort of cheap tart. I take my job very seriously. I thought I was doing her a favour filling in at the last minute too. Her threats didn't matter after then. I had to leave, and Carm came out with me, didn't you Carm?"

"I did," Carmen affirmed.

"And that was when you called the police?" asked Pawel. "Officers collected you from a few streets away at around half past ten."

"Not quite," said Carmen. "First, we had to escape because a couple of the guys from the club were following us. They may have just been naively trying to get to know us. Some get confused and think they can become friends with models, or

24

even ask us out on a date. Letting them down is hard, but you have to be professional. But sometimes they get a bit grabby and forget that there's a hard limit to what their money can buy, especially outside the venue."

"I tell you, running in these heels is a skill we learnt through a lot of practice," Blossom added.

Owusu leant forward and waited to be sure she wouldn't be interrupting. "Were either of you assaulted at any time? We will do all we can to address that if so."

"No. Luckily, we managed to avoid it," said Carmen. "But that manager, Mrs Sumun, she put us at high risk, and if she carries out her threat, we'll be at even higher risk. She has our personal phone numbers and copies of our ID."

"What about the other girls from the club? Can we hear from them?" said Pawel.

"I can give you the stage name and mobile number of one girl who was there that night. She's a regular at the main club. She might be able to tell you something. That's all I have, I'm afraid."

"That would be appreciated. Please write it down here, Ms Panadero," said Owusu, passing Carmen a pen and piece of paper across the table.

"Thank you, both of you. We appreciate you having the courage to come forward and giving us your time, especially after a traumatic evening. We will investigate this fully and contact Mrs Sumun. We will also put you in touch with a legal advisor, and of course the first thing we will do is ensure that you both get home safely. Is there anything either of you would like to add?"

Blossom looked pensive for a moment, and then shook her head. "No, nothing else, Inspector. Thank you for listening to us."

"Thank you," Carmen added. "Please don't let her ruin our careers and our lives. We're professionals, just like you."

"I understand," said Owusu. "Interview terminated at 11:35 pm."

The two detectives escorted the girls out of the interview room and led them along a corridor towards a group of officers patiently waiting for them. "Please see that these two young ladies get home safely," said D.S. Krol.

"Yes, Sir," said the nearest officer, standing and gesturing to the female officer in the adjacent seat to join him.

"We've passed on your contact details to a legal advisor. If you haven't heard from her by the end of tomorrow, you can call me directly on this number." Owusu handed each of the models a card. "Thank you again, for trusting us. We will do everything we can. I promise."

As the girls were led away, Owusu and Krol turned and walked in the opposite direction, back along the corridor that had taken them from the interview room. "Thanks for staying late, Sergeant," she said. "It was really important to me that these girls see two detectives listening to them. I wanted to make them feel as heard as possible, even before we heard what they had to say, if that makes sense."

"Of course, Sir. Just do me a favour."

"What's that, Sergeant?"

"Don't let my wife find out that I spent the evening with a couple of strippers."

Owusu groaned.

***

Friday was bin day on Edith Road, W14. In fact, there were two bin days on Edith Road. Every week, every Tuesday and Friday, all of the bin bags – whether transparent and full of recycling, or black and full of general waste – would be collected. Other boroughs and the rest of the country settled for one collection a week, alternating between the two. But not here in Hammersmith and Fulham. This was luxury land when it came to rubbish disposal.

On this particular Friday a poor unfortunate bin collector ran into Jason Bampton, tripped over him, and then almost gave himself a back injury trying to collect him and carry him away. With considerably less effort than he had needed to leave prison, Jason Bampton tore through the bottom of the black bag in question and lay sprawled across the pavement, and he continued to lie there until the police arrived.

The often grossly underappreciated employees of the council were long gone by the time D.I. Owusu and D.S. Krol arrived. However, the officers securing the scene and gathering forensic evidence still had much to do.

"What do we know so far?" asked Owusu as she and Krol approached the body.

"It's the body of Jason Bampton, Sir. A dustman found him concealed in a large black bag this morning, at about eight o'clock. Residents of the surrounding houses said they noticed it here as early as six when they brought their own rubbish out this morning. Others said it definitely wasn't here at eleven o'clock last night when they brought out theirs."

"Do we have a cause of death? A murder weapon even?"

"No," replied the young officer, suppressing a yawn. "We have evidence of a blow to the back of the head, but it doesn't appear to have been what killed him, Sir."

"Sir," said Pawel. "Lance's email."

"You're right, Sergeant. B for Bampton. B for Bin day."

"I'll call him."

"He definitely needs to know, but he doesn't need to be at the scene. He'll just be getting out of bed now. Swing by his office on your way back to the station. You can show him photos. This is clearly relevant to Lance's own conundrum, but we still have to follow our mundane leads. We can't just ignore all the enemies that Bampton's made recently."

"I agree. I'll make a list of known associates of those he sold out to get free and we'll work through them. Knowing our luck it'll probably turn out to be Lance's nutter instead."

"Probably. But we have to do it anyway."

"Yes, Sir."

Chapter 3:

"Come in, Pav mate. Yeah, I've already seen it on the news." Lance was sitting looking composed but pensive, like a bohemian Bond villain, behind his office desk.

"Look, you and Owusu, you have your leads already. Bampton's enemies, local gangs. It could even have been an impatient loan shark, for all I know. Yeah, we've got this email, and it's screaming at us to say that whoever wrote it is behind this, but that's all we have so far. It doesn't get us any closer on its own. So all we can do is what you're already doing, plus hope I get lucky and spot something in another email, which I'm sure I'll be receiving pretty soon, mate."

"You're right, Lance. There's still the post-mortem to come. Maybe Dr Grappa will have something for us."

Lance nodded. "He's got to have something. No obvious cause of death, from the scene investigation, did you say?"

"That's right, just a bang on the head that should not have been fatal."

"OK, then. One love, Dombattu."

Pawel frowned and folded his arms. "It's a game to you, too, Lance? I'm not comfortable with that," he said, shaking his head.

Lance tried to defeat Pawel's frown with an exaggerated smile. "Come on, Pav, after what his men did to you, the cunt can afford me a bit of cold detachment while trying to figure out how the fucker died."

"Lena would agree, that's for sure." The frown's defences were showing signs of weakening.

"Oh, for sure. That could have been you, if you'd forgotten the bins, mate."

"Or to clean the kitchen, I know." Frown defeated.

Lance loved how Pawel saw his wife's intense and oddly specific bursts of aggression as reasons to adore her even more. "At least you get to enjoy the look on her face when you tell her the news."

"Yes, there is that. A light at the end of a tunnel of number crunching and phone calls at the station."

"Have fun, Pav, mate!"

***

Pawel was lost in his mundane but important task. He fought the urge to tear himself away from the repetition of dialling number after number, and ticking each off his list after the fruitless conversations ended one by one, each demoralisingly similar to the one before. The main weapon he had at his disposal in this fight was his sense of duty, and frankly he needed a bigger one. He did however have a pair of invisible sidekicks in this battle in the form of familiar sounds and smells.

The background chatter coming from the other desks in the room no longer registered, although he would certainly have noticed if they suddenly stopped. The chatter comprised a familiar set of voices, in a particular room's acoustics all coming from mouths positioned just so. Similarly, the large room's familiar smell of stale coffee and cheap spray-on deodorant – in the latter case most of which could be attributed to one particular officer's internal battle of time management versus appearance consciousness, albeit consciousness that Pawel imagined was induced by certain other officers repeatedly 'having words' – was an important cue to Pawel, as an almost Pavlovian trigger to enter 'work mode'.

Lost in his task though he had been, the change in air movement around Pawel's desk prompted him to look up just in time to make eye contact with Owusu before she began to speak.

"All right, Sergeant. What do we have?"

"I began with the obvious, from the burglaries around the time of the Jane Alder case. We'd arrested Jason Bampton along with Jordan Forbes and Charles Smith. Forbes refused to co-operate with us and is still inside."

"Yes, I remember that. Sad story really."

"Smith had a longer sentence due to possession of various illegal drugs and stolen pharmaceutical products in addition to his burglary convictions. He had an older brother, Frederick, who we suspected to be part of Charles's supply chain, but we couldn't prove anything . . ."

"Until Bampton shared a few text messages with us, of course." Owusu had seamlessly caught the baton of Krol's sentence. "So, who's on the outside who might have acted for the Smiths? Don't you dare say Morrissey."

"That's the brick wall I'm hitting, Sir. Bampton gave us Fred. Fred's giving us nothing. He's probably realised he needs his friends on the outside to stay on the outside for him. What about that postman they recruited for distribution? His name was Jim Sawbridge, wasn't it? Is it worth talking to him again?"

"I doubt it, Sergeant. He was completely out of the loop. Bottom end of the food chain for a bit of extra cash. He's done his time and learnt his lesson. He'd have no motive now and probably doesn't know anything."

Pawel scratched his head. "Yes, you're right, Sir. Then before I move on to Bampton's other enemies, perhaps I should talk to Smith's family members. If I suggest that whoever got Bampton might be after them, perhaps."

"Be careful, Sergeant. I don't want you doing that on your own. Sometimes I think you overestimate everyone's sense of humanity. It's a rare and precious trait to have in the police, especially when it comes to our public image, but catching Bampton's killer is actually second on my priority list to keeping you from a second hospital stay. It is a good idea though. I'll come with you. I suggest you spend the rest of the afternoon working through the rest of the list of people Bampton managed to incense."

"None of this is going to be easy though, is it, Sir? I mean we put them away. We're the weapon that Bampton used against them."

"No, Sergeant. They did it to themselves. Do not forget that. They might have grievances between each other that seem legitimate in the context of them being on the same side of the law together, but before any of that, they chose that side. We're the cliff edge over which they push each other, that's all. And for some of them, we're the convenient handholds and tree branches with which they might be able to climb back to safety, if they're clever enough about it. But if they lose their temper, and hack away at those branches and loosen those rocks, they will fall all the way down."

A cough came from behind Owusu's back. Owusu stepped aside as she turned to face the young cougher, whom Pawel was now able to identify by her face.

"Excuse me, Inspector, Sergeant," the cougher said nervously. "Sorry to interrupt, Sir. Could you both come down to the front, please? There's an overexcited Irish woman asking for you by name."

Owusu gave an uncontrolled sigh of exasperation. "Did she happen to be waving a press pass, and did you wince as she trotted in wearing ridiculous high heels?"

"That's why I didn't need to take her name, Inspector."

"Deep breaths, Sir," said Krol, more to himself than his superior as the two of them headed downstairs.

***

"Mrs Gallen. What a pleasant surprise. How can we help you?" Owusu's tone could have been used as quality control for most high-end spirit levels.

33

"Good morning, both of you." Ciara Gallen's, on the other hand, had an edge of expectation to it, as she tapped the tall thin heel of her left shoe on the hard floor of the police station. "You're investigating another local murder, I hear."

"Are you here to confess? We would never have guessed." Owusu might have shown some restraint had her day not begun quite as early.

"What have you guessed so far?"

"No guesses," said Pawel.

Ciara Gallen rolled her eyes. "Fine. What can you tell me?"

"We can confirm it was murder, on the basis that suicide victims don't put themselves out for the bin men. We can tell you the name of the victim. Jason Bampton. Male, aged thirty-one. Grew up locally."

"Bampton. The burglar from a few years back? He was just released from prison, wasn't he? For reasons that might have reduced his popularity among his associates, perhaps?"

"He was released in exchange for some very useful information, yes," Owusu replied.

"There's the motive then." Ciara's tone had an air of conclusiveness.

"Very likely. That's the lead we're following at least." Owusu's did not.

"Is there anything else we can do for you Mrs Gallen?" D.S. Krol had spotted a vacancy in the conversation for some diplomacy. "Would you like a cup of tea perhaps?"

"No, that's everything. Thank you." She seemed to have taken the hint.

Owusu smiled and nodded gently. "Do pop in again if you discover anything before we do."

"Aye." Ciara Gallen returned the smile, though somewhat curtly, before turning and almost clattering into an onrushing hurricane wearing Cousin Itt cosplay, complete with a squeal that was knocking on the door of the ultrasonic band.

The columnist stepped back from the quivering dark-blonde hillock and cast her eyes slowly downwards to see a face, complete with wide-open bright-blue eyes, adorned with a pair of red circular-framed glasses, sitting atop a round nose. The nose in turn protruded above lips wearing a lipstick bright enough to match the shade of the frame, all clearly visible through a parting of the long flowing hair, now settled in place as the hurricane came to a complete stop.

"Oh my wow! It's you, isn't it? Oh wow! Ciara Gallen of the *Daily Mail*. You wrote up the Jane Alder story. It's one of my favourite cases. Bo Fulgar, so honoured to meet you!" Cousin Itt extended her right hand, eagerly expecting a firm and professional shake.

Ciara Gallen looked at the white gloves on her own hand for half a second, momentarily tilted her head, and then gave the handshake as if accepting a manageable loss.

"Looks like you've made a new friend. We'll leave you to it and get back to work," said Owusu, having decided she'd seen enough. She turned away and began walking back towards the corridor from which she and Krol had entered. As the D.S.

caught up with her, she whispered impatiently to him, "Milk and two. Please!"

***

Ciara Gallen took a further step back away from her aspiring groupie.

"Bo Fulgar, did you say? This is very flattering, but I don't have time to stop, I'm afraid. I'm guessing that you came here for the same reason as I did, since you're fascinated with murder cases."

"I am. I run a true crime podcast. Yes, I came here to ask the police for information, but I'd much rather invite you on as a guest speaker."

"Not a chance. I mean, I'm far too busy, sorry. But I'll do one thing for you. The police haven't been able to tell me very much. So I can save you some time by advising you to do all the digging yourself. But don't lose track of the time and miss your hair appointment."

"Are you sure you can't? It would be so wonderful. An actual suspect from the Jane Alder case. You knew her well, didn't you. Of course you did, through the school. Her lesson with your work. You know I've just moved into her house in Lysia Street. The immersion in that story I get from it. It's amazing. If I could have your memories of it all for my podcast, oh my wow!"

"Yeah, that's not happening. I'll be off now. Good luck."

***

Dear Mr Lance,

Do you find yourself frustrated by people who say they're going to do something, insist on it even, as if it's their top priority? And then just don't? I don't think anything frustrates me more than that. I'm so pleased to have been able to demonstrate to you that I am not one of those people. Never have been. I said what I was going to do, and didn't waste any time. You don't want to be wasting time either, as we're just getting started.

I do hope you're having as much fun as I am.

Ever your opponent,

Malcolm Dombattu

Lance had been expecting this email and was not surprised that it had come just twenty-four hours after he'd first heard about Bampton's body, though he had been hoping he'd have more time. He still needed a cause of death before he could even begin to speculate on what might be going on. That's if Dombattu even intended to give him any clues at all. A horrifying thought occurred to him. It might only be possible to deduce anything at all once enough murders had taken place for either connections to be made between them, or for Dombattu to get complacent and make silly mistakes. He didn't want to think about any more people having to die before anyone could be saved. But he needed more information no matter what.

So, he decided that wasting time was indeed in no-one's interest. Taking a while to reply might delay things, but he would learn nothing new from it, and so he and Dombattu's subsequent targets would be no better off than if he replied immediately.

He hit the reply button.

Malcolm.

No this isn't fun for me. I'll take your word for it that it's fun for you. How much fun are you going to need? How many people do you intend to murder?

He hit send. Dombattu must have been waiting for his message. Lance barely had time to scratch his head before he received a response.

Maybe it's an acquired taste for you, Lance. That's OK. You'll be tasting it often. We're certainly not going to be stopping any time soon. I think we'll start with at least 26, no, make that 25. Letter A was done for me, I remember now. Then I might even let you choose which alphabet to go with after Z. That's exciting, isn't it? Anyway, that's a long way off. For now, all you need to think about is this: C is for Cheder.

Shabbat Shalom

***

Lance closed his laptop and picked up his phone. He sent a message to his WhatsApp group chat – titled *The Genius Crew*, with D.S. Pawel Krol and jazz trombonist Sahana Acharya – hoping they'd both be free on a Saturday afternoon. He put his phone away and went through his warm-up stretches preparing for another run. When he loaded his running app, it presented him with what in normal circumstances would have been a shock revelation – that he'd be doing a continuous twenty minutes, when the previous sessions didn't have him go any longer than eight at a time.

Instead of shock, however, what he felt could almost be called relief. He stepped out of his front door and began the brisk warm-up walk that took him to the junction of Goldhawk Road and King Street, and on to the entrance of Ravenscourt Park.

The pavement beneath his bare feet still felt pleasantly warm, but the air was crisp and refreshing, in contrast with the brightness of the sun, which was almost directly above him yet just far enough in front to be a nuisance to his eyes once he was heading east along the main road. He had his music and the dulcet Scottish tones of Sanjeev to keep him busy for twenty more minutes, plus a warm-down walk. And that would surely have been enough time for his two friends to reply to his message.

**

A couple of hours later, Lance, Pawel and Sahana had a pint each in front of them around a small table upstairs in the Swan pub between the two Hammersmith tube stations. Usually rammed on a Saturday afternoon, when at least one of QPR or Fulham would have a home match, the pub on this occasion had an air of tranquillity to it, particularly upstairs, with plenty of clear paths between the light fittings, the polished mahogany furniture that matched Sahana's hair colour, and the mirrors that covered some of the walls. The background noise around the three of them was minimal, as the majority of it came to them via a gentle simmer up the staircase from the busier bar area below.

"What's the goss then? I heard about that burglar," said Sahana as she scanned the QR code to load up the online ordering system on her phone.

"It's pretty heavy," Lance admitted. "But it's what I wanted to talk to you both about. Pav knows a lot of it already, but as of this morning, there's more."

"Another email?"

Lance nodded. "Another email."

"What emails? Are you about to inherit a Nigerian fortune?" Sahana's chuckle was cut short by the sight of four eyes widening in sync across the table from her.

"Funny you should say that." Pawel was first to respond.

"At least that's what it looked like at first," Lance added.

"Don't tell me you thought it would be real, Lance. You, of all people," said Sahana.

Lance's eyes said the words 'What do you take me for?' so that his lips didn't have to.

Sahana shrugged. "Care to start at the beginning, chaps?"

"Lance has a new online pen pal," said Pawel.

"Someone's messing with me," Lance elaborated. "Started out pretending to be a 419 scammer, but turns out he's a psycho, making a game of being a serial killer. He's basically giving me his take on *The ABC Murders*."

"B for Burglar? Who was A?"

"Yes, but he started at B, for some reason. Mr Bampton the Burglar. Probably as part of his attempt at getting in my head, he mentioned the Jane Alder case and said we could call that A."

"Is he moving on to C, or is he going to play Happy Families and do Mrs Bampton the Burglar's Wife next?"

"Glad you're taking this seriously, Sahana! But yes, that's what's in the next email."

"Did you get another clue?" said Pawel.

"Here, have a look for yourself." Lance loaded up Dombattu's latest email onto his phone, which he then passed around the table. While Pawel and Sahana each read through in turn, he recapped.

"The previous clue was B is for Bin day. And then Jason Bampton turned up in a bin bag left out for the dustman on Edith Road yesterday morning. Any news from Gianni Grappa yet, Pav? Do we know the cause of death?"

Pawel shook his head and said, "Not yet," as he received Lance's phone from Sahana. He scanned down the short but menacing missive and raised an eyebrow. "What does that say? Is that supposed to be Cheddar? As in the village or the cheese? Do I want to imagine how you murder someone with cheese?"

"You lock them in a small room with 'Dancing Queen' playing on repeat until they beg you for a means to end it all, Pav, mate."

Sahana laughed at either or both of her friends. It wasn't clear which. "No, Pawel. Cheder is where Jewish children are taught their cultural things, it's like a sort of Sunday school, except it takes place on Saturdays, of course. It's where they learn Hebrew and prepare for their Bar or Bat Mitzvah."

"Looks like we need to check out the local synagogue then," said Pawel, still feeling slightly embarrassed.

"There are a couple of well-established ones in Holland Park and Kensington," said Sahana. "What? Don't look at me like that. I have many friends. I learn things from them. None here in Hammersmith or Shepherd's Bush as far as I know, though."

"Yeah, I checked," said Lance. "But there is an informal synagogue congregation that hires out a community hall every Saturday morning and for the highlights of the Jewish calendar."

"Do you know what times the normal Saturday service runs, Lance?" said Pawel.

"Yes, I did look it up. Ten am to one pm, and then they tend to hang around a bit afterwards for the kiddush."

"Grub," Sahana translated.

Pawel relaxed. "So, we wouldn't be able to speak to any of the members there now, even if we rushed over. They'll be long gone and the building will just be a community centre again until next time."

"So," Lance summarised, "we've got a vigilante who might also be a nice Jewish boy, or who may be neither nice, nor Jewish . . ."

"Nor a boy," suggested Sahana.

"Indeed," said Lance, without loss of momentum. "Either way, first move has to be to see if we can link Bampton with any member of the local Jewish community. Perhaps some of them reported burglaries in the last five years or so?"

Pawel nodded.

"And Pav, you get the fun job of deciding whether to call Owusu and tell her she doesn't have the weekend off after all now, or to just send her a quick text saying the fellas on duty will take care of things until she's in again on Monday."

"Very funny, Lance. You know that's not a choice by any stretch. I'll phone her now."

Lance and Sahana exchanged amused looks as Pawel called his superior.

"OK, Sir, we'll take care of it," said Pawel into his phone. "I take it at least this means we can stop looking into Bampton's former associates for now. See you on Monday. Enjoy your trip. Bye." Pawel ended the call and put his phone back into his pocket. "She's currently driving around the Peak District with her parents over from Ghana. Excuse me, I'd better head to the station and fill them in. Can you forward me the email, Lance?"

"See you again soon, then, I suppose, Pawel," said Sahana.

"Hope so. Lance, I'll get Gianni to come over to your office with his report on Monday, shall I?"

"That would be great, Pav. Thanks. I'll send you the email right now. Hope you get some of your afternoon back, mate."

"Not holding my breath. Cheers, anyway," said Pawel as he stood up from the table and made his way towards the stairs.

"Oy vey," said Lance.

Sahana looked at him calmly for a moment before speaking again. "Everything else OK, Lance? You usually take this sort of thing in your stride. I don't know how half the time, but you do."

"It's a bit different this time, Sahana. Whoever it is, is making a game of it, playing with me. Making my part in it affect how many people die. And now I've got to go to a bloody synagogue."

"Is that a problem? I didn't know you were that politically minded, Lance," Sahana teased.

Lance feigned offence, clutching his chest and making an exaggerated gasp, which smoothly transitioned into a gentle laugh as he relaxed his hand. "No. It's just that some of those Jews, lovely as they are, remind me too much of my mum."

"Shit, Lance! You're a chosen person? How did I not know this?"

"I never committed. Never believed any of the beliefs, was never keen on any of the rituals. The food's fine, but I'm not enough of a hypocrite to go through all the motions just for that."

"Mazel tov!"

"Your chicken and bacon sandwich, Sir."

Lance stretched his legs out in anticipation and a Cheshire-Cat-sized grin possessed his lips. Almost immediately the grin had vanished and he was sitting straight upright, as Sahana, unable to control her fit of laughter at the waiter's timing, had managed to stamp on his outstretched toes under the table.

"Sorry, Lance. Did I hurt you?" Lance's reaction had also pulled Sahana back into a state of sensibility.

"For all of half a second. I'm fine. Mind if I start eating though? I'm starving. You can have Pav's too, when it comes."

Chapter 4:

Owusu and Krol had agreed to meet in Lance's office near Brook Green at ten o'clock on Monday morning. Lance stood up as they entered, stepped around to the front of his desk and crossed the sea of thick black fluffy carpet to meet them, gesturing towards the comfortable armchairs he kept for visitors as he sank into one of them himself.

"Hi, Lance."

"Good weekend, was it, Inspector?"

"Yes, thank you. Parents suitably entertained, and my sons both grateful for a couple of days' breather from them."

"Glad to hear it. OK, where are we at with the synagogue so far?"

Owusu looked to her left. "Sergeant?"

"Yes, Sir. The synagogue at the Grove Neighbourhood Centre is led by a rabbi named Jeremy Cotton. The centre gave me his number and he's agreed to speak to us at his home this afternoon at two."

"Do we know anything else about him, Sergeant?"

"He's not a full-on out-and-out rabbi, if I understood correctly. It seems he does it just for devotion to his faith. I don't know if there's such a thing as ordination in Judaism, or whether he's been ordained as such, but it's all very casual. As he put it to me, he's Jew . . . ish."

"Very droll, Sergeant."

"You can tell him that yourself, Sir. Other than that, all we know about him is that his day job is teaching trumpet and directing the brass ensembles at three schools in the area."

"OK, very good, Sergeant." Owusu took a breath. "Lance, I've seen the emails and I must say I've not seen anything like this before, aside from when I read *The ABC Murders*, that is. Our would-be serial killer seems to be quite a fan of yours and is taking a lot of pride in toying with you, wouldn't you say? Do you think it could be someone you've dealt with in the past? Someone with an axe to grind against you perhaps? Maybe even someone who's followed you here from Australia?"

"I wouldn't rule it out, Inspector, though I can't think of anyone specific. As I see it it's one of two possibilities worth considering. Either it's someone who has chosen to involve me because he knows me personally, or used to, and wants to beat me in a contest, or it's someone who fancies himself as a master killer who's familiar with my professional reputation and hence wants to beat me in a contest.

"If it's the latter, we need to determine whether the killer has chosen to operate in this area because it's where I'm based, or the killer has chosen me because this is where the killer wants to operate. And again, that one can be split further, because we'd need to determine what the killer's reason for wanting to operate here is. Perhaps he's based here, or perhaps his highest-priority target or targets are. Or it could be another reason altogether."

Owusu nodded, as if to say 'Go on'.

Lance hesitated for a moment, and then the resignation in his tone revealed why. "Just so many unknowns at the moment. At least we know where to begin, even though it means jumping through the hoops that have been put in front of us."

"I agree Lance. Let's hope that the post-mortem reveals something else." Owusu looked up at the clock on the wall and then heard a knock on the door behind her. Just fourteen minutes later than expected. That counted as commendable punctuality for Doctor Gianni Grappa.

"Come in, Doc," Lance called. Dr Grappa pushed the door open and slowly approached them, his cane doing much of the work.

"New suit? Mustard suits you, mate."

"Thank you, Lance. Good morning, detectives. Yes, I bought it just last month. Very nice, no?" Dr Grappa took the remaining empty armchair and then lifted his black briefcase onto his lap and opened it.

"Can we attribute your chipper demeanour to anything in particular?" said Owusu.

"I've just heard from my brother. He's got us tickets to see Roger Glover in Milan on the seventeenth."

"Who?" said Lance.

"No, not The Who, Lance," said Dr Grappa, shaking his head like a schoolteacher met with sarcasm. "He's from Deep Purple."

"I don't know," said Lance. "All these bands sound the same to me, and they all have a Roger."

Gianni Grappa tapped his cane on the floor, even more like a teacher, and one from a bygone era.

"Even I've heard of Roger Glover," said Owusu. "Anyway, getting back to business, what can you tell us about Bampton, Dr Grappa? It wasn't the blow to the head that killed him, was it?"

"Correct, Inspector. Jason Bampton was hit on the head with the surface of a flat object, likely made of metal, probably a kitchen utensil of some sort. Maybe a wok or frying pan. But there was no skull fracture or indication of physical brain damage. What killed him was the large amount of chemicals in his system. Hints of his nose being squeezed firmly, and corrosion on his lips, suggest he was knocked unconscious and then forced to ingest some liquids and the internal organ damage that followed was the clear cause of death."

"What chemicals? What kind were they?" said D.S. Krol.

"Sodium hypochlorite, sodium hydroxide, various surfactants and solvents and fragrance chemicals."

Owusu's jaw dropped. "Bleach? Dishwasher powder? Is that right?"

"Or possibly kitchen spray, but basically yes, Inspector," replied the pathologist. "Ingredients of cleaning products, and

49

very likely the victim was fed directly from bottles of products bought in a supermarket."

"How can you tell that?" said Owusu.

"I ran a comparison with some of the things I use at home. Not just chemical composition, which was extremely close, but even the bottle apertures were a good match to the impressions left on the victim's lips."

"Pav, mate. You know those products intimately – which ones do you use at home? Where do you buy them from? I bet you can't wait to tell your wife that actually it is possible to die from cleaning the kitchen." Lance's levity was poorly pitched as D.S. Krol stood absolutely still, looking as pale as a Hollywood star's incisors.

"Pav? You OK?"

"Not funny, Lance. You know how Lena's felt about Bampton ever since my stay in hospital. And now he's barely out of prison a week before he turns up dead by means of cleaning the kitchen and putting the bins out? It's as if someone's trying to grant her wish. Or troll her. Or frame her."

"As a part of messing with me, no doubt."

"Yes, there is a doubt. How did he know? It's not as if you put it in the emails – 'Oh Mr Dombattu, yes, here's the £100 Apple gift card to unlock the funds from the dead philanthropist, and by the way, my friend in the police is terrified of what his wife is capable of whenever he leaves the kitchen messy or forgets bin day.' Or did I skim too lightly and miss that bit?"

"Someone's been spying on her. Or you both. Shit, sorry Pav. You're right."

"Language, Timothy," said Owusu involuntarily.

"Sorry, Inspector."

"It's fine, Lance. Force of habit."

"Hold on, Inspector. I need to get my head around something. When did you meet up and talk about Bampton? Was it Monday evening? Tuesday?"

"It was Wednesday," said Pawel. "I remember which games were on. Why?"

"It's just that I received my email with the clue before then. Nearly a week before. What day was Bampton released, Inspector?"

Owusu thought for a moment. "Thursday the 29th."

"I got the email with the clue that evening."

"Which means," said D.S. Krol, "that the killer was already planning this long before Lena knew that Bampton was out of prison."

"Exactly," said Lance, eager to lift his friend's mood. "And already intending to involve the bins."

"That makes it worse," said Pawel. "Someone could have been stalking Lena and me for a lot longer."

"Or overheard your conversations with other police officers. Assuming you have the same running joke with some of them as you do with me, your adorable little marital idiosyncrasies are hardly up there with the identity of Banksy."

"I can assure you, Lance, that D.S. Krol does indeed have those conversations," said Owusu. There was no smile on her face but her tone of voice did the same job. "I think even D.C.I. Murphy keeps a bottle of kitchen spray under his desk, which he's saving for just the right prank."

"Feel better, Pav, mate?"

"Not really," said Pawel, wiping moisture from his hair and still-pale face.

Owusu acted quickly. "Is there anything else you can tell us, Dr Grappa?"

"Yes. There were some bumps and scratches on the body's back and dirt on his clothes, suggesting it had been dragged by the feet a very short distance on a pavement, while unconscious but not dead."

"How short a distance?" said Lance. "Like off the pavement and into a parked car?"

"I didn't find any trace of carpet fibres or car upholstery, but yes, that sort of distance."

"What, are you thinking, Lance?" said D.S. Krol.

"I'm thinking blow to the head with a frying pan, let's say. Suppose the killer has come out of nowhere in the dark, catching Bampton unaware while he's on his way home from the pub, or something. Drags his unconscious body to a nearby parked car, probably with plastic covering everything. Maybe used a dolly or something to make it easier to move. Holds his nose and force-feeds him the cocktail, from which he never wakes up. Drives around to somewhere no-one will be looking and pulls the large bin bag around the body there. Then drives around to Edith Road and dumps him in the street next to the more conventional rubbish and recycling."

"It's something to go on for now, certainly," said Owusu. "Let's check CCTV for suitably large vehicles spotted by the Cock on Thursday night."

"That's where he was drinking, Inspector?" said D.S. Krol.

"Yes, Sergeant. Police officers saw him there, and saw him leave at closing time, just after eleven o'clock."

"So, this can't have happened too close to any of the officers," said Lance. "And what was Bampton's typical journey home after a night like this?"

Owusu let a subtle smile escape. "You'll like this, Lance. His address as of release was on Burnfoot Avenue. It's off Munster Road, near where it crosses Fulham Road. Just to the north of there."

"Hmm, remind me to put the name to the test next summer. I'll send a letter to the council if it doesn't meet my standards. Anyway, bit of a walk from the Cock, isn't it?"

"Yes," said Owusu. "Quite a wide area to search and to check CCTV for, unfortunately."

"Let's see if we can narrow it down. Bear with." Lance skipped over to his desk and turned his laptop around to face him at the near side. He loaded Google Maps on his browser and looked up the walking route between the Cock Tavern and Burnfoot Avenue.

"OK, says it's a seventeen-minute walk, but most of it's on Bishop's Road and Munster Road. Far too unlikely not to have been witnesses there. We can put out a general call for information to the public in case it did happen on one of the larger roads, but for our fine-tooth comb efforts, let's prioritise that hypotenuse road across that corner." He pointed at the road in question and then zoomed the map in to read its name. "Filmer Road," he read. "I'd ask the neighbours if they saw anything there, and check for vehicles that were parked there at any time that evening."

D.S. Krol was beginning to look more like himself again. "Good shout, Lance. We'll do that."

"Can you tell us roughly when the chemicals were ingested? And is there anything else we should know?" asked Owusu, turning once again towards Gianni Grappa.

"An hour or so either side of one in the morning would be my best guess. And that's everything I have, I'm afraid. I have to agree with your speculation so far. It fits well."

"Thanks, Gianni, mate."

"Thank you, Dr Grappa," said Owusu and Krol in turn.

Owusu turned to address Lance and Pawel. "OK, gentlemen. We have much work to do. I'm going to make a quick call to the station and get a team started in Filmer Road. Sergeant, you can decide where we're having lunch, before we visit the rabbi's warren. You have his address?"

"Glad you're still in the mood for jokes, Sir. Yes, I have the rabbi's address."

"Sorry, Sergeant. I should be more sensitive. Tell you what, lunch is on me."

"It'll be OK, Pav, mate. We'll catch him. Anyway, if he's done his research on Lena, he'll know not to fuck with her. Plus, she's got you keeping an eye on her as well."

***

So short was the delay between Owusu's release of the doorbell button and the opening of Jeremy Cotton's front door, that the rabbi must have been standing behind it in wait when she and D.S. Krol arrived at his home on Gastein Road.

"Please come in, Officers. Let me show you through to the living room." Rabbi Jeremy Cotton led them through the first door on the left, just up the narrow hall and into the well-heated and lavishly decorated front room. It looked less like the home of a man who worshipped God, and more of a shrine to Louis Armstrong, a colourful portrait of whom loomed large above the mantelpiece in a forty by thirty-inch brass picture frame.

Jeremy Cotton was a tall and wide man in his late forties with a round face encrusted in a thick black bush of untamed hair, and an enormous beard to match. It was as if John Lennon had sworn off hairbrushes and healthy eating in his later years, while attempting to hide any trace of his Liverpool origins. His voice was a penetrative baritone, whose dynamic range appeared to be simply on and off, and it seemed to bring him much joy when set to on.

The rabbi gestured towards the black patent leather sofa beneath Satchmo's omnibenevolent gaze, and to the assortment of fresh fruit and cake accompanied by two empty plates, which were unambiguously positioned for them on the coffee table in front. "Help yourselves, please. The kettle's boiled. Tea or coffee?"

"Tea please. Milk and one," said Owusu.

"Coffee, milk no sugar, please," said Krol.

"I'll be back in a sec. Make yourselves comfortable, Officers."

Owusu and Krol silently and independently observed the room during the two minutes before the rabbi's return.

"Thank you, rabbi," said Owusu, as he handed her a mug of tea. The black text on the plain white mug read 'I'm not yelling. I'M JUST JEWISH'.

"Call me Jeremy, please." The rabbi somehow managed to combine haughtiness and humility in the same tone. "And coffee for you," he said, handing Pawel a mug with a blue Star of David and the words "JUST JEW IT!"

"Thank you," said Pawel.

"Let's begin," said Owusu, transferring what she gauged to be an appropriately appreciative but not gluttonous amount of cake and fruit onto the plate in front of her. "I'm Detective Inspector Esi Owusu, and this is Detective Sergeant Pawel Krol."

"I'll do my best to help you both. Was it you I spoke to on the phone, Sergeant Krol?"

"That's right, yes. We're hoping you can help us with our investigation."

"An investigation that concerns my congregation . . ." Rabbi Cotton paused for a moment. "And a burglar?"

"I'm afraid it's somewhat more serious than that, Jeremy," said Owusu. "You see the burglar was found murdered, rather brutally and elaborately."

"In a manner that reflected Jewish symbolism I take it?"

"No, that's not the connection."

"Then you suspect one of the members for some other reason?"

"I think it's best if we ask the questions. I appreciate you're just trying to help, but we'll get to the answers much more quickly this way around."

"Of course. Please ask away."

"Thank you," said Owusu, taking a sip of tea before continuing. "First of all, are you aware of any of your members being burgled around five years ago, give or take one or two?"

"I can't say I am. That doesn't mean it didn't happen. Yes, we do live up to the stereotype of being top of the list at keeping up with the goss, and right down at the bottom for keeping secrets, but that long ago, I don't know. I started running the synagogue here three years ago when we, that is the trustees and myself, established it at the Grove Neighbourhood Centre."

"The trustees?" said Pawel.

"Three of them. The four of us decide everything that happens, in co-operation with the management of the venue that is, and we also co-ordinate with other synagogues in West London to make sure we don't miss anything important."

"Can you provide their details?"

"Sure, Sergeant. There's Simon Levy, Rebecca Freedman and my mother, Sheila Cotton. Here are their phone numbers, printed on a recent newsletter."

"Thank you, Jeremy," said Owusu. "Next, can you tell us if the name Jason Bampton means anything to you? If you know of any connection between him and any of your congregation?"

"I'm not God, I'm afraid. I just work for him. Haha." The rabbi gave the two detectives time to respond in kind. They declined the opportunity, though Pawel gave a courteous nod. Without looking defeated, Jeremy added, "You'll have to speak to the members yourselves."

"We'd rather not wait until Saturday. I'm afraid we haven't yet revealed how serious the events are so far. Before Jason Bampton, the burglar in question, was murdered, an associate of ours was taunted with an email, most likely from the killer, stating an intention to kill someone, giving a single clue that was eventually reflected in the way that the body was discovered."

"I heard the news story about the dead body in the bin bag. So that was him?"

"And there was also a . . . ." Pawel stopped when he felt a subtle but firm stamp on the top of his foot.

Owusu continued, "And there has since been another email, with a one-word clue: cheder."

"I've heard the phrase 'death by cheder' often enough. But this puts a different spin on it altogether. Are you suggesting we suspend the cheder classes for now? It'll mean a few disappointed twelve-year-olds and a few difficult conversations with their parents, but now I think about it, that actually wouldn't be a fate worse than death."

"Quite. And you now must understand why we cannot wait until Saturday for a chance to speak with your congregation."

"You won't have to. It's Sukkot this week. That's why I'm not at work today. We usually take the first two days off. Most synagogues would have something going on every day, though since our premises aren't ours during the week, the best we could get was one evening slot on Wednesday. But you can expect to see almost as many people there as you would on a Saturday."

"Thank you, that's most fortunate," said Owusu, before taking the remaining piece of cake from her plate.

"In the meantime, please could you put the word out with as many members as you can reach, especially parents of children attending cheder? Ask them about recent burglaries, and the name Jason Bampton."

"Of course."

"And forgive me for asking this question – I have to, I'm afraid – but where were you on Thursday night between eleven pm and three am?"

"I see. Well, I had a band rehearsal that finished around ten-ish, and then I was in The Half Moon having a few beers with the rest of the trumpet section until closing time. Must have left around quarter past eleven. After that I came home, went through my usual bedtime routine, and slept."

"Well, thank you very much for your time, and your generous hospitality, Rabbi Cotton," said Owusu, standing up and handing him her card. "If you think of anything else worth mentioning before Wednesday, please give us a call."

He pocketed the card without breaking eye contact. "Don't mention it. Let's hope you catch this meshuggeneh. I tell you I won't be inviting him to *my* funeral." He went ahead of the two detectives, out into the hall and to the front door, which he held open for them.

"I see the postman's been," said D.S. Krol, stepping over a small parcel on his way out.

"So he has. Shalom, detectives."

***

The Grove Neighbourhood Centre was fairly busy on Wednesday evening. No children were present, as once the word had got out about the cheder clue, parents immediately decided not to bring them at all, but there were at least a hundred adults in attendance. They had built a sukkah in the forecourt in front of the main entrance to the building and were adding further decorations in the form of plants and artworks made by the children. Parents were stood around the sukkah aiming their phone cameras, each strategically positioned to catch their own child's masterpiece in the centre of their frame.

"Inspector! Sergeant! Welcome!" The lavish and brightly coloured garments loosely draped around Rabbi Cotton's substantial frame were surprisingly inconspicuous in front of a scenery of children's paintings and papier-mâché sculptures, but the rabbi's voice could be heard south of the river during times of light traffic.

Owusu wove her way through the congregation towards him, with Pawel Krol following just behind. "Thank you for allowing us to conduct our investigation during your festival, Rabbi Cotton."

"Jeremy, please, Inspector."

"Thank you," Owusu repeated. "Did anyone you spoke to have any information to share at all?"

"Not exactly, but when everyone had arrived not long ago, I mentioned that you would be coming this evening, and a few people seemed keen to speak to you. I told them they could approach you directly. Can we get you anything to eat or drink?"

"Do you have any fruit juice?" asked D.S. Krol.

"There's punch!"

"Not while we're on duty, but thanks all the same."

"Come on, Sergeant. Let's find somewhere to stand and look approachable."

Pawel nodded and Owusu led him away towards the edge of the forecourt where it met the pavement of the street. She reached into her pocket, pulled out a Twix and handed it to him. "Stress affecting your blood sugar, is it, Sergeant?"

"Feels like it, Sir. Thank you!" he said, accepting the bar and unwrapping it immediately. He ate it quickly under the cover of Rabbi Cotton's booming vocal pronouncement.

"IF I MAY HAVE EVERYONE'S ATTENTION FOR JUST A MOMENT. THE TWO POLICE DETECTIVES ARE NOW HERE AND YOU MAY APPROACH THEM IF YOU HAVE ANY INFORMATION TO HELP WITH THEIR INVESTIGATION. THANK YOU. MOADIM L'SIMCHA!" He followed this with a laugh, indicating that he may have used the phrase ironically.

"Chagim u'zmanim l'sasson," responded the crowd.

Within one minute a frail-looking elderly lady approached. "Excuse me, Officers," she said gently but with a piercing timbre to her voice.

"Thank you for speaking to us. I'm Detective Inspector Esi Owusu, and this is Detective Sergeant Pawel Krol. Are you able to tell us anything about burglaries in your area, or a man named Jason Bampton?"

"Jason Bampton, yes. That's the name of the man in the news. He was murdered."

"Yes, please continue."

"They found him in the street, in a bin bag. I saw it on the news. Only I'm afraid I didn't get a good look. I haven't been able to find my glasses for a while."

"That's OK, madam. What else can you tell us?"

"My name is Sarah. Sarah Hamberger."

"Very good, Ms Hamberger. And what's your connection to Mr Bampton?"

"Connection? Oh no. I saw it on the news. I thought you should know."

"I see. Well, that's very thoughtful of you, Ms Hamberger. Can you remember where you were that night?"

"I was at home in bed, just the same as every night."

"All right. Please do let us know if you have any more information."

"He was a burglar. The rabbi told me. You should ask him if he knows anything else."

"Yes, we certainly shall, Ms Hamberger. We won't keep you from the festivities any longer."

D.S. Krol was clearly feeling more himself, as evidenced by his barely suppressed sniggers, which became significantly less suppressed once Sarah Hamberger had turned her back to them.

"Go and get me a glass of punch, Sergeant," said Owusu. "Stop. I was joking."

Pawel set his raised foot back down next to the other. "You handled her very diplomatically, Sir," he said.

"The next one's yours, Sergeant. Here she comes now."

"Hello detectives. My name's Sheila. I'm Jeremy's mum. I'm so proud of him. He could lose some weight though. I'm a bit worried about the size of his belly, and he definitely could do with a haircut."

"He's been a very gracious host, Ms Cotton," said Pawel. "We're looking for more information that might connect members of the community here with the deceased Jason Bampton. I imagine that you would have already told your son if you knew something."

"You're very kind, but a gracious host would have offered you a drink by now. Let me get you some wine or some punch."

"We're on duty, Ms. Cotton."

"Please, call me Sheila."

"Thank you, Sheila. Might you have been burgled at all? Would you remember anything about it if so?"

"Actually yes, I was. It must have been about four years ago now."

"What was your address at the time, and what was taken?"

"I was living in the same place I do now. I've been there for decades."

"Where's that, Sheila?"

She pointed directly between the two detectives' heads, out into the street, behind which was a T-junction. "Right there. Lamington Street. It's a bit far to see with my eyesight, but you can probably make it out with your young healthy vision."

"What was taken by the burglars, do you remember?"

"Not a lot, oddly. They went through every room, left it all in a terrible state. Things were thrown around everywhere; books swept off shelves; drawers all opened. But the only things I noticed missing were some small pieces of jewellery. They were quite valuable, and I'd had them a while. But the computer, the TV, my passport, and even Jeremy's spare trumpet, were all left behind. It was the violation that upset me more than the material loss."

"Fits the profile," said Pawel, turning to Owusu, and back to Sheila Cotton. "Do you know if other houses in the neighbourhood were burgled around that time?"

"Oh no. I only spoke to the police." There was a dip in the confidence conveyed in Sheila's voice. It was momentary. "They wouldn't have told me even if I'd asked probably."

"Probably," agreed Pawel, to save time.

"I know my next-door neighbours were left alone on both sides. I didn't speak to anyone else here about it, I'm afraid. We only founded this synagogue three years ago, you see. I used to travel to Holland Park for shul every Saturday before then."

"And no-one mentioned a burglary here once this synagogue was established?"

"I'm afraid not."

"And can you tell us where you were that Thursday night?"

"I was at home. I phoned my friend Lisa from my landline at around nine. We must have spoken for at least an hour. Then I made myself a hot water bottle and went to bed."

"Was anyone there with you?"

"Oh yes. My husband. He was there all night. He stayed up a bit later than me watching telly."

"Well, thank you, Sheila. You've been very helpful."

"Oh, jolly good."

"Enjoy the rest of your evening."

"Righty ho," she said as she turned to walk away.

D.S. Krol turned to Owusu with a grin. She allowed a small smile to crack. "If I'd known that chatting with old ladies was enough to pick you up, I'd have hung onto my Twix, Sergeant."

"I appreciate it, Sir, I really do."

"Excuse me, detectives. You're here asking about burglaries, I understand."

Facing forwards again, the two police officers found a short woman standing where the rabbi's mother had previously been. She appeared to be in her early forties, with long dark hair tied into a ponytail, her frame concealed beneath a thick brown woollen coat, the hem of which hung below her knees.

"I see you've been speaking to my neighbour, Mrs Cotton."

"Does that mean you also live just over there in Lamington Street?" asked Owusu, pointing her thumb back over her shoulder with a jabbing motion.

The woman nodded carefully.

"I'm D.I. Owusu and this is D.S. Krol. May we have your name, please?"

"Sophie Dimsdale."

"And were you burgled as well?"

"Yes, about three years ago, not long after I'd moved here from Hendon."

"And when you mentioned it to the congregation, did anyone else say they'd had a similar experience, Ms Dimsdale?"

"I didn't. I mean, I didn't know them then. I was still attending shul in Hendon out of habit for a year after I moved. This place had just been established, as I understand it now, but it didn't occur to me to look."

"Of course, it's funny how our habits blind us sometimes," said Owusu, before going quiet instead of asking another question.

Pawel took the reins. "Did you report the burglary? Do you remember what was taken?"

"Yes, I did. Police recommended some new security measures. There's no way I can remember the crime number now though I'm afraid. The only thing I remember actually going missing was a gold and sapphire necklace that I kept in my sock drawer."

"Thank you. Don't worry about the crime number. We can look up the report from your name, street address and date range."

"Can you tell us anything else? Perhaps the name Jason Bampton rings a bell?" said Owusu.

"Jason Bampton, no. Oh maybe. No. It just sounds like the name of someone who'd go on *Strictly*, but that's not it, is it?"

"I'm afraid not, Ms Dimsdale. Thank you for your help, anyway."

"Not at all, detectives."

"Ah, detectives!" Sheila Cotton had returned, almost barging Sophie Dimsdale to the floor, and narrowly avoiding launching the contents of the enormous tray she was carrying into the air. "I've got you some nice non-alcoholic fruit punch, and some bagels and some of my homemade cakes." She appeared to use the word 'some' to mean an amount that would defeat even a stereotypical New York police detective from American television. "Here, now you take the juice, and let me plonk down these two plates next to you. Can't have you going without, just because you're on duty!"

Owusu and Krol had no choice but to accept a glass from the tray as it was thrust towards each of their chests in turn. At this point Owusu noticed that Sophie Dimsdale was no longer standing near them. "That's very kind of you, Mrs Cotton. We definitely appreciate the fruit juice. We'll do our best with the food. There is rather a lot of it."

"Righty ho," seemed to be Sheila Cotton's catchphrase.

"Oh, and if I were you, I would make sure you speak to him," she said, turning and indicating to a tall thin lightly tanned man towards the centre of the forecourt, with a large afro extending from the top and back of his head, supporting a small white kufi hat riding atop his hair like a novice surfer at high tide. He was handing over a glasses case to Sarah Hamberger, who looked confused at first, before gratefully taking it and placing it in her handbag.

"Any particular reason? What can you tell us about him?" said Owusu.

"His name is Rayan Chelouche, and I don't like him."

Owusu waited for more. More wasn't forthcoming, so she gave a prod. "And why's that, Mrs Cotton?"

"I don't like him coming here when he isn't even Jewish, for a start. He seems to know everyone, tries to be everyone's friend, and is suspiciously well-connected for a bingo caller."

"I see."

"Plus, he's a cheat."

"You could have led with that, Mrs Cotton, but please continue."

"Last week I was sure I was about to win the bingo, when suddenly out of nowhere, that Sarah Hamberger, who couldn't find the numbers on a calculator on a good day, had a full house. I'm sure he helped her cheat. I hope you can find out why."

Owusu nodded gently but earnestly.

Sheila continued. "He's also very pro-Palestinian, which I think is very unfair. And he's such a smooth-talker. Everyone thinks he's so amazing. He calls the bingo and he smiles and looks pretty, and I don't like him."

"Well thank you for that information, Mrs Cotton. It could prove invaluable," said Owusu, channelling her inner Alan Rickman. "And thank you very much for the food and drink. That was very thoughtful of you." This second thank you was delivered with due enthusiasm. The D.I. took the opportunity to back up her statement by grabbing a cupcake and immediately peeling away its paper case. She raised it as one would a champagne glass before inserting it between her teeth.

"You're very welcome. Wish you health to wear it!"

"Excuse me?" Owusu held up the empty paper case in puzzlement.

"I do beg your pardon. I mean, B'tayavon!"

"Indeed," replied Owusu. "Sergeant, why don't you go and have a word with Mr Chelouche over there, while I tackle this workload just presented to us here."

"Yes, Sir. Save me some, Sir."

Chapter 5:

D.S. Krol knocked back the contents of his glass and found a table on which to discreetly leave the empty receptacle, as he made his way to introduce himself to Sheila's scapegoat, still standing among the crowd in front of the sukkah. He felt especially uneasy about picking out the one Muslim in the middle of a Jewish crowd, approaching him with questions, when he and Owusu had been waiting for the others to approach. Nonetheless, a lead was a lead, and it would be a mistake not to follow it.

"Hope you're not racial profiling, Officer," Chelouche said, smiling, in a gentle teasing tone and a disarming North African accent with a rich blend of Arabic consonants and French vowels.

Pawel hesitated for a moment.

"Relax, I'm joking!" The accent had evaporated. Chelouche was a Londoner. He appeared to be in his mid-fifties. He was certainly tall, though his hair added an extra seven or eight inches, giving him the stature of a basketball player. "Rayan Chelouche," he said, extending his right hand. "How can I help you?"

"Detective Sergeant Pawel Krol," Pawel replied, shaking it. "I'll be honest, Mr Chelouche. I don't have any reason to single you out at all, but a lady we spoke to suggested you might know something that would help with our investigation."

"How so?"

"She seemed to believe you're well-connected across multiple sections of the community, and given your presence here, her prejudice notwithstanding, I thought perhaps you might indeed know something useful."

"Ah, Mrs Cotton. Yes, I'm afraid she and I aren't on the best of terms. Actually, I was just here to return Mrs Hamberger's glasses. She left them behind at the bingo last week."

"You're the bingo caller, is that right?"

Chelouche nodded.

Pawel felt somewhat more relaxed. "And when and where does that take place?"

"There's a small community college on Queen Caroline Street, just up from the primary school. I teach a couple of evening classes there. French on Tuesdays. Arabic on Wednesdays. I need to get going soon as I start my class tonight at seven o'clock. They also offer courses for GCSE and A-level retakes to adults, some BTECs too. On Thursdays I run the bingo evening. It's exactly what you might imagine. Old ladies getting fiercely competitive, with all the enthusiasm of a crowd of drunk football fans but only ten percent of the violence."

"Mrs Cotton said something about you helping one of her rivals to an undeserved victory."

"She called me a cheat, yes. Look, as I say, they get fiercely competitive. I just call the numbers and follow the health and safety rules. Other than that, it's up to them to play fair. But I didn't see anything untoward, and all of Mrs Hamberger's numbers had been called by then. Seemed a fair win to me."

"Don't worry. The Met tends not to encroach on the territory of the European Bingo Union, or whatever the governing body of the game is called."

"The National Bingo Game Association. It does exist."

"Very good. So you teach languages, call bingo, return lost property to little old ladies. Anything else?"

"I'm a freelance handyman. I get booked for odd jobs in the local area during the day and work three evenings a week, as I said. Tomorrow I'm installing some outdoor lighting in a garden in north Ealing, ahead of Diwali and Guy Fawkes night, for example."

"And whereabouts do you live?"

"North Acton."

"I see. Have you been burgled at all in the last five years or so?"

"No, I haven't."

"Everything OK for you and the inspector, Sergeant?" boomed Rabbi Jeremy Cotton as he glided around members of the gathering with more agility than seemed plausible for a man of his volume. "I see my mother's been inundating you both with food and drink. Please don't feel obliged to finish it all. I've made that mistake repeatedly and I'm paying for it now."

He gave a deep and deafening laugh that masked what ought to have been harsh transient *thwack* sounds as he firmly slapped his belly with alternating hands. Rayan Chelouche stood still, patiently. If he was waiting for eye contact with the rabbi, it never came. Pawel blinked and the rabbi was gone, vanishing just as smoothly as he had appeared.

Pawel decided it best to pretend they'd never been interrupted. "Does the name Jason Bampton mean anything to you?"

Rayan Chelouche appeared to agree. "Only that I heard it on the news recently. I thought that might be what this is about."

"And may I ask you where you were on the night it happened? Thursday before last, that is."

"I see. The bingo session ended at nine o'clock as usual, and then I stayed late to mark some homework from my two language classes. I must have said good night to the site staff at around eleven. Then I went home, where I live with my wife and youngest son who's in sixth form."

"OK, well thank you for your time, Mr Chelouche. I really appreciate it. I'll let you get off to your French class now."

"Arabic tonight, but thank you. If I were you, I would hurry back and get some cake before your colleague polishes the last of it off."

Oh to be that tall, Pawel thought to himself as he headed back towards Owusu, wondering if and how she'd managed to get on the outside of so much cake in so little time. *The observation powers it would bring.*

When he reached her, he found he had a rival for Owusu's attention. Not in the remaining food, the immediate threat to which had been somewhat exaggerated, but in a young woman of medium height with shoulder-length light-brown hair and blue eyes, already in mid-conversation with the detective inspector.

"Yes, I'm doing my postgrad there, a master's in Artificial Intelligence and Data Engineering. If everything goes right, it should be completed by the end of April next year."

"What's your project on?" said Owusu, while Pawel reached for a cake.

"I'm creating an audio chatbot, which will, if I'm successful, be able to learn to identify and distinguish different personality types. In theory there would be two major practical applications. One would be to simulate good personality fits for human interaction, for example to function as effective colleagues in a professional environment. And the other would be to be able to predict compatibility between pairs or groups of humans based on their individual personalities."

"I suppose you've considered the implications of outsourcing judgement of character to machines?" said Owusu.

"I'm still considering them. This is just research after all. I'm not working for Google or anything like that just yet. There'll be a whole PhD's worth of work to come before that becomes a conversation worth having."

"And how long have you been attending here?" asked Pawel.

"Just a couple of years. My godmother's sister attends here. I don't know if she's here tonight. I've only just arrived. I was working on my code all afternoon."

"I wasn't aware godparents were a thing in Judaism," said Owusu.

"They're not an explicit part of the faith, no. But they're not exactly excluded from it either, and they are a British tradition."

"Like Christmas?" Pawel suggested.

"You could say that, Officer."

"D.S. Pawel Krol, sorry, I should have introduced myself."

"Anyway, lovely chatting with you both. Sorry I couldn't give you any more information about the burglar. I'd really like to see if there's any booze left – I know I've pushed my luck with the timing."

"Of course. Go for it. Thank you," said Owusu.

"Did I miss anything important?" asked Pawel, with half an eye on the young lady's quest for the last glass of punch.

"Just now? No. Did Mr Chelouche have anything useful to say, Sergeant?"

"He gave his side of the story between himself and Mrs Cotton. And he is fairly well-connected, with his fingers in a few different pies. Freelance handyman. But I'd say he's a well-adjusted member of the community. The West London community, I mean."

"You seem quite charmed by him, Sergeant."

"Perhaps, Sir. Also, the rabbi completely blanked him."

"Mummy's boy, perhaps?"

"Perhaps, Sir."

Owusu raised her right arm, gesturing sideways and turning her head to match. She led Pawel out towards the street. Once they were less likely to be overheard, she resumed their conversation. "Did you notice anything odd from any of the conversations we've had this evening?"

"I noticed you react to something, Sir, and then I realised what it was when you pretended not to have. Sophie Dimsdale said she lived just down the road from here for a year before she started coming, and never apparently in that time did she notice a synagogue on her doorstep. When you didn't question her on how she could have missed it for that long, I nearly asked her myself."

"And I would be having strong words with you now if you'd done so, Sergeant. Good. There might be an innocent if unusual explanation for it. Perhaps she's extremely introverted, or neurodivergent in a way that accounts for it. But it has certainly got my attention."

***

Peter Owusu put down his copy of Friday morning's *Guardian*. "Have you seen this, Esi?"

"Obviously not," replied his wife.

"There's an interview with the manager of a strip club. Didn't you say you had dealings with strippers last week?"

"Let me see," said the inspector, holding out a hand for her husband to hand over the newspaper. She found the piece in question and began to scrutinise it. "Yes, that's the manager we had to speak to about safety of some of the strippers."

"So you wouldn't recommend that particular club, then?" He knew what was coming. He couldn't resist.

"I can recommend a very comfy sofa for tonight, if that's what interests you my dear. And for the foreseeable."

Peter chuckled. "Love you."

"You have no choice, husband."

"I know. You're far too attractive for me not to."

His wife growled both abrasively and affectionately at the same time, in a manner perfected by few other than Marge Simpson.

"That's odd," said the inspector.

"What is?"

"The writing style looks familiar. It looks like rage bait, but flipped upside down. It's pro-sex-worker but designed to make people angry at the same time. It's more like a mirror universe *Daily Express* than a progressive piece."

"Who's the columnist?" Peter asked.

"Someone called Angela Clair."

"What's she written before? You know I'm not a big reader of the papers."

"Nothing I remember," he replied. "She must be new. Anything in there to shed any light on your case?"

"Not really. She doesn't even mention the ticketed party that the two girls I interviewed discussed. The security blunder is mentioned in a lot of detail though. Looks like those girls went to the press. No matter. The case was already resolved. I hope they got some money for their trouble."

Peter nodded in agreement and then went to retrieve his breakfast from the toaster.

***

Saturday began for Rabbi Jeremy Cotton just like any other Shabbat. Sukkot had been a success, despite limited access to the premises during the week. Despite all of the complications it brought, especially when it came to keeping half a dozen fiercely proud and generally fierce mothers and grandmothers from making him the poster boy for paracetamol, he was grateful for the cancellation of the day's pre-service cheder session. The opportunity to spend the early morning at home in peace, working on his Dizzy Gillespie transcriptions instead of in the company of entitled little shits, made him feel that he was somewhat up on the deal.

"Baruch atah adonai eloheinu melech ha olam," he began, holding the full attention of the congregation. He felt dizzy, but continued. ". . ." But the words wouldn't sound. In their place came a dry cough. He spluttered and managed an underwhelming, "Excuse me." Looking over to the table at the side, he was relieved to see the water jug full, just as it was every week.

He turned towards it and took two steps. Again he coughed. His next step didn't land. He found himself staring downwards as his left foot slipped behind him, passing underneath his groin. His right knee gave way. The rabbi's shortness of breath gave way to a searing burst of agony in his chest, and another in his left knee as his patella smacked against the hard wooden floor. He didn't feel his forehead do the same, though no-one could have missed the sound it made. He never felt anything again.

Chapter 6:

Sheila Cotton was right up in the faces of Owusu and Krol as soon as they entered the forecourt. Most of the congregation had conglomerated by the end of the building furthest from its entrance, led there by the officers already present as they roped off the site of Rabbi Cotton's collapse and prepared to begin the investigation. Onlookers would certainly, however, have had no difficulty in making out the rabbi's mother's every word.

"Why didn't you stop him? I warned you! He was right there, and I warned you about him and you should have stopped him!"

Owusu drew a deep breath and told herself to keep calm. "I'm sorry, Mrs Cotton. What do you mean? We've only just arrived."

"On Wednesday. I told you I didn't like him. I told you he was a bad man. That Rayan Chelouche."

"You told us he was a cheat," Owusu said, maintaining her calm delivery. "I'm sorry about your son, but what does that have to do with bingo? What are we missing?"

"I asked Jeremy to have a word with him. He said he was going to go to the community college and complain about the cheating, and about Mr Chelouche's bias towards Palestinians as well. He thinks all Jews are in the wrong. You can just tell he does from looking at him. And he was there on Wednesday and you talked to him. Why didn't you stop him? Will you be going to arrest him now?"

"We'll be speaking to everyone with the potential to have been involved. That includes Mr Chelouche and everyone who was present here this morning. We'll discover what happened as quickly as we can."

"Well, I'm sure you can find his address. Go and arrest him now. Quick, before he flees the country! I'll make him confess myself if I have to!"

"That won't be necessary, Mrs Cotton. But you could help us immensely by describing what you saw this morning."

An expression of mild delight made a very brief appearance on Sheila Cotton's face. It had completely vanished by the time she spoke again, only seconds later. "The service began as normal. Jeremy began a prayer about ten minutes in, and then he lost his voice and was coughing. Then he collapsed and didn't move. We called for an ambulance, but even if there'd been one already in the building I don't think it would have made a difference. It looked like he had a heart attack."

D.S. Krol looked up at the energetically grieving mother from his notebook as he scribbled on an empty page. "So, he collapsed spontaneously. Possibly had a heart attack, yes? Was anyone near him when it happened?"

"No. We were all stood back from him. We were watching him and joining in with the responses. No-one went near him once the service had begun."

"Was Mr Chelouche in attendance?" he said.

"No, he's not one of us."

"So why do you suspect him? How do you believe he could be responsible?" said Owusu.

"In fact, why would we suspect anyone at all?" added Pawel.

"I don't know. That's your job to find out. Maybe he poisoned the water when he came here last week."

"We'll be sure to look into that, Mrs Cotton."

Owusu took over once again. "Did you notice anything unusual before the service began?"

"No, it was all normal. Oh. It's probably nothing, but Jeremy did say something odd. He thanked me for a present I'd sent him, but I didn't remember sending one. It could be my memory. I do find nice jumpers for him in M&S and pop them in the post. Maybe he hadn't opened one for weeks and had just got around to it. It probably is nothing after all. I still think you need to arrest Rayan Chelouche."

"We'll be investigating fully, Mrs Cotton, you can be certain of that. And thank you for the information. Once again, we're very sorry about your son."

Sheila's fingers rigidly curved around an invisible cricket ball in each of her trembling hands held out in front of her as her chin bobbed up and down, synchronised with her elbows. She took in a harsh whistling gasp, rising in pitch and volume. "My grandchildren! What about my grandchildren?"

"What about them? Were they left at home alone?"

"No, of course not! I've lived my whole life working hard towards two things in a happy retirement: bestowing loving abuse upon my grandchildren, and being able to get Radio 4 anywhere in my house. And now I will never have grandchildren. Oh God!" She followed with wails that undulated in pitch and volume evocative of the most enthusiastic amateur performers of classical theatre.

Then before Owusu or Krol could add another word, Sheila Cotton turned and strode away from them, wailing towards a small crowd of men and women, most of them roughly her age. "Oh my God! Oh my Jeremy! Oh my God! Oh my Jeremy!"

Owusu walked in the opposite direction, gesturing to Pawel to follow her until they were a far enough distance away to be able to hear themselves think again. "I'll call Lance now."

She pulled out her phone and dialled. "Hi Lance."

. . .

"I'm afraid so. The rabbi. We're told he collapsed in the middle of the community centre just after the service began. His mother said it looked like a heart attack. Scene investigation is underway, and in light of your email correspondence I'm already treating it as a murder. Obviously, we do not want the punters or anyone else to know that yet. We'll get the body sent over to Gianni as quickly as possible. D.S. Krol is about to get a warrant to search the deceased's house. Please let us know if you're sent anything else. We'll share what we find with you too, unofficially for now."

. . .

"Yes, I'm sure we can do that again. OK, we'll be in touch. Bye for now."

As she ended the call her stomach colluded with her brain to recall memories of the feast served to her and the D.S. almost right where they were currently standing. "OK Sergeant. Let's get some witness statements. And I could murder a tea. Or at least observe it die from what appears to be a heart attack suspiciously close in time and location to a confirmed murder."

"Yes, Sir. Do you want me to see if the kiddush food is still available?"

***

"And that's everything we have so far," said Pawel to Lance as they walked together into the Hammersmith Ram.

They strolled right through the atrium, along the bar and into the larger open area that extended behind the neighbouring shop fronts on the eastern end of King Street. Sahana's waving hand was easy to spot by a table at the back. Sitting next to her was a young Indian man wearing an outfit that would be consistent with most people's interpretations of the term 'smart casual', albeit with only minimal heed paid to casual. Indeed, his attire would have satisfied a lot of workplaces' professional dress codes.

85

He stood up offering an eager handshake both to Pawel and to Lance in turn, while Sahana skipped round from behind the table, extending both arms for big hugs. She waited patiently for the handshaking to conclude before she homed in.

"Vineel Eshwar," said the handshaker. "Nice to meet you both."

"Yes, sorry, I should have said." Sahana released the second of her temporary captees and moved to make proper introductions. "This is Vineel. He's a friend of my brother's, over from Bangalore on a work trip."

"Hi, Vineel. What kind of work, mate?"

"I do data analysis for an insurance company. And you must be the famous detective Lance Pomegranate." Vineel spoke with complete sincerity.

"I don't know about famous, mate. The rest is accurate though."

"Sahana told me a lot about you. You're very good, she says."

"Well thank you. And did she tell you anything about Pav here?"

"Police detective, is that right?" Vineel turned to face Pawel. "You put two criminals in hospital, I heard. It must have been like a scene from a Tamil film."

"Actually, those two criminals put *me* in hospital," said Pawel. "But I put three of them in prison afterwards. Detective Sergeant Pawel Krol."

"Oh. Very good. And at least you are showing no sign of your injuries, Detective Sergeant."

"You can call me Pawel."

"So, what's the latest?" Sahana said, sitting back down, cueing the others to follow suit. "Did you find out anything from the synagogue? Any more emails?"

"Thanks for this, Sahana," said Lance, sipping the pint that had been waiting in front of his seat. "We found out quite a lot from the rabbi. And now the rabbi's dead."

"Shit!"

"His name was Jeremy Cotton."

Sahana sat up straight with a judder in her neck, rippling through to her hair. "Hold on. Big bloke? Lots of dark hair and a big bushy beard?"

"Yes actually."

"Fuck. I know him. I can't stand him, to be honest, but that's weird."

"Oh yes, he was a jazz trumpeter too, wasn't he?" said Pawel.

"He definitely fancied himself as one. But if you ask me, he thought he was a lot better than he is, er was. Arrogant twat, to be honest. Sorry. Little bit sorry he's dead, I suppose. Sorry."

"Small world, but yeah. We couldn't stop his death in time. And no more emails yet. Not even to gloat."

"Emails?" asked Vineel.

"Oh, sorry, yeah, Lance. Is it OK if we tell Vineel about this? I think we can trust him."

"I can tell you a few things anyway," said Lance. "I was contacted by the killer, posing as a 419 scammer at first, before he started taunting me, telling me he was going to kill, before killing. And he's done it twice. Using the alphabet for clues."

"Like *The ABC Murders*?" said Vineel, looking excited.

"Just like *The ABC Murders*," Lance replied, shaking his head. He was already bored of mentioning that book title, and it had been one of his favourites until very recently.

"Nigerian, is he?"

"Who knows? Picked a name that could be Nigerian for all I know, but that wouldn't guarantee much even if it were."

"What's the name?" said Sahana.

"Malcolm Dombattu?" said Pawel, whose tone implied he was questioning his own memory.

"Yeah," confirmed Lance.

"And a 419 scammer, did you say?" said Vineel.

"Posing as one at first anyway," said Lance. "He was never after my money though. Literally said as much, a couple of replies in."

"He's Indian."

"And I thought Jews were the champions of putting their own down."

"No. Well yes, you're probably not wrong – I mean strictly I'd have to say you are, since you were leaning towards Jews rather than Indians – but yeah, you're probably not wrong to make the comparison."

Lance looked at Pawel and, reassured by a blank expression that could easily have been his own, offered a shrug, which Pawel gladly reciprocated.

Vineel appeared to have suddenly realised that he was expected to make a point and to make sense. "But no, that's not what I mean."

"What do you mean, then?" said Sahana, her heritage offering no more insight into Vineel's train of thought than Lance's or Pawel's.

"The name. It's a joke on the numbers four one nine in Kannada. Naalku Omdu Ombattu. Say it quickly and it sounds really close. Your killer is from South India, maybe even Bangalore, I guarantee it."

"Do you agree, Sahana?" asked Pawel.

"Don't look at me," she said. "I only know Hindi and Marathi and my Marathi is shit."

"Shit," said Lance, though the repetition was entirely coincidental. "Can't argue with that I suppose."

"Oh, you two are back here again," said a gentle and slightly provocative feminine voice from behind Lance's back. He turned around to face Laura the waitress, who appeared to remember him and Sahana as the semi-regular visitors that he would have to admit they were.

"Let me see," she said, stooping down, "are you still . . ." she peered underneath Lance's chair from behind. ". . . yep." Laura had a look more of satisfaction than surprise on her face. "Even in this weather!"

"All weather," said Lance, pride emanating from his enlarged cheeks.

"Fair play," she said, standing up straight. "Will you be lining up the tequilas again tonight? Are you all playing?"

"Not tonight, thanks. Got a lot of work to do tomorrow. Just the eight pints for me, then I'm setting a hard limit."

The two people at the table who knew he was joking exchanged a chuckle, while Vineel showed intense admiration on his face. Laura simply rolled her eyes, picked up their empty glasses and carried them away.

***

There might eventually come a day when Dr Gianni Grappa's entrance into the office of Lance Pomegranate would not be greeted by two police officers and one barefoot Australian breaking their impatient stares at the door, but this would not be that day. This was just another October Monday morning, on which nothing that threatened to break the universe would take place, and today certainly presented no threat to causality on the scale of Dr Grappa arriving within a few minutes of the time he agreed to.

Lance wasn't keen on any more silence. "So, while we're waiting, what are we thinking? Poison?"

"He dropped dead in the middle of the room with the service already underway, according to the witness statements. No-one was near him. So, if it wasn't just his dietary history then yes, I'd say poison," replied Owusu.

"Was anyone else showing any symptoms at all?"

"No, although once it happened, they were very careful not to touch anything."

"Shrewd bunch. Or experienced, perhaps?"

"What, all of them in on it at once?" asked Pawel incredulously.

"Never mind," said Lance, only then realising that what he'd said wasn't that funny after all.

"Regardless," Owusu said, keen to continue, "somehow someone got some poison into his system."

"Unless he had a spontaneous heart attack without any help from anyone," suggested Pawel. "Spherical people are prone to it."

"As I said, it could just be due to the rabbi's dietary history," Owusu repeated. "But while we're waiting it wouldn't hurt to get brainstorming on the other possibilities."

"I'd be very surprised if it turned out to be drawn-out suicide by cholesterol," said Lance. "Not in a synagogue, right after we've been tipped off by a killer, Pav, mate," said Lance.

"Unless there's anyone else that email clue could be referring to?"

"No, Lance. You're right."

The knock on the door came at last.

"Come in," said Lance in that no longer exclusively Australian tone of ending sentences that clearly aren't questions with a raise in pitch usually associated with questions. The hand holding the cane with the bone carving of the god Asclepius came into view first, then the burgundy suede shoes, and finally the rest of Gianni Grappa's body, dressed in a navy linen suit and bright-yellow cotton shirt. The lights from the ceiling bounced off his hair gel directly into Lance's eyes.

"Sorry I'm late," said Dr Grappa, carrying none of the promise to avoid a recurrence that is the entire function of the word *sorry*.

"You're here now at least, Dr Grappa. Glad you could join us," said Owusu.

Lance leant to his right, reached over and patted the side of the empty armchair. "Come on, Doc, I'm itching to know what you've found out. I'll just go and re-boil the kettle for you."

Dr Grappa showed no urgency, but with the assistance of his cane he approached the chair and sank into it with more dignity than one would typically associate with sinking into a large comfortable armchair.

"Cause of death was heart failure induced by potassium cyanide, with the victim's underlying health issues also a significant factor."

"How did the poison get into his system?" said Pawel.

"Absorption through the skin and hair."

"His hat thing?" Pawel asked.

"Not exactly. We found traces of it on the kippah, but it was mostly on the hair grips used to attach it to his head."

"So he would have got it on his fingers, when putting it on, and then it would have soaked into his hair and scalp the whole time he was wearing it," said Owusu.

"Yes, and depending on when he next washed his hands, it could have been all over his fingers for some time too," said Lance.

"We also know the time of death from the witnesses," Owusu added. "So can you tell us how long the poison might have been in his system?"

"I don't think he would have put his kippah on the night before, Inspector. He'd have been dead before leaving home anyway if he had, wouldn't he Doc?" Lance scratched his head in an attempt to dismiss his awakening childhood memories of painfully attached hair grips.

"Yes, Lance. You're correct. It would have only taken one or two hours for him to die after attaching those hair grips to his head, whether with the amount I found, or even a smaller amount."

"So, someone poisoned his hair grips? They got into his home and went through his drawers?" said Pawel.

"No, mate. When would they have the chance to do that?"

"Sergeant, don't you remember what his mother said to us?"

"About Rayan Chelouche, Sir? Or her life's ambition to inflict low-level cruelty on her grandchildren?"

"No, Sergeant, about an M&S jumper, if I remember right. Or so she thought."

"He'd thanked her for a gift, Sir!"

"Yes, Sergeant. What if someone posted him a new kippah, and for convenience included some hair grips with it. The killer managed to convince him the package came from his mother, so Cotton decided to wear it for the first time when she'd be there to see him wearing it, leading a Saturday service."

"You're right, Inspector!" added Lance, excitedly. "And when he opened it up, he would have used the grips it came with. Let's say they came sealed in a separate packet, which he wouldn't need to open up before putting the thing on before heading out on Saturday."

"We need to search the rabbi's house again," said Owusu.

"And I know exactly what to look for," added Lance.

"Do I still get to have my cup of coffee?" asked Dr Grappa.

***

Lance and Pawel walked up Gastein Road until they reached Jeremy Cotton's house. Pawel still had a key from their previous search on Saturday afternoon, and their warrant was still valid.

"So, we're looking for an envelope from a parcel delivered in the post recently, yes?"

"That's right, Pav, mate," said Lance. "And any plastic bags or other containers that the hair grips might have come in. He might have put them away in a drawer before leaving home."

"OK, gloves for us each." Pawel offered a pair of light-blue disposable gloves to his friend.

"Cheers, Pav." Lance was wearing them only seconds later, though he had no intention of touching anything. He was quite content to offer a pair of eyes and let the trained police officer deal with the practicalities.

"I don't believe it," said Pawel, looking at the small table to the far end of the hall, next to the kitchen door. On it were the remnants of a medium-sized package. "I've seen this before. I nearly tripped over it on my way out of this place last week."

Next to the familiar-looking envelope was a handwritten note, which read:

"WISH YOU HEALTH TO WEAR IT! LOVE MUM"

"Ironic," said Lance. "Pav, see that little bin in the corner? Have a rummage through it."

Not exactly rummaging, D.S. Krol carefully leafed through the contents of the bin with a long set of forceps. Most of what he identified consisted of receipts, chocolate bar wrappers, a few tissues soaked in Olbas Oil, and paper cake cases, but there was also a screwed-up letter from Rabbi Cotton's bank, and a clear plastic resealable bag, empty but for droplets of liquid clinging to its inner surface.

"Bingo!" said Lance as Pawel held it up for them both to examine. "Take the bank letter as well. Might be helpful to know if there was any awkwardness in his financial situation."

"We're done? That easily?"

"Maybe. But we're going to check the rest of the house anyway."

**

Dear Mr Lance,

Having fun, yet? I certainly am, even though some so-called experts wouldn't even say I count as a serial killer yet. Let them worry not. Yet is the operative word here, of course. By the time I've finished, they'll be inventing a new term just for the elite-level masters of the art like me.

But what about you? Have you figured anything out yet? A connection from A to B to C, perhaps? You'll get more pieces of the puzzle the further we get of course, though you have to buy each one at its full price. Ellemenopy is a five-volume bumper edition. Got to be honest, I'm looking forward to that one. You've had two clues. Ready for your next? They say a picture is worth a thousand words, so if this isn't enough of a help, then I'm afraid that's what the young people refer to as a 'skill issue'. User error to you and me.

Happy sleuthing,

Lots of love,

Your friend Malcolm

Lance was still on his way home when he'd received the email. He opened up the attachment. It was a photo of a Cavalier King Charles Spaniel, and a very familiar-looking one at that. The photo was captioned in Times New Roman solid black capitals against the sky towards the top of the image. It said 'D is for Doggy'.

He put two fingers against his phone screen and zoomed in. Could that be him? It wasn't easy for him to tell, but he had a lead at least.

Chapter 7:

Las Cucharas Grasientas wasn't the sort of place to stay open too late into the evening, and Martina would almost certainly not be awake by now, so Lance had no choice but to sleep on his idea and head there early in the morning. As he got off the 220, walked along Fulham Palace Road and turned the corner into Lysia Street for the first time since the COVID pandemic had hit, a flood of memories of the Jane Alder case washed over him, triggered by the feel of the paving stones beneath his feet. They had been warmer and drier before. Now they felt cool and almost slimy, a sensation perfectly pleasant in other contexts.

Lance crossed over to the south side of the road earlier than he needed to. He wasn't feeling especially nostalgic for a close view of Jane Alder's house opposite his destination. There weren't many empty tables visible as he passed along the windowed front of the café towards the door. He absentmindedly scanned across the sea of serious faces and hands holding either cutlery, newspapers or phones. Not that he needed to stop and eat, and he didn't have time to stop and chat either, though he very much would have liked to.

Only when he entered through the front door could he see the red-tipped spiky hair of the café's proprietor and manager, Martina Vongola.

"Lance!" she called to him in her breathy Argentinian accent. "Long time!"

"Good to see you again, Martina. Do you have a moment?"

"Oh, you're here on business then. I suppose I might, if you can bear with me for another ten minutes. Half of these people should be on their way to work by then. I'd say take a seat, but I don't seem to have one at the moment."

"No wuckers, Martina. I'll just hover in the corner, out of your way for a bit. But I'll have a coffee if that's OK?"

"Sure. You will have your coffee. Thanks for being patient, Lance. It's good to see you too!"

Lance turned and wove his way around the busy tables, and stood in the far corner. He pulled his phone out of his pocket out of habit, but he wasn't really looking at his screen. He was rapidly becoming far less interested in social media these days. It all seemed so dull, repetitive, sometimes infuriating, and rarely related to any of the content he'd actually signed up for. And yet it was an involuntary action that he performed whenever he had completed any other task: to pull out his phone, load one app or another, and idly scroll through it until he saw something irritating enough to remind him that he had the option to close the app, or even put the phone away.

He kept his phone out because staring at your phone was so normal, whereas idly standing still and being patient alone in a public place was very rarely perceived as such, even when there was nothing surprising about the way you were dressed. Rather than any particular platform's mind-numbing-cum-incendiary feed, Lance was really watching the people – partly to keep his observation muscles in shape, but mostly because it was significantly more interesting than anything that any of the tech giants were willing to digitally present to him at the moment. He was playing a game with himself to see if he could find any correlation between the food and drink various people were consuming, their approximate ages and their work attire.

Most straightforward to observe was the size of the bellies of those with a full English in front of them. Those tucking into little more than a toastie and a coffee tended to wear a pair of glasses that might have weighed more than their arms. The same people turned out to be more likely to have the most expensive phones and Bluetooth earbuds as well.

There were one or two suits being worn as well. Lance usually would expect to see laptops out in front of them, but the café was incredibly busy this morning. Either they feared getting baked beans spilt on their precious Apple machines by a well-meaning but clumsy construction worker – a fear Lance didn't entirely distance himself from, his intense dislike of Apple notwithstanding – or Martina had kicked out all of the selfish suits long ago, only admitting those willing to share table space with everyone else.

Martina stepped out from behind the counter carrying a large tray she'd been handed by one of the kitchen staff. She navigated the tables, just as Lance had done. In fact, her motions and gait looked to be just the same as Lance's own walk just minutes earlier. He wondered. *Surely not*, he thought. He cast his gaze down towards the floor. His view was obscured by legs of tables and human beings, but there was a glimpse of a colour matching that of her face and hands.

Lance was excited, eager to see if this hint delivered on its promise. Visibility continued to be intermittent as she wove between tables, chairs and ambulatory clientele, who were presumably in search of the facilities. But then, when the bottom half of the café owner was in view once more, where he might have expected to see an elliptical border from the exposed skin into the coloured material of closed pumps, he saw five distinct toes on each foot, healthily spaced apart, and the underside of an arch as she raised her left heel to step forward. Martina Vongola, a friend he'd gladly have made had she not been a suspect in a case three years earlier, was working barefoot in her café.

Martina's bare feet stepped towards him and it occurred to him a fraction too late that he might have benefited from looking at the rest of her at the same time.

"Hey, my tits are up here!" she said, holding out a mug of coffee for him. "Milk and one, if I'm not out of date?"

"Yes, that's right, Martina. Thank you, and er, sorry. I feel like I've travelled to Mars and met another human there all of a sudden."

"It's fine. You don't have to explain. I was just teasing you. Really, you inspired me. I tried it in the park, and I liked it. And then I found I didn't like not doing it. I'm not you. I still own shoes. But I like getting to decide when to wear them and when not to."

"That is awesome. I wish I had all day to talk all about it with you."

101

"Your favourite subject, I know! But come back another time. We'll have a proper catch up. You should have come back years ago, really."

"I know. I'm sorry. And I'm afraid I only came today for a case, but I promise I'll be back soon."

"A case? A case I can help with?"

"Yes."

He loaded up the photo from Dombattu's last email onto his phone screen and showed it to her.

"Is that . . .?"

"That's what I wanted you to confirm, but I think it is."

"It is. It's Stanley. I'm sure it is. But how can I help?"

"You oversaw his re-homing, didn't you? I remember you took care of him for a short time before handing him over to another family. Is that right?"

"Yes, it is." Martina couldn't give Lance her full undivided attention, but he could tell she wanted to. In the short gaps where neither he nor she was speaking, her eyes were scanning the room.

"I need to find him. He, or his owner, might be in danger."

"Seriously?"

"That photo was sent to me by a killer, teasing me about what he's going to do next. Help me find Stanley, please. Who took him?"

"You've cleared it with the police, I take it? I'm not going to get into trouble for breaching confidentiality, or anything?"

"Shit. Let me make a quick call. I'll sort it out."

"OK, I need to get back to my customers. Give me another five minutes."

"That should be all I need."

Lance turned his attention back to his phone and dialled Owusu's number. His gaze automatically followed Martina Vongola's graceful movements around the café while he waited for the D.I. to answer.

"Hi, Inspector. I have another lead and I'm following it now. It's Jane Alder's dog. Just checking that I can ask Martina Vongola for the contact details of the family who took him. That won't get her or me into trouble, will it?"

**

A slim and well-dressed Korean woman in her early fifties answered the door and invited Lance inside with emphatic hand gestures.

He wiped his feet just as emphatically, relieved to see dark hard floors in the house instead of delicate pristine white carpet. Fortunately, this was not a house whose beauty his lifestyle threatened in any way. He followed his host inside and allowed her to usher him enthusiastically towards a very comfortable-looking sofa.

"Wait, one moment," she said, before disappearing further back into the house. Barely more than a minute later she returned with a large mug of tea and an even larger plate of biscuits. He had no idea how she managed to prepare that tea so quickly. Did she have a tap that produced boiling water on demand?

"Thank you, Mrs Bong, that's very kind of you. And for seeing me too. As I said on the phone, I'm investigating a very serious case, and it's related to the dog you adopted a few years ago. A café owner did the handover. The dog's name was Stanley. He was a Cavalier King Charles Spaniel. Does that ring any bells?"

"Oh, yes of course. Our young son adored him, but he's no longer with us now."

"No longer with you? May I ask what happened?"

"Our boy caught leukaemia a while back. He's fine now, but we couldn't keep the dog while he was being treated. His immune system, you see."

"I see. Do you know where the dog is now?"

"Our son's babysitter adopted him. It was a while ago now, so we're no longer in touch. She was called Mandy and came from an agency. I'm sorry, that's all I know."

"No need to be sorry, Mrs Bong. Thank you for your time, and especially for the tea. This is great. Is it Korean?"

She nodded. "You're welcome. I hope you find what you need. But I'm curious. Why do you have no shoes?"

***

"Hi, Inspector," said Lance as soon as Owusu answered her phone. "Yeah, I'm just on my way back from the family that took Jane Alder's dog."

. . .

"Yeah, he changed hands again. Their babysitter, name of Mandy. That's all they knew."

. . .

"A couple of years ago, according to the lady of the house."

. . .

"Yeah, I've already called the agency. She doesn't work for them anymore and they've deleted her contact information, so this is all we have for the moment. This and the photo. Looked like the dog might have been in Ravenscourt Park when it was taken, but I'm only about forty percent sure, and anyway, Photoshop is a thing."

. . .

"Yeah, the letter D might narrow it down. Then again, our killer's a fan of *The ABC Murders*, and the pattern was broken at the letter D in that story. So maybe the D is the second syllable of Mandy."

. . .

"I do have one idea. Vets in the local area might be able to give us something. Maybe start with the ones closest to Ravenscourt Park?"

. . .

"OK, great. Let me know if you come up with anything. Cheers, Inspector. Speak soon. Bye for now."

***

"I'm on my way," said Pawel Krol, who'd been just about to leave home for an early morning gym session before work when he received the call.

He ran south down North End Road to the large crossroad with Talgarth Road, the lights of which seemed to take forever to change and allow him to cross. Then he took the first westbound District line train from West Kensington, three stops over to Ravenscourt Park. The sun had put a short distance between itself and the horizon by the time he arrived at the park entrance, where officers were recommending other open green spaces to disappointed members of the public. Standing with them was a short stout Caribbean gentleman who looked to be in his early sixties, holding his dog's leash and waiting patiently to be interviewed.

"Thanks for waiting, Sir," said Pawel. "I'm Detective Sergeant Pawel Krol. I take it you discovered the body?"

"I did, Officer," said the man in his gentle Caribbean accent supported by a rich baritone timbre.

"May I ask your name?"

"Albert."

"OK, Albert. Tell me everything you saw and the rough time you saw it."

"Sure ting, Officer. I was walking my dog around six am in the park, like I do every morning. He's only little, not very fast.

So, we take our time. We entered the park and walked round anticlockwise. About ten minutes in, little Dwayne here must have smelled something. Him got all excited, tugging at his lead. I picked up my pace and followed him to a tree, and there was another dog just sitting there. A spaniel it was. And then I saw the body and called 999."

"Thanks, Albert. So that would have been around, ten past six? Is that correct?" Pawel was scribbling in his notebook.

"I'd say so, Officer. She could have been sleeping. I thought it was just some poor girl passed out after a bad night. Then I asked myself why the dog? And then I saw her shoes. She had too many shoes, and she weren't dressed for no night out in town!"

"Thanks," said Pawel again. He turned his notebook to a blank page and handed it to the witness. "Would you be so good as to write your full name and contact details here, in case we think of anything else to ask you?"

"Sure ting, Officer." Albert filled half a page with large letters of clear handwriting. "Poor girl," he said as he handed the notebook back.

Pawel gave a solemn nod and then entered the park. He walked his way anticlockwise, around to the crime scene. After six or seven minutes he came to the tree in question, impossible to miss from the forensic team milling around it. He approached the body. Standing next to it was a very familiar dog. He checked the pendant on the collar. Yes, it was definitely Stanley.

Pawel then went to look at the body of a young woman, lying flat on her back. It didn't take long for him to understand what the witness had meant about there being too many shoes. She was wearing a pair of light trainers on her feet, with a pair of dark jeans, a blue turtleneck jumper and a black leather jacket. But lying on her chest was another much fancier shoe; the sort that would normally have a tall sharp heel. Another was beside her neck, above her shoulder. Changing out of heels into comfortable shoes after a night out was common enough. But her other clothing was ideal for dog walking, not clubbing.

Pawel took another look at Stanley. "Here you are again. Poor thing. This might start to feel normal to you now." He addressed the dog with a mix of sympathy and disbelief.

He looked at her face and then had a shock of sudden recognition. "I've met her before!" he exclaimed, either to whoever happened to be standing nearby, or to the trees, with no qualms about letting them decide for themselves as to which the case may be. He started taking photographs of the face, the dog and the body.

There happened to be a young trainee, who had hesitated for a moment, wondering if the sergeant might be talking to her. "You have, Sergeant?"

"Sorry, I was just talking to myself. I didn't mean to interrupt you."

"No problem, Sir. Did you say you recognise the victim?"

"I spoke to her at the synagogue last week."

Chapter 8:

"Yes, Sir, the one who was studying for an AI master's we spoke to at the synagogue. I missed her name," said Pawel.

. . .

"Amanda Dawson," he repeated, writing the name into his notebook. "OK, yes, I'm positive it's her. And you won't believe who was with her."

. . .

"Oh, Lance told you, did he? Didn't mention anything to me. He's on his way over now, though. Yeah, I know, at this hour! OK, thanks, Sir. Anything else I can do while I'm here?"

. . .

"All right then, Sir. See you then. Bye."

Pawel put his phone away and took another look at the dead body, whose name he now knew. He took a moment to process how young she was, how much of her life had been yet to happen and all of the things she wouldn't experience. Though the only two facts he knew about her were that she was an academic of the computer nerd variety, and that she attended a local synagogue on Saturdays, thoughts of the person she would now never become were flooding into his mind entirely under their own weight.

Those spare shoes drew his attention again. Not only did they not match her outfit at all, but they seemed far too small compared to the trainers on her feet, deceptively chunky though they may have been.

"Definitely not her shoes, Pav, mate," said the familiar voice of his best friend, complete with the customary cocky Antipodean tone.

Pawel turned around in momentary surprise, interrupted by realisation. "Vampires don't have reflections, and Lance Pomegranate doesn't make footsteps," he quipped, with none of the joviality that requires a civilised number of hours' sleep and at least one cup of coffee.

"No-one makes footsteps in this grass, Pav. Sorry if I startled you."

"Whatever. Glad you're here. Really, even if I don't sound like it."

"There aren't many people I get up at stupid o'clock for, but you are one of them. Although the song and dance I did to persuade your mates to let me in the park was fun. Fortunately, one of them isn't that new to the borough."

"Are you lamenting the fact that you aren't more famous? That some of us haven't heard of the great barefoot detective yet?"

"No, mate. Not looking forward to that when it happens. I'm quite content with the number of selfies I'm asked for as it is. Right then. Shall we?"

"Have at," replied Pawel, gesturing to the body in front of him. "Not her shoes, you said. I agree."

"Let's have a look. You got gloves for me? I'm guessing bringing my own doesn't count."

"Yes, here you go."

Lance took the gloves from D.S. Krol and put them on before bending down to examine the shoes. Just as was the case at Rabbi Cotton's house, Lance had no intention of touching anything, but it was a sensible precaution anyway. He made two immediate observations. The shoes weren't simply lying on or beside the body, and they weren't flats.

"They're the murder weapon," said Lance.

"Heels?" said Pawel, leaning in for a closer look.

"Heels. Of course forensic could have told you that. Will they get here soon?"

"Any minute. They're unusually late in fact."

"As soon as they clear it, I'm going to get this dog out of here and back into familiar hands, poor little sod. Mind if I take some photos for myself?"

"You know the drill, Lance."

"Discreet is my middle name."

"Fuck off, Lance. Your middle name is Ernest."

"And on duty as well," said Lance, shaking his head in mock consternation.

They heard several sets of heavy footsteps approaching across the dewy grass. "You were saying, Lance?"

Lance raised his hands in an exaggerated show of surrender as he and D.S. Krol parted to let the forensic team through. "OK Pav, not messing with you any more today. Promise!"

***

Lance had one reason to be grateful for the early start, and that was by the time he and Stanley had trotted around from Ravenscourt Park to Las Cucharas Grasientas, a pleasant half-hour route on foot along the Thames Path, the café was open but nowhere near full. A couple of corner tables were occupied by pairs of legs whose attached heads and torsos were obscured from his view with broadsheets. The rest of the space was pristine and peaceful. He pulled out his packet of wet wipes and removed the mud from his soles and toes, and then did the same for each of Stanley's paws.

His memories of a somewhat messier entrance to the place were still vivid, and he shuddered as they once again surfaced. Rather than everything that had led to that moment, it was the mud he'd had to traipse into the café, marking the shiny chequered lino floor – and the thought of Martina hurriedly cleaning up after him as if it were no bother was what had hurt him the most that day. It was far enough in the past not to matter. He had every reason to believe it didn't matter to her at all. But it still troubled him.

112

"Twice in a week! I'm honoured," teased Martina Vongola, stepping out from behind the counter to meet him. "And what's this? You've found him! Don't tell me he's yours now?"

"No. I'm definitely not the right person for him."

"I see. So are you here on business, or can I have a hug?"

"I sort of am, Martina, but you're not tied to the case, and to be honest I think it's overdue."

She moved in, arms wide and closing. "Good. Don't stay away so long again. I've really wanted to catch up, and share my experience, and make sure I'm doing this barefoot thing right."

"It's really awesome. I love it. I mean I love that you're doing it. There's no right or wrong way though. Does it make you happy? Do people give you hassle about it? Is it affecting your dating life?"

"You have more questions than I do, Lance. I wasn't expecting that," said Martina, releasing Lance from her determined embrace.

"I hope we have time for a nice long chat, in that case, but first I need your help with Stanley. He's just witnessed another owner's murder."

"Not the Bongs! Oh no."

"No, not the Bongs. They're fine. I spoke to Mrs Bong the other day. Stanley hasn't been with them for a while. This was a young woman. You'll hear about it on the news soon enough, but she was found dead in the park a few hours ago, and Stanley here was with her."

"I don't think I can take him again, Lance, I'm sorry."

"I don't expect you to. Can you help me find him a new family?"

"Why not take him back to the Bongs?"

Of course he'd already thought of that, but that would be the end of his reason to visit his new kindred spirit.

"Oh my wow! Oh my wow oh my wow!"

Neither Lance nor Martina had seen Cousin Itt float in through the front door.

"The famous Lance Pomegranate! Here, in my street! This is so exciting! I'm a huge fan! Huge!"

"You know it's so funny," said Lance, dryly. "You're the fourth person this week who's mistaken me for this Pomegranate bloke. I don't even know who he is!"

"Oh, my gosh! I'm so sorry! I'm so, so sorry! I just saw your feet, and your hair and I . . ."

Lance hadn't intended to give himself up, but he did not want tears on his hands, and they seemed imminent. "Relax, I'm just winding you up. It's me. And I'm genuinely flattered. And you are?"

Tear alert aborted. Cousin Itt reverted instantly into bubbly mode. "Oh my wow! Oh my wow!"

"Is that really your name?"

"Oh. Sorry, no. My name is Bo. Bo Fulgar. I've just moved in across the road."

"OK, Bobo, well nice to meet you. Don't let me keep you from ordering your breakfast here."

"It's just Bo. Sorry, I'm not normally like this. I'm normally so cool."

"Like if the Fresh Prince and the Fonz had a baby?"

"Who?"

Lance had no comeback for young people with insufficient exposure to culture.

"So why are you here? Are you like Einstein? Is this your equivalent of his Patent Office job?" Bo was already affecting a giggle before she'd finished her sentence.

"Can I get you anything to eat or drink?" said Martina, breaking the ice.

"Do you have gluten-free toast?"

"I'm afraid we don't. This is an old-fashioned greasy spoon café."

"Clue's in the name," added Lance.

"How about a vegan fry-up?" Martina suggested. "I can do that for you, and a black coffee."

"Oh, I'm not vegan. Just gluten free and proudly unvaccinated. I'll have a full English without toast please. And a normal coffee with cow's milk."

"Sure, take a seat," said Martina, casually scratching her right calf with the toes of her left foot. Lance found himself wondering if he did similar things more often than he was conscious of, and whether other people noticed.

"Thank y— Oh my wow! You're barefoot too! Is that a rule here? Should I take my shoes off? I'm so sorry, I must have missed the sign."

"There is no sign. You're fine as you are. Please, take a seat and I'll bring your order over soon." She turned and retreated behind her counter from where she issued instructions towards the kitchen.

"Waaaaaaiiit. Is that? It is, isn't it! A King Charles! Just like Jane Alder's dog! Rodney was his name, wasn't it?"

"Stanley," said Lance.

"Stanley! He looks just like him! What's his name?"

"Stanley," said Lance again.

"*The* Stanley? What's he doing here? Did you keep him?"

"You ask a lot of questions, just Bo."

"It's what I do. I run a true crime podcast. I'm fascinated with murders in the local area. Have been ever since I moved to London. The Jane Alder case was incredible. That's why I had to move into her old house across the road."

"You had to," said Lance, flatly.

"You kept the dog, I took the house," she offered, in a tone that was the Peak District to Lance's Fenland.

116

"I didn't keep the dog," admitted Lance. "If you must know, I came here to ask for help to rehome him."

"Oh my wow! That's perfect!"

"Come again?"

"I can take care of Stanley. He can live in his old home. It will be an honour!"

Lance accepted defeat. "I suppose, as a temporary measure at least, it wouldn't be a terrible idea."

"Her house, her dog, it's like I'm living the case. My listeners will lose their shit over this!" The last few words were Lance's best interpretation of her accelerating and ascending squeal.

"All you need now is to be stabbed and locked inside your front room, and then your life will quite literally be complete," quipped Lance.

"Oh, would you? It would be an honour!" said Bo, followed by a laugh that died a sad lonely death. Eventually she broke the silence "Would you do a feature for my podcast? Spelt with a double E of course."

"When I'm less busy perhaps," offered Lance.

"Oh, you're working a case? Is it the murders I saw in the news? The burglar and the rabbi? Are they connected?"

"Here," said Lance as a substitute for *No comment*, handing her Stanley's lead. "The two of you can bond over a shared fry-up."

117

Martina Vongola's re-emergence from behind the counter, carrying a tray supporting a steaming mug and a plate loaded with an array of cholesterol in an assortment of shapes and colours, prompted Stanley's newly assigned carer to pick a table.

After delivering the podcaster's fry-up, Martina silently stepped back towards Lance. "About those many questions we both have. I might have a few minutes before we start filling up with hungry people."

"I might have a few minutes too, Martina, but I'd rather we do it in front of people who aren't poised to record every word I say."

"I understand. We'll do it another time. Come back and have a lunch on me."

"Sure thing, Martina. Bonus points if you're barefoot."

"I couldn't say no to bonus points now, could I?" She flicked one big toe against the floor and then gently tapped her foot.

"Really touched that you got into it. Wish I'd come back sooner!"

***

Lance spent the whole of his bus journey back to his office staring at his phone, specifically at the photo of Stanley from Malcolm Dombattu's email. He continued to stare at it from the chair behind his desk long after he'd sat down. Of course, there was now no need to suppose the location wasn't in Ravenscourt Park. The image file size was large. Plenty of

118

pixels, but the content wasn't especially clear. It had to have been taken from quite a distance, but most likely with a high-quality phone camera. From the light level and shadows, it was taken late in the afternoon. The dry weather and overcast sky might help to identify the date, but only in conjunction with more information.

He lay his phone flat on the desk so that he could rotate the image without it automatically righting itself. Perhaps there was something to be gleaned from where the image had been cropped. What might have been cut out? And why?

His train of thought was abruptly derailed by a knock on his office door. "Come in, please," he said, looking up. He hadn't been expecting anyone.

A long thin leg was first to become visible from behind the open door, balancing itself precariously on the ridiculously impractical heel of a shoe that somehow counted as professional dress, at least for those born into a certain kind of body. As the leading leg was joined by its other half and the familiar owner of the pair came into full view, her unmistakable Belfast accent completed the picture.

"Please tell me you don't expect me to take my shoes off," said Ciara Gallen sincerely.

"Relax, Mail-on-Sunday. I would not want to see the damage they've done for all the coke in Colombia."

"I always had you down as more of a stoner-drinker type."

"Well now we've got the formalities out of the way," said Lance, up on his feet and walking around to the front of his desk, "how may I help you?" He walked towards the armchairs in the middle of the room and gestured towards one of them, while choosing another to sit in himself.

"Thank you, Mr Pomegranate. It's about the dead girl in Ravenscourt Park."

"You know about that already, then?"

"It's my job to know."

"It's reassuring to know you do actual journalism from time to time. Must make a nice change for you."

"What can I say? Sometimes I get writer's block and need inspiration. I need to be serious with you, though." She hesitated for a few seconds. "I'm actually scared."

"Scared of what?"

"I heard about the murder weapon." She lifted her left leg and tapped her shoe with the fingertips of her right hand.

"You think it's about you? Because of the heels?"

Ciara Gallen returned her foot to the floor. "I know it is, and it's more than the heels. I had a personal connection to the victim."

"Go on," said Lance.

"She used to babysit my son for me a few years back."

"OK," said Lance.

"No, that's not all. Now please, this is very hard for me to admit. It's almost as hard as admitting that I need your help.

I'm not proud of what happened. But I need you to hear it from me, before it gets out."

"Why me? Why not the police?"

"Please. I'd prefer the police hear it from you. I can't face making what's tantamount to a confession to them directly. I can't lose face like that and then go back there the next day asking them for information on the next big story. Can I trust you to tell them for me?"

"OK, I'm listening." Lance understood immediately. He never imagined seeing her this vulnerable, and he was surprised at himself that he wasn't enjoying it the way he would have expected. It was all too real. He could see why she wouldn't want to expose that side of her to the police officers she dealt with on a daily basis. Flipping a power gradient that you're used to seeing sinking away from you must be pretty daunting.

"OK," she said, and took a few deep breaths. "It didn't end well, our arrangement with the babysitter, and I am not proud of it. You know how famous my husband is."

"I saw the start of his new series on Netflix only last week," said Lance.

"Aye, exactly. Well, I am sometimes prone to jealousy, especially around younger models with a tendency to be star stricken."

"You wanted her dead? Buyer's remorse? Didn't wish carefully enough?"

"As if. You know what I'm like by now. No surrender, no regrets. My heartless bitch side is genuine. It's nothing like that."

"What then?"

"I'm being set up here. The murder weapon. My personal connection. The girl was pregnant when she died for fuck's sake. How much more of a motive do you need?"

Lance momentarily froze, hoping that the columnist hadn't noticed. Getting info on a case he was personally involved with from a tabloid journo would not be a good look. He'd been so fixated on the dog photo, not to mention his newfound kindred spirit, he'd not even checked the news reports since leaving the park in the morning.

"I can see what conclusions people might jump to, yes," he said, doing his best to sound pensive.

"The things I said to her, and to Samuel over the years, especially on her last night working with us. I wanted to take them back the next day, and I don't think there's any record of any of it, but I'm scared, as I say."

"You're worried about your readers turning on you?"

"No. Well yes, somewhat, but not to an extent I couldn't handle. No, I'm worried that I'll be next. Whoever did this, I don't think framing me is the endgame for him or her. And if the connection between me and the killer works both ways, if I can find out who it is – and make no mistake, I am going to follow every avenue there is –if the killer thinks I can get close, who's to say I won't be next?"

"You won't be next," said Lance.

"What makes you say that?"

"Are you aware of the names of the recent murder victims in the area, Mrs Gallen?"

"The burglar. Jason Bampton. The rabbi. Jeremy Cotton. And then this babysitter, Mandy Dawson."

"Correct. Do you see the pattern?"

"A couple of names beginning with J. Two men and a woman. No, I don't see . . . oh! Alphabetical order by surname?"

"So, you won't be next."

"My name's not that far down the list. Please, don't make light of this, Mr Pomegranate. It's all right for some, isn't it?"

Hearing his professional name spoken made him suddenly all too aware that his birth name began with the same two letters as that of the trembling woman seated opposite him. "Of course, you're right. Relax. I'll talk to the police. You'll be in good hands. I recommend you talk to Lena Krol as well, the D.S.'s wife. She's going through similar right now, though Pav's taking good care of her. Much better than I can offer you myself, I'm afraid."

She appeared to need more convincing, and was not in a hurry to stand up with him as he rose from his seat. He gently lowered his gaze towards her and said, "Now don't you worry. You and I are going to be annoying the fuck out of each other for a very long time."

A wry smile broke through, and with it the will to rise to her feet. "Too fucking right," she said, carefully, before taking another slow deep breath. "And you're still barred from my house with those dirty bare feet of yours." She forced a small laugh out, as if to hide the sniff that had immediately preceded it, and then whispered, "Thank you."

Chapter 9:

The next morning, Lance strode into Hammersmith Police Station. This was his first visit there since his regular associates had moved following the closure of Shepherd's Bush Police Station. He didn't see anyone he recognised on the desk. The three officers in his view must have been based here since before the closure, about two years prior. The police hadn't needed his help since the Jane Alder murder case a year before that, so the turnover in that time may also go some way to explain the lack of familiar faces. The pandemic of 2020 and the lockdowns put in place to contain it had made murders significantly easier for the police to solve, since nearly all of them had been literal domestic cases, perpetrated by one household member against another. That didn't explain the past eighteen months, though D.I. Owusu's competence certainly did, and Detective Chief Inspector Kieran Murphy's icy – slowly melting though it was – disposition towards Lance's unyielding aversion to footwear completed the picture.

By chance, as Lance opened his mouth to introduce himself to the first officer to make eye contact with him, D.C.I. Murphy happened to stride into reception and broke the silence.

"Mr Pomodoro! To what do I owe you presence here? You've come to see the D.I. I take it?"

"Yes, Chief," said Lance to the man still saved in his phone contacts as 'Chief Grumpy Fucker'. "Good to see you too."

"I'll let her know you're here. She's not in yet, but will be any minute, if you'd care to wait in her office."

"Eager to get me out of the view of the public, Chief?" said Lance, only half-joking. "Sure, lead the way. Cheers."

"Keeping well, I hope," said D.C.I. Murphy as he led Lance through a set of double doors and began to climb the staircase. His shiny black shoes squeaked against the firm floor with every step.

Lance followed behind him, his steps making no sound at all. "Not bad, considering I'm getting personal emails from a serial killer. But I didn't catch COVID or lose any relatives, so can't complain. Yourself?"

"Similar. Apart from the emails. Then again, the ones I receive from the Chief Superintendent on a daily basis aren't especially pleasant, I'll admit."

They continued along another corridor from the top of the stairs until Murphy stopped outside a door to their right and turned to face Lance.

"Go straight in, make yourself comfortable. I'd recommend stopping short of putting your feet up on the desk though, Mr Poppadom."

"Sure thing, Chief. Thanks. I like your new haircut, by the way. Suits you."

"Thank you. Do excuse me. Snarky replies to the Superintendent's emails do not write themselves."

"May the muse inspire you, Chief," said Lance, before proceeding through the door into Owusu's spacious office. The furniture appeared to have been arranged with extreme mathematical precision. Lance would have put money on there being extensive use of a tape measure and several protractors. Mondrian copies were hung on the walls.

The floor was unchanged, with respect to what he had just walked over on his journey from the front entrance, but everything else suggested the involvement of Owusu's personal touch; not least of all the one deviation from a sense of perfection in the form of a number of biscuit crumbs on her desk, next to the neatly arranged piles of paperwork, sorted by page size into a pleasing tessellated arrangement towards what would be the top-left corner in a plan view from where her chair was positioned.

Lance looked at the other two chairs in the room and then pushed the one to his left a distance of three or four inches further away from the other, and then sat in it, pulling his phone out of his pocket to examine the photo of Stanley further while waiting for Owusu to arrive. The photo's file size was nagging at him. For the size and resolution of the image, it shouldn't be this small, even accounting for the distance at which the photo appeared to have been taken. The photo also looked to have been cropped, most likely to remove crucial information. Perhaps the full-size image was still contained within the file somehow.

He started browsing the Google Play Store for apps that could allow him to investigate this further, but he'd barely read three reviews of the first app on the list of search results before he was interrupted by the sound of Owusu's footsteps and a polite cough.

"Sorry for keeping you waiting, Lance. I really thought I'd get here before you when you called me this morning."

"That's OK, Inspector."

"Did Murphy give you any trouble? He let me know you were here after he showed you in."

"By his standards he was the embodiment of hospitality. We had a lovely little natter on the way up here."

"Life is full of surprises," said Owusu, raising her hands in a gesture of mock resignation.

"Anyway, I thought now would be a good point to have a proper back and forth and go over everything we know so far."

"I agree. Let me dig out my notes."

"Sure. I'll do the same." He opened his briefcase and pulled out his tablet.

Owusu took two steps towards her desk and then turned around, pausing in thought. "Put that chair back, Lance!" Her fierce parental tone came out of nowhere, such that Lance was almost vibrating like a cartoon character who'd just been whacked in the face with a broom handle. He'd forgotten he'd done it while lost in thought about the photo cropping.

He attempted to reverse his earlier nudging of the chair, the precision of which he'd not paid any real attention at the time. His attempt did not satisfy Owusu.

"Left a bit. No, not that much. OK. Now rotate it very slightly clockwise. No. Now back towards the door a couple of millimetres."

"You're just messing with me now, aren't you Inspector?"

"You started it." Owusu gave him another two seconds before finally breaking into a smile and letting a small chuckle out.

"All right, touché," said Lance, his sigh of relief beyond audible, almost a pant.

"Let's get to work. I'll get some tea brought in. Still milk and one?"

"Yes please. Thanks, Inspector. And I should add, you are wicked!"

"You're very kind. To work now." Owusu picked up the landline handset on her desk and said, "Can we have some tea and biscuits for two in my office please?" before replacing the receiver and taking one of the notebooks from the corner. She sat down while Lance loaded the page of his own notes on his tablet.

"OK, let's summarise. Three victims, two of them connected by the synagogue, a third perhaps connected by burglaries in the area. Each one in the order of their surnames, beginning with consecutive letters of the alphabet – B, C and D. And someone is claiming credit for the murders in advance, in emails sent to me personally, under the name Malcolm Dombattu. Whoever it is, he fancies himself as the guy from *The ABC Murders*, except he believes he won't get caught."

"Not an uncommon trait in murderers," said Owusu. "I've not read *The ABC Murders*, but I've seen the David Suchet adaptation. Wasn't the true aim of the killer in that story to embed one particular murder in a group of them, to misdirect everyone's attention from the motive?"

"It was, Inspector. It was never about trying to outsmart Poirot. The killer wanted him to think it was, but really, there was one person he wanted to kill, and all the others were just cover."

"Do you think that's what's going on here?"

"It would be stupid to rule that out. We definitely want to be compiling a list of possible reasons anyone might have to kill one of these victims, something that stands out more than any other. But there are a couple of complications."

"I can see one already, Lance. We don't know if the murder that's especially important to the killer has taken place, and we can't be sure that it isn't planned for much further down the line. The killer didn't get to choose any of his victims' names."

"That's right, Inspector, but he did get to set the pattern. So if this is what he's going for, he would only have chosen the alphabet theme if it fits."

"OK, Lance, what's the other thing?"

"The other thing is that the killer has chosen methods of execution for each crime to match someone specific, and that person has at least some sort of motive."

"You mean like Lena Krol?"

"Exactly. And that's a really personal thing. Pav and I joke all the time about her killing him one day for failing to clean the kitchen or take out the bins. But who else would be in on that? Sahana? Yourself perhaps? Maybe Pav talks to the other officers here too, but beyond that I've no idea."

Owusu paused to think, but if she was looking for a suggestion to add she didn't find one. "What about Jeremy Cotton? The killer used something iconically Jewish as the murder weapon, but does that point anything at anyone?"

"Not especially, but the weapon was disguised as a present from the rabbi's mum, and one person in particular had made something of an enemy of her, and by extension her son, recently. And he's pro-Palestinian too. That's somewhat poetic to the untrained eye."

"Untrained being the operative word, Lance."

"Sure, Inspector, only a child would think it's that simple, but our killer is clearly toying with us. And then we've got Mandy Dawson."

"The artificial intelligence researcher. Did you know she was pregnant?" Before Lance could answer her, there was a knock on the door. "Come in, please," said Owusu. The officer carrying the tray was clearly sufficiently experienced at this particular task. In a matter of seconds the tea and biscuits were on Owusu's desk, the door was closed and the two of them were alone again.

"I found out from the most unlikely of sources yesterday evening," said Lance, watching Owusu pour.

"Oh?" Owusu looked up from the rapidly filling teacup, but not for long enough to risk any overflow.

"Yes, Inspector. A source who also happens to be our killer's scapegoat." He grabbed a biscuit from the desk.

"Oh, of course. The heels." Owusu rolled her eyes as she spoke.

"The heels. Surprised the killer didn't go all out and roll up a copy of the *Daily Mail*, shove it into the poor girl's mouth and drown her with a liquid poured from a can cartoonishly labelled 'vitriol'."

"Maybe even a psychotic serial killer wouldn't stoop to buying a copy of the *Daily Mail*, Lance." *Crunch*. The sound of Owusu crunching biscuits was satisfying, even from as far away as where Lance was currently seated.

"Good point. Anyway, I need to pass this on to you: the victim used to babysit for Ciara Gallen a while back. The arrangement did not end amicably. Gallen got jealous, saw Dawson as a threat. There was some serious drama around it. Not sure how much was covered in the press, but I'll be checking for that next."

"I see. So, our dear Ciara is in the same situation as the sergeant's wife. Which means that, apart from Rayan Chelouche, with each murder the killer is taking a shot at someone connected to us."

"To us, yes, but also to me in particular. I'm the one getting the emails after all, Inspector. The wife of one of my best friends—"

"And of my partner," Owusu interrupted.

"Sure." Lance let a moment pass in acknowledgement of his unfortunate bout of solipsism before continuing. "And then a sort of enemy."

"She's everyone's enemy, Lance. Everyone with a conscience and an IQ above sixty, at least."

"You're not wrong. Sorry, I really shouldn't be making this all about me. OK then, if it's not necessarily about me, and honestly, I really hope it isn't, can we find an equivalent connection between anyone in the police and Mr Chelouche?"

"That is a good shout. If we can't, then he has to be our main suspect for now. Have you spoken to him at all, Lance?"

"No, not yet."

"Neither have I, though D.S. Krol has. I've read his notes. Charming, he said he was. Not that that adds any weight in either direction."

"OK, I'd like to speak to him myself. Can I do that without Murphy tasting piss on his cornflakes?"

Owusu spat out her tea. She took a second to recover her composure. "You can if I go with you, Lance."

"It's a date, Inspector! Oh, and is there something we can do for the tabloid tart?"

"Gallen?"

"Yeah. She came to see me, told me about her prior connection with the victim. Asked me to fill you in so you didn't find out in a less delicate way. Didn't have the guts to tell you herself."

"I'm sure. She loves being able to feel superior around us."

"She admitted as much to me."

"Of course she did. OK, I'll see to it that she feels protected until this whole thing's over."

"She's got a two-letter buffer for now, Inspector. We're not desperate yet." He put his empty cup down on the desk and took one more biscuit.

"Cold, Lance. Very cold," said Owusu, laughing nonetheless.

"All right, our next move is to suppose that the rabbi's murder is particularly special to the killer, and to treat Rayan Chelouche as our main suspect. Let's see if we can connect him to the other murders as well."

"Yes, OK that's our position on motive for now, Lance. What's next to go over?"

"As well as Rayan Chelouche, we really ought to check out anyone else who might have a connection to the babysitter and the rabbi, and talk to them. And I'd rather not wait until Saturday to do it."

"The venue doesn't keep a list of names, but the group of trustees might. I suppose we'll have to talk to Sheila Cotton again."

"If she's anything like my mum, that won't be fun."

"She's already convicted and sentenced Chelouche anyway, so she'll take some persuading that exploring any other avenue isn't a complete waste of time. But I'll take care of it. Leave it with me."

"OK, thanks, Inspector. And that leaves just one more thing I wanted to ask. What did the CCTV reveal regarding cars that could have been used to transport Bampton's body?"

"We have a few. We're still going through the list and contacting owners."

"Were there any hired cars, Inspector?"

"Yes, two as it happens."

"See what you can find out about who hired them. I seriously doubt our killer would use their own car."

"Yes, thank you for that remarkable insight. We're contacting the other drivers in case they might have witnessed something."

"Sorry, of course, Inspector," Lance said somewhat sheepishly. Then he added, "Sure I never doubted you," in his best impression of D.C.I. Murphy's voice.

Owusu continued unmoved. "I'll let you know what we learn once we learn anything, Lance. Top up?"

Chapter 10:

Lance was already back in his own office by the time he had remembered to check for cropped parts of the image that Malcolm Dombattu had emailed him. He picked a promising-looking app and installed it on his phone. Navigating a minefield of ridiculous banner ads encroaching on every button within the app that anyone might want to tap, he managed to find a way to load the photo and assess whether there was a full image that could be restored.

He made one last tap to execute the process, narrowly avoiding a guerilla link to an online casino, and watched the progress bar make its way from the left to the right of the screen. It didn't cross the midpoint. A message popped up: *Error: Unable to Process File. The application encountered an issue while processing the selected file. Please ensure the file format is supported and try again.*

Lance hadn't expected everything to work perfectly first time. The app's reviews had been consistently positive, but maybe it was just a bit fussy about file formats. He tried another app. This time the banners he dextrously evaded would have taken him to an insurance aggregator, a cheap Chinese marketplace, and a porn site offering content eerily suited to his personal taste. The progress bar this time was a bit thicker and blue instead of grey, but there wasn't much difference beyond the superficial between this app and the one he'd previously tried. No error message this time. The process simply aborted, leaving no evidence that he had tapped the button to begin it.

He tried two more apps, with no change in outcome. Not feeling inclined to believe that there was a problem with this many apps – all reasonably well-recommended, with the only complaints being about the placement of the ad banners and the small size of the buttons – he considered that it might be the file. He conducted the obvious experiment, opening up his phone's camera app and taking a selfie. Next Lance went to edit the photo, cropping out everything below his chin as well as his right ear.

He took his cropped selfie into each app and, albeit via an accidental detour to a T20 World Cup betting page in one of them, succeeded in reversing his virtual van Gogh complex and restoring his torso in every single one. He said the name van Gogh aloud to himself several times. Therapeutic though the sensation on the back of his throat was, it didn't prevent his demoralising return to square one. If there were any more to learn from this file, it would take someone with far more expertise than he had to access it.

He decided it was time for a distraction, and dialled Sahana's number. She answered within one ring.

. . .

"Hi, Sahana, yeah, not bad, thanks. Just need to come up for some air. Are you busy tomorrow? Want to watch some cricket? I've somehow managed to put a bet on Scotland to beat Zimbabwe."

. . .

"Yeah, it's part of the investigation. Sort of. Are you OK?"

. . .

"Oh yeah, how's he getting on?"

. . .

"Sure."

. . .

"Oh, tonight? No, I don't think I can tonight, but if you're OK to catch up tomorrow, that would be great. Cricket optional."

. . .

"Of course you fucking are. OK, looking forward to it! Cheers! Enjoy tonight. Bye for now."

***

The Old Sergeant on Garratt Lane, Wandsworth was about half-full by the time Sahana and Vineel walked in. It was a pub she liked enough to regret not visiting it more often, lamenting not acquiring more friends who lived nearby. It made more sense for her to travel to Hammersmith and Fulham, or Tottenham, or even Newham, than to bring people to Wandsworth. Except when she was conscripting Lance to accompany her for her Bollywood cinema fix. She was grateful for that.

But this week she had a temporary lodger with her and thus an ideal opportunity to visit her local without the indignity of drinking alone in front of witnesses – something that only the most asocial of old people, usually old men, seemed cut out for. Of course, it wasn't just about the pub. Sahana had a reason to be particularly excited, as for the first time in years an old friend was free and in the mood to travel across town.

She left Vineel at the table they'd claimed and went straight to the bar to get the first round. He'd told her he wanted to try some traditional English beer, trusting her to recommend him something he wouldn't be able to find at home. She ordered a pint of Young's Special for them each and was sipping hers at the table only a few minutes later. By that time the table next to theirs had been occupied by a solitary drinker. *Perhaps it's not just old men after all*, she thought to herself.

"I heard that you drink warm beer in England. Do they have that here as well?" said Vineel, looking surprised, as if disappointed by the cool touch of his pint glass.

"This is it," said Sahana.

"This is warm?"

"It's room temperature. We have cold refrigerated beers, and then we have real ale like this, which isn't served chilled. Foreigners call it warm because it isn't ice cold."

"Oh," said Vineel, more embarrassed than disappointed.

"Well, try it then!"

He took a sip. "That's a lot of flavour. Very strange."

"It's an acquired taste, but you've got a whole week to acquire it, haven't you."

"Let me get through one pint first," said Vineel. "What time's your friend joining us?"

"Five minutes ago. She's late. I don't think she'll be much longer."

"And how did you guys meet?" He took another sip, making amusing faces during the protracted gustatory analysis he performed before he swallowed.

"Divya and I go way back. I think we were both nineteen when we first met, working part time in the same supermarket while we were students."

"Long-lasting friendship! So precious."

"They are. We don't see each other as much as I'd like to, but yes. She is very special to me. I actually really fancied her for a while. It hurt when I realised she wasn't capable of feeling the same way. Do *not* mention that in front of her, OK?"

"Lips sealed," said Vineel, miming a zip across his mouth. "Is it also a secret that you like girls? I didn't know, you see." Another sip. The puzzlement was perhaps beginning to give way to a hint of satisfaction, though that may have been wishful thinking on Sahana's part.

"Not really. People don't assume it, because I dress like a typical straight woman, if there is such a thing. It's a good look for the stage, and it also feels right for me. I like boys too. Just not as many."

"So the Australian guy we met the other night, not him then?"

"His type, yes. But him, specifically, it would be such a seismic shift from being friends. I don't think either of us would be able to land on our feet."

"Well, if it's feet you want, he's your man, surely."

Sahana couldn't tell if Vineel had a weak sense of humour, or just wasn't familiar with the idiom. "What I really want is a really big pair of tits, but unaccompanied by a massive belly. Probably why most men don't do it for me. No offence."

Vineel held his hands up in surrender. "Don't worry about me. I have no stake here. I want to marry a rich Indian girl, with an engineering background and an unhealthy obsession with cricket and crypto."

"If she's well-endowed enough I might steal her from you and bring her to London."

"Bring whom to London?" said a familiar voice from behind Sahana, startling her, which resulted in beer spilling from Sahana's raised glass and splashing on the table in front of her.

Sahana firmly planted her pint glass back on the table and pushed her chair backwards so she could stand up and turn to face her friend.

"Divs! So good to see you!" Her hug was preceded by no warning at all, and several seconds passed before it occurred to Sahana that it might be in her interest to allow Divya to breathe.

Divya took a moment to relax and take a couple of breaths before replying in kind. "Really great to see you too! It's been too long! What are you drinking? And who's your friend?"

"I'm Vineel," said Vineel, standing up and offering a handshake. "I know Sahana's brother from his time in Bangalore. I'm in London on a work trip and Sahana's kindly hosting me for my stay this week." He retook his seat after Divya released his hand. Sahana took her cue to sit back down as well.

"All right for some. I wish my work would send me thousands of miles away for a week. Though I don't think I want to go back to India in a hurry. I was born there."

"You don't miss home?"

"Let's just say all of my best memories were made here. Now what am I getting you both?"

"Young's Special again for me. Was that all right for you, Vineel?" said Sahana.

"It was," said Vineel, and his face showed that he meant it. "But can I try something different this time?"

"Such as?" asked Divya.

"Surprise me. I like surprises."

"OK, then." Divya walked over to the bar.

"You and I seem to have a similar taste," said Vineel.

"Hands off," said Sahana, abruptly withdrawing her own hands from the table. "I mean it. It's not for me to divulge, but she had a difficult time in her teens. She doesn't respond well to even the gentlest approaches. Charm will put her off. Manners will make her question a man's sincerity, and confidence will frighten her away."

Vineel leant a few inches backwards to signal his retreat. "You seem very protective of her."

"I am. When you've been in love with someone and seen them hurt, it's worse than being hurt yourself, because both of you are hurt at once."

"OK. I'm sorry. I'll drop it."

"Let's just have fun tonight, OK?"

"Sure."

"Here you go, Vineel. Try this one," said Divya as she passed a pint over his shoulder and placed it down in front of him."

"Thanks. What is it?"

"It's a porter."

"It's very dark."

"Yes, and fairly strong. Drink it slowly."

"Oh, don't you worry about me. I have a good constitution." He took his first sip. Divya's face reflected Sahana's own reaction perfectly to watching Vineel betrayed by the false sense of familiarity that his experience with the ale had given him.

"You'll need it," said Sahana, grinning. "Thanks, Divs." She received her own pint from Divya's hand and seconds later a fifth of it was already inside her.

Divya returned to the bar to fetch her own drink and at last pulled out the third chair from under the table and joined Sahana and Vineel properly.

"Tell me then. How is everything, Divs? Are you still working for British Gas?"

"I still am. I don't get much sleep, but I am on the property ladder at least. And yes, I have been badgering marketing to get you involved. No luck yet, but I'll keep trying."

"Tell them I'll accept payment in credit against my heating bills," Sahana said earnestly.

"Payment for what?" asked Vineel. "Music? You want to shoot their advertisement video songs?"

"Would be nice. Musicians don't work for exposure, but there are some degrees of exposure that actually would pay the bills. Although in this case I'd want my bills paid as part of my fee as well."

"I like jazz," said Vineel. "But I don't think it would bring customers to a gas company."

"Then you clearly haven't heard Sahana sing," said Divya defensively. "Don't be so quick to judge."

"OK, OK. I admit I don't know what I'm talking about," said Vineel, retreating into his pint. "This beer is really strong. Is it like five or six percent?"

"Try eight or nine," said Sahana, grinning again.

"OK, OK, that's fine. I don't have to do anything tomorrow morning anyway. Just one meeting near Marble Arch at two in the afternoon. Anyway, eight or nine percent is not so much. It's less than wine still." He took another sip. This one much larger than the first. The entire top half of his body juddered.

"But we don't drink wine by the pint, Vineel," said Divya. "Take it slowly. Enjoy it. We don't want to have to carry you home."

"But you don't say that meanfully," said Vineel, taking an even larger gulp of his porter.

"Come again?" said Sahana. "Divs, we should have given him the porter a bit later. Never mind. You and I are due a good time." She took another sip of her own drink.

"Divs? What's wrong?"

Divya was motionless, as if she had just made eye contact with Medusa.

"Divs?" Sahana repeated.

Divya slowly lowered her jaw, which undulated as she drew in a slow deep breath. Then her shoulders trembled as she exhaled, followed by every part of her body visible above the table. "Excuse me. I'm really sorry. I need to go."

"But you've just got here? Seriously what's the matter?"

"I'll tell you later. I'm so sorry. Really. Really sorry. I'll call you." Divya knocked back the remainder of her drink, stood

145

up, slid her chair back under the table, picked up her bag and began to walk away.

"Call me when you get home safely, Divs! Hope you're OK. Love you."

Divya nodded without turning to face her and continued walking to the exit.

Sahana and Vineel looked at each other. He opened his mouth. She shook her head. He closed it again.

"I'm really sorry, Vineel. I'm not blaming you at all, but my evening is rather ruined. Do you mind if we bin tonight off? I think I just want to go home. Would that be all right?"

"Yes OK. Can I finish my drink first?"

***

"What's up, Pav, mate?" said Lance into his phone.

. . .

"Yeah, it's fine. I'm at home now, trying to figure out a few things, but I'm free to talk. Did you hear anything back about the hired cars?"

. . .

"OK, so can I come with you when you talk to the two drivers?"

. . .

"Sure. I won't tell Murphy if you don't."

. . .

"OK, and let me know if the car companies get back to you. I don't suppose they told you whether either of the drivers were obscuring their faces at all, or what kind of ID they showed?"

. . .

"Yeah, please do that. We've got so little to go on at the moment. Owusu and I are going to interview congregation members again tomorrow, although I might have double-booked myself, now I think about it. I need to make a grovelling phone call to Sahana now."

. . .

"Sure. Cheers, Pav, mate. Speak soon. Love to Lena."

Lance ended the call and was about to dial Sahana's number when he saw an email alert.

He tapped the notification and read Dombattu's latest taunts.

How much is that doggie in the window? The one with the two deceased former owners? How much is that doggie in the window? I do hope his next ones aren't goners.

How do you feel this is going so far, Mr Lance. Are your exhibitionist toes tingling with excitement? Or are you just feeling impotent and embarrassed? Speaking of which, I think it's time for the next round, don't you?

You didn't do so well on the picture round, so let's give you a multiple choice this time. Fifty-fifty. Is E for a) Exciting or b) Embarrassing?

147

Remember: we skipped A.

Best wishes,

Your darling Malcolm, who longs to be with you, if you can just send me the £50 Apple gift card to pay for my sick grandmother's shopping, etc. etc. etc.

Lance contemplated sending a reply, but before he could think of a sufficiently sharp-tongued opening line to make it worthwhile, his phone started buzzing and Sahana's name was on the screen. His ringtone began two seconds later but only played for half a second before he'd answered.

"Sahana. I was about to ring you. I've fucked up I'm afraid."

***

"No, Lance," said Sahana through a stream of tears, her voice unwilling to pick a register and stick with it. "I'm the one who fucked up. I have fucked everything up. Fuck, Lance! Fuck! Everything has gone to shit, and it's all my fault!"

Chapter 11:

Sahana had hoped to feel a little bit more in control of herself by the morning, after a good sleep. Unfortunately, she hadn't managed to get that sleep. Her night had been a mess of barely begun television series – half a dozen first episodes, each abandoned around the twelve-to-fourteen-minute mark – cups of tea that both relaxed her and reinforced her insomnia, heavily buttered slices of toast, and a distracting if not especially artistic attempt at turning her troubles into a set of song lyrics.

The latter was usually a helpful way of converting a problem of emotion she didn't know how to solve, into a task of rhythm, metre, rhyme and catchiness; exactly the type of problem she excelled at solving. By the time she finished she would have a piece of work she was proud of, and the subject matter wouldn't be hurting her so much. At present, her feelings were still far too raw for that to work. She promised herself, certain that she owed it to Divya, that she would come back to this song and make it great one day.

But she still needed to talk through everything, and now she might at least be able to get the words out. Not onto paper, but into the ears of a friend. She wasn't particularly sure that even now she could hold herself together for a phone call, but she needed to try. It was almost eight o'clock. Lance would be awake and in front of the telly for the cricket by now. She dialled his phone number.

"Hi, Lance. Sorry I couldn't get through a single sentence last night. But I still need to offload. Can I try again? Have you got some time?"

. . .

"The cricket, of course. I'm afraid I'm not in the mood for that, but fuck, I need your ears right now. Do you want to go for a walk?"

. . .

"Oh thank fuck you're not Indian. You'd never hear an Indian say 'it's only cricket'. OK, Bishops Park? One hour from now?"

. . .

"Thanks so much. I really need this!"

Sahana put her phone in her pocket, grabbed her bag, and double-checked that her keys, purse and Oyster card were all inside it. She then put her bag down to free up both arms so she could put her coat on.

Sahana looked at the array of shoes by her front door, wondering which to wear. For a moment she considered leaving them all behind, for an additional distraction. The feeling of the pavement beneath her bare feet wouldn't have been a brand-new experience for her, but she didn't feel like being stared at between her home and the park, and from what she could see through the window it probably wasn't going to get much warmer today.

Still, as she stepped into her simple black ballet-like pumps and stepped out onto the street, she was chastising herself as a coward. However, the chilled air rushing between her fingers as she pushed her front door closed behind her went some way to mitigate that, even while she was squinting to avoid being blinded by intuition-defyingly bright sun that could somehow burn retinas without bestowing any warmth.

**

Lance was waiting on a bench a short way from the Fulham Palace Road entrance to the park, looking up from his phone in between reading text messages coming in from Owusu, each one to confirm a name and address that the two of them would be visiting that afternoon. Sahana was over ten minutes late. That was all too easily explained by the buses, not to mention her fragile state, which would likely be causing her to underestimate how much time she needed to get ready and get there. Lance and Owusu had the whole afternoon's worth of meetings planned by the time Sahana entered his view.

He stood up, slipped his phone into his pocket and ran towards her, in the same light jog he'd been practising over the past few weeks. If she hadn't clamped her arms tightly around him the moment he came within their range, he might have knocked her flying backwards upon contact.

As soon as she released him and stepped back, tears streamed down Sahana's face towards the sharp corners of her wide enthusiastic smile. He reached into his other pocket and produced one of the two clean handkerchiefs he'd brought in

151

preparation. Sahana gratefully accepted it and wiped her eyes and cheeks.

"You're a lifesaver, Lance. I don't know where to start."

"It's cool, Sahana. It's nothing you haven't already done for me, more than once. Let's start walking first, and then you can figure out what you need to say once we're on the move."

"Yes OK. You lead the way. One second though," said Sahana, unzipping her handbag.

"Sure."

She lifted one leg after the other in order to pull the black pumps off her feet and unceremoniously dropped them into her bag before zipping it shut.

"OK, I'm ready now," she said, scrunching her toes in the grass. Her breathing was already much gentler.

"Yeah, that'll make you feel better, I promise. I was thinking of suggesting it myself but I've preached enough to you for a lifetime."

"You have, and not all of it went out the other ear, clearly. Don't get used to it though," she teased. "OK, lead on, my good Sir!"

Lance began walking, his full attention on Sahana to his left, in step with him. "Your toes look like they need a re-paint."

"Are you offering?"

"I suppose I am. My nail varnish collection is at your disposal at any time."

"And your steady hands too, I hope."

"Of course, my lady."

"That is binding, Mr Pomegranate. OK, but let me say what I need to say. I've run it over in my head a few times now. It doesn't make it hurt any less, but I should be able to get it off my chest at least."

"Fire away."

"Sure. I'll start from the beginning. You remember Divya, don't you? She remembers you anyway, so you've definitely met."

"Well yeah, and you invited me to join you both last night, anyway."

"Right, so there are a few things that you don't know about her. Personal stuff I wouldn't tell anyone, except now it's all come to the boil and I need to talk about it."

"It won't leave this park," said Lance, looking around in case there might have been anyone near enough to overhear.

"We became close friends really quickly. That much you know already. But she soon confided in me about why she moved here, and it wasn't just about getting her degree. She'd been, erm, *assaulted* in her teens."

"I take it you're not just talking about someone raising a hand to her."

"Correct. Not just beaten up. The other kind. She never knew who did it. She never saw his face and it wasn't someone she already knew."

153

"And this happened in India, yes? Their track record for convictions there is even worse than here, isn't it."

"Yep. There was no-one to press charges against anyway. No-one she could identify. So, for her sanity she chose to escape. She's been in London ever since. I'm one of the first people she got to know after she arrived, and I really liked her."

"Really like, as in . . .?" Lance finished his sentence by gesturing with his hands.

"In that way. Yes. She was the first girl I'd really liked, too. I'd been looking for a way to come out to her, to see if I could do it without scaring her off. We were nineteen. It was all so new to me."

"You own it so well now. I'd never have thought you had any trouble."

"Yeah, thanks, but it took effort to become that confident about it. Not too different from you, really. Anyway, we were in a pub one evening, and it looked as if she was about to throw up after a man had flung a chat-up line at her. And I made a little dig at men, as you do."

"Yeah, we're bastards, the lot of us," said Lance, smiling.

"Indeed. I suggested she bin you all off and pick from the other half of the population. I was heartbroken at her reply. She said how she wished she could ever feel that way about a woman. I'm not sure if at any point she came to know what I was getting at. She knows exactly who I am now, but I don't know if she has ever connected it back to that conversation, or if she even remembers it. Needless to say, I was crushed. We've stayed good friends, but we only catch up a few times a year at most now. By the time I'd adjusted to the heartbreak, I'd also got out of the habit of keeping in regular touch. I love her to pieces though. Always have."

"She'd have been very lucky to have you, Sahana."

"Thanks, that's sweet. Wait. Watch out for that glass." Sahana veered left, away from Lance, then looked shocked as Lance continued in the same straight line they'd been following. "What the fuck, Lance? Seriously, do not show off like that! It's not funny."

Lance plodded nonchalantly through an assortment of green and colourless pieces of broken glass, large and small, that littered the concrete path separating the soft moist grassy area behind them from another ahead. "I have to," he said, sincerely.

"You do *not* have to, Lance Pomegranate! For fuck's sake!" Sahana returned to his side after he reached the grass beyond the path and locked her pace and step to his once again.

"What would it say about me if I didn't? That it was really fortunate someone was there to point out the danger. That I would have hurt myself otherwise, because I don't pay enough attention to where I step. That what I do is reckless and irresponsible and it's just a matter of time before I cut my feet to shreds."

"I suppose."

"Look," he said, lifting his left leg and bending his knee, allowing Sahana to inspect the damage. There was none. He very gently brushed off two small pieces of glass that had clung to his skin using the mud on his feet as an adhesive, and one more that his skin had closed around, like an amoeba's food vacuole, just as leather would around a knife, indenting instead of tearing. "I'm not saying you should go and dance on it. Or that I'm especially inclined to either. But walking through it is a doddle and it's really rare that I ever have to pick anything out of my foot, and when I do, it's only because it feels annoying stuck in there. That's all it ever is."

"OK, fine, Lance. You win, as usual."

"Of course, if people don't say anything, I often walk around the glass anyway."

"You can be such an arsehole sometimes."

"You're welcome. You're enjoying the grass, though, I'll bet?"

"I'm loving the grass." She wiped one foot after the other through the thick damp green-and-brown carpet beneath them. "And the mud. Not looking forward to getting it all over my floor between my front door and the shower, but fuck it. That's a problem for future Sahana."

"Future Sahana is welcome to use some of my wet wipes," said Lance. "But present Sahana was just getting to the important part, I think."

"OK, yes."

"So, you were heartbroken, but you stayed friends. All worked out fine, yes?"

"Yeah, so far. Until last night. She came to meet me for drinks, and I fucking ruined everything."

"Seriously? How did you manage that?" Lance angled in towards her and put his arm around her as they continued walking.

Sahana ducked away from his arm and restored the small gap between their inner shoulders, but turned her head and gave him an appreciative look while doing so. "I didn't know at first. She'd not even finished her first drink before she suddenly froze, made her excuses and left. I checked with her to make sure she'd made it home OK, and then she called and told me everything."

"So what was it?"

"It was Vineel. My brother's friend you met a few days ago. Something he said. A weird phrase that I thought was just a quirk of Indian English, but turns out it's not. Divya had only heard it once before, and it was the response she got when she was saying no to her rapist."

"What phrase?"

"He said 'You don't say that meanfully'. Now I think about it, no-one in my family over there has ever used it."

"*Meanfully*? Never heard that one before. Where do you think he got it from?"

"You'll forgive me for not having the least inclination to ask him."

"Sure. Sorry."

"Lance, I brought her fucking abuser to the pub to meet her and undid nearly twenty years of therapy and recovery. What a shit friend I am, eh?" The tears were coming back, far from tentatively, perhaps given additional momentum by her hundred-mile-an-hour speech.

"You kicked him out, I take it?"

"Yeah, he's gone. I made an excuse about an impromptu visit from a landlord who doesn't allow unmarried men and women together. He's already packed, gone and presumably checking into a hotel by now."

"Your landlord must have no idea what really goes on at your place."

"I knew you'd say that, and you're right. But it's not true about the landlord, though I admit it would be barely an inconvenience for me most of the time if it were."

"Come here," said Lance, stopping and turning to face his friend. She turned and faced him as well, and rested her head on his shoulder. He was caught off guard, first by the wetness of her tears seeping through his shirt and onto the skin of his chest, and then again by the feeling of Sahana's muddy toes gently brushing over his own as he held her tightly. He returned her niche gesture of affection with his other foot against hers.

More than a whole minute passed, and Lance wondered if she might be falling asleep. He wouldn't have complained if she were. When she at last withdrew from him, he felt almost disappointed to release her, but relieved to see her smile return.

Sahana pulled out the handkerchief Lance had given her and wiped her face once again.

"Listen, Sahana. It's going to be OK. This wasn't your fault. It was pure bad luck. I mean, fuck me how many people are there in India, and those two managed to make friends with you and your brother independently? It's either pure chance on a lottery-winning scale of improbability, or Vineel tipped the odds in his favour so he could track her down. You can't blame yourself, either way."

"Oh, shit! You don't think he . . ."

"No. Divya knows who he is now. She wouldn't let him get near her."

"You're right. I said that to her on the phone. She's strong, resourceful and bright. Fucking terrifying thought though."

"Yes. But speaking of terrifying people, I'm really sorry Sahana, but I can't give you the whole day. I've got plans with the inspector this afternoon. We could go for breakfast first at Martina's place if you like."

"Martina's place?" Sahana teased. "I told you she liked you, didn't I!"

"You did, but I'm not ready to believe it just yet. Turns out she and I do have something in common though." He winked and tapped his toes against Sahana's bare foot again.

"It must be love!" The return of Sahana's sarcasm was the best sign Lance could have hoped for at that moment.

"Anyway, thanks, but I'll pass on the food. I really needed this talk. I don't have much of an appetite though, and to be honest I need to spend some time alone again, before I turn into really shit company. I'm just going to lock myself in my studio and practise. I'll need another hug and a big drink soon though. I'll call you then. Would that be OK?"

"Of course, Sahana. I'm really happy to be able to help."

"Thanks, Lance. I want you to know how much I appreciate you."

"I feel the same. Always have. Here, take these." He pulled out a small packet of wet wipes and handed it to her. "I'll walk with you back to the bus stop."

***

An hour later, Lance Pomegranate stepped outside Las Cucharas Grasientas, still wiping the grease from around his lips and on his fingers with his remaining handkerchief. His meal had been heavy, but he could justify it now as fuel for his runs instead of the calorie surfeit that he had previously been eager to avoid. In principle, that was. He doubted that he'd be able to fit a run in this evening.

He took the 220 bus up Fulham Palace Road, through Hammersmith bus station and on towards Shepherd's Bush, where he caught the 260 all the way to Gypsy Corner in North Acton, where D.I. Owusu was standing at bus stop, making a show of looking at her watch as he alighted the bus.

"Good timing, Lance. Spot on in fact. I've been here twenty minutes already. It was that or risk being so late that there'd be no point."

"Good to see you, too, Inspector. How are you?"

"Sorry, yes, I'm very well thanks. How are you?"

"I'm OK. Sahana's been through a rough time, so I spent the morning offering moral support."

"Is she OK now?"

"She will be, if there's any justice in the world."

"OK, let's go, Lance. Cloister Road is just round the corner."

"So the map said, Inspector."

"Of course. Sorry again." Owusu led the way around to Cloister Road and a short distance along it to the front door of Rayan Chelouche's house. Lance stood behind as she stepped up to ring the doorbell and then stepped back.

Rayan Chelouche answered the door himself. "Hi, can I help you? Oh, aren't you one of the police detectives who were at the synagogue when I was there?"

"Yes, I am. Detective Inspector Esi Owusu. You spoke to my colleague D.S. Krol that day I believe. And this is my associate, Private Detective Lance Pomegranate. May we come in and ask you a few questions? I promise we won't take much of your time."

"That's absolutely fine, Inspector. Come in, both of you." Rayan Chelouche stopped himself as he was about to turn away to lead them through his hall. "Oh, you don't need to take your shoes off, Mr Pomegran— Hold on. Where are your shoes?"

"Lance doesn't wear shoes," said Owusu, bluntly.

"Oh, that's fine then. You must save a lot of money that way. Anyway, please come."

Owusu and Lance followed Rayan Chelouche into his living room.

"Just one moment," he said. "But have a seat." He gestured towards the dark-coloured sofa contrasting with the colourful room decor, the gentle green carpet, red-and-black ornaments on the mantelpiece and framed artworks hanging on the white walls.

Owusu and Lance made themselves comfortable while Chelouche stepped out of the room and shouted towards his wife in Arabic. He walked away and returned a moment later carrying a lighter and some incense sticks, which he set to work in the elephant-shaped, hand-carved holder on the coffee table in front of them.

"My wife will bring us some Moroccan tea shortly. I'm supposed to treat those Moroccans as fierce rivals according to my family's idea of national pride, but I must admit they make amazing tea. Anyway," he continued, while sitting down in a chair on the other side of the coffee table, "what would you like to ask me?"

"You'll remember D.S. Krol asking you about the burglar and murder victim named Jason Bampton, yes?"

"Yes, of course. Why? What else have you discovered?"

"What we've discovered, is that his murder was just the first of several. We believe they have all been committed by the same person, and we're trying to establish a connection between them all."

"How many people are we talking about?"

"Two more so far, and both of them were present at the synagogue when the sergeant spoke to you."

162

"Had you not heard about them on the news?" said Lance.

"I've had rather a lot on this week. I've missed a lot of the news I'm afraid, and I've been focusing more on the Palestine conflict than anything local anyway."

"Or from any of the bingo players?" added Owusu.

"Come to think of it, the two Jewish ladies missed bingo this week. It didn't occur to me to wonder why. Nor has Sheila Cotton followed up on her complaints, which is unlike her. Why, what's happened?"

"The rabbi Jeremy Cotton, and a young woman named Amanda Dawson have both been murdered," said Lance.

"And we're working on the hypothesis for now that they and Jason Bampton were all murdered by the same person," Owusu clarified.

"What happened? When?" Chelouche's expression of surprise seemed perfectly genuine.

Lance jumped in quickly. "Could you tell us your whereabouts on Saturday morning, Mr Chelouche?"

The Algerian gentle giant responded just as promptly. "I had work appointments for the whole of that day, spread between Richmond and Alperton. My first began at nine in the morning, and I was either working or travelling between them until at least half past five."

"The rabbi collapsed in the middle of his service last Saturday in front of all of the attendees," said Owusu, puzzled by Lance's seemingly redundant question.

"We've since discovered that he had been poisoned," Lance added.

"That's awful. I'm sorry to say, but this is the first I've heard of it. I have been fairly busy. I was booked all day for various odd jobs around Ealing and Acton for all of this week as well, including Sunday. And I had my evening commitments at the community college too, of course."

He stopped speaking abruptly as the door opened and Mrs Chelouche entered carrying a tray containing a beautiful glass teapot displaying a delightful golden transparent infusion and emitting a healthy ejection of steam from its spout. Around the teapot were three robust-looking glasses, with a thick heat-insulating layer of asymmetrical thickness elegantly preventing the temperature from being a problem for eager fingertips.

"Do I need to give you client details to verify?" Rayan Chelouche resumed the conversation, while his wife silently smiled at Owusu and Lance in turn, gently placed the tray onto the coffee table in front of them, and then delicately walked back out of the living room.

Owusu managed a gracious "Thank you" in Mrs Chelouche's direction before she closed the door behind her. The inspector looked at the woman's husband once more and said, "We may ask for them at another time, but we'll take you at your word for now."

"We believe the murder weapon was sent to him by Royal Mail," Lance clarified.

"Then anyone could have had the opportunity to post it, I suppose."

"Anyone in the area, yes," confirmed Owusu. "Amanda Dawson, though, was attacked and murdered in Ravenscourt Park just before dawn on Wednesday this week."

Rayan Chelouche picked up the teapot and filled each of the three glasses. "Please," he said, gesturing at the tea in front of his visitors.

"Thank you. Smells great. And what about early morning on Wednesday the nineteenth?" said Owusu.

"How early?" said Mr Chelouche.

"Before dawn," said Lance, in between sips of his tea.

"I would have got out of bed very slightly after dawn. Around seven-ish. I went to the gym for an hour before visiting my first client of the day. I had a lot of jobs to do this week, as I said. Hence all of this being news to me."

"So, your wife can account for your presence in bed, and gym staff can corroborate your time there, I take it?" said Lance.

"Certainly."

"OK, that's fine," said Owusu. "How well did you know Amanda Dawson? Or Mandy as you may have known her."

"I'm afraid I didn't at all. My only connection with anyone at the synagogue was through the bingo. If Mrs Cotton hadn't raged against her perceived injustice the other week, I would never have encountered her son. And if Mrs Hamberger hadn't forgotten her glasses, I wouldn't have set foot on the premises. I only went there to return them."

165

"Might you have overheard anything – there, or during a bingo session – that could point to a connection between these three victims?"

"I'm afraid not. I can only speculate as you did, that they'd been burgled, and they knew each other through their religious events."

"I see. Well, Mr Chelouche. One thing's for certain. You're absolutely right about the Moroccans and their tea." Owusu handed him a card. "Please call me on my direct number if you remember anything else. And thank you very much for your time, Mr Chelouche."

"You're very welcome. Both of you."

Chapter 12:

Once they'd turned the corner away from Cloister Road, Owusu broke the silence. "Why did you ask him where he was on Saturday morning, Lance?"

Lance had to stop and think for a moment. "Oh, yeah. Of course we know the poison was delivered by post and sent days or more before that, and so would our killer. But an innocent party, especially one who wasn't present to see what happened wouldn't know that, and would give a more direct answer to the question. If Mr Chelouche had been puzzled by the question in the same way you were, that would have given us another reason to suspect him."

"Clever. But we didn't get that clue, did we?"

"No, we didn't. So we keep trying, Inspector."

"Indeed, we do."

"Where next?"

"Sophie Dimsdale. Lamington Street. My car's parked just up the road. It's about a twenty-minute drive."

"What do we know about her so far, Inspector?"

"She moved to the area from North London three years ago and was burgled around that time. I've looked into the report of the burglary at her address. Unfortunately, we weren't able to attribute it to Jason Bampton or any of his associates." Owusu unlocked her car, and they were both soon seated and strapped in.

"But he didn't take kindly to rivals encroaching on his territory, I imagine," said Lance.

"A reasonable supposition," agreed Owusu, as she pulled out of her parking space. "And we've got prison staff trying to learn more from those inside at the moment. We just haven't come up with anything concrete yet."

"Can't hurt to assume that Bampton was connected to every burglary in the borough at the time," suggested Lance.

"No, but for motive we would need the homeowners to hold Bampton responsible, justifiably or otherwise, and it would be a stretch to assume that Sophie Dimsdale, Sheila Cotton or anyone else is making that assumption too."

"So, if we can't find a way to link Bampton to a burglary, we can't really expect anyone else to?"

"That's how I see it, Lance."

"I agree, Inspector. OK, what else is there?"

"Not much. She said she started attending the synagogue only a year later. Claimed not to have noticed it at the end of her street for over a year."

"Well I suppose the building doesn't look especially religious from the outside."

"No, but people would have been walking in and out in appropriate attire every Saturday."

"It's something, I suppose. There are people who never look out of their windows. Did you get a sense of what kind of personality she has? Any hint of neurodivergence or spectrumminess?"

"Spectrumminess? Is that an official term?"

"I dunno – there are so many different identifiers and I'm not qualified to diagnose. I hope you can't go too wrong by suggesting someone's a bit spectrummy."

"You can always go wrong, Lance. Even someone who spends as little time on social media as I do figured that out years ago. One of the perks of sharing a house with teenagers."

"I'll be keeping the term between friends in that case."

"Very wise, Lance. Though I will say I'm honoured to be included as such."

"Of course, Inspector! Do we know what she does for a living? What kinds of people she comes into contact with?"

"Actually, we don't. That's one of the things we need to find out today. Our chat with her at the synagogue was terminated prematurely by an old lady determined to feed D.S. Krol and myself. Ms Dimsdale was not prepared to wait for the interruption to pass."

"No-one's stalked her online?"

169

"If you mean what I think you mean, Lance, we tried. We didn't come up with much."

"At least she's consistent then. She could be just very shy, secretive, paranoid or whatever."

"Spectrummy?"

"Spectrummy, Inspector, or maybe just shy."

Owusu turned off the A40 and onto Old Oak Road. "Traffic could be worse. A lot worse," she said.

Lance nodded. "While we're at it, what else do we know about Mandy Dawson? Any connection with the other members?" He had nearly said parishioners.

"We know one thing. Her godmother's sister also attends. But we don't know who that is. Dawson wasn't able to identify her there when we spoke to her."

"And she didn't give her name?"

"Unfortunately not."

"Do I need to have a word with Pav, Inspector?"

"In fact, that one was my fault. I was asking the questions, and I didn't manage to push for the name. Sergeant Krol was interviewing Mr Chelouche for most of that time."

Lance was already primed from his morning conversation with Sahana to offer sympathy and forgiveness wherever he felt it might be helpful. "We had no idea she'd be next. We didn't even know that the rabbi was going to come first at the time."

"Indeed, Lance. And by the time it became urgent to ask, she was dead."

"And I take it you couldn't find out from anyone else, Inspector?"

"Only if the trustees asked everyone on our behalf and the person in question came forward. And we don't even know if the sister is an elderly lady, or a minor, or anything in between."

"Nor how regularly she attends, I suppose," said Lance. "Let's take every opportunity to find out though."

"Agreed," said Owusu, parking her car in the gap in front of her own house. "We can walk the rest of the way."

***

Sophie Dimsdale opened her front door after a wait of several minutes, punctuated with repeated knocks and rings, but showed no sign of having rushed to answer. "Inspector Owusu. I'm sorry, were you waiting long? I had headphones on, so I've no idea how many times you rang the doorbell."

"That's quite all right, Ms Dimsdale."

"Please, call me Sophie."

"Very well, Sophie. This is my associate, Private Detective Lance Pomegranate. May we come in and ask you a few questions?"

"Erm, yes. Yes, you may. I'm sorry, I'm not really fit for visitors at the moment. I don't have anything to offer you. But I do have some time to talk. Let me show you in." She glanced down at Lance's feet and momentarily shuddered at first, and then visibly relaxed.

"Is something the matter, Ms Dimsdale?" asked Lance, trying perhaps not quite hard enough to avoid sounding provocative.

"I thought there was for a moment, but no," she replied. "Sorry I have this weird thing – I just can't handle the sight of open-toed footwear. I thought you were wearing a pair of Jesus sandals when I saw your toes. Then I looked properly. It's fine. I'm fine with bare feet. Phew!"

"Phew!" Lance mirrored, with an unmistakable tint of kindness in his tone.

"Shall we?" said Owusu.

"Of course. Follow me." She led them into her lounge. It was simple, but neat. There was no table of any kind in the room; not even one supporting a television, for there was no television. There were bookshelves full of non-fiction. They were mostly texts on computer science, coding and linguistics, and the remainder represented a variety of scientific fields, apart from a handful of tutorial books on foreign exchange, makeup and learning Korean. There was just one picture frame in the entire room, hanging on the wall to the right of the door, facing the front windows, whose plain white curtains were currently drawn.

The frame contained a print of a cartoon featuring Marie Curie, Steve Jobs and John Coltrane. Lance felt the message must be pretty bleak, if he understood it correctly. The expression on Owusu's face suggested she might be thinking the same thing.

There happened to be three empty chairs, forming an equilateral triangle whose centre was also the centre of the room. Owusu's face showed approval at this. Lance sat very carefully so as to avoid even slightly moving the chair he'd chosen.

"Thank you for giving up your time, Sophie," said Owusu. "We will aim to take up as little of it as possible."

"You're following up on the Jason Bampton murder? Or is this about Rabbi Cotton?"

"Both, in fact. And more. Hold on." Owusu paused to gather her thoughts. "Are you aware that there's been a third murder?"

"No. Is there a connection to the others? I'm still processing the rabbi's death. I was there when it happened. Most of us were. Horrible. His poor mother."

"I'm afraid there is. One of your congregation members has also been murdered. Amanda Dawson?"

"Amanda . . . Mandy? Oh no! That's horrible! My sister. She'll be destroyed."

"Your sister?"

"My sister Elizabeth. She's a close friend of Mandy's parents. They sort of made her a kind of godmother. Will she have been told? Do you know that?"

"The victim's parents know. Whom they would have subsequently informed is none of our business. But it was also on the news. Your sister may have discovered it that way instead."

"Could be. I don't follow the news myself. I'm in the Mark Twain camp. But Elizabeth might."

"Mark Twain?" said Owusu.

"Those who don't read the news are uninformed," said Lance. "And those who do are misinformed." He then added, in a weak imitation of a Belfast accent, "More relevant today than it was in his time."

"Yes, thank you, Lance," said Owusu curtly. "Sophie, can you tell us your whereabouts on the night of Thursday the 6th of October, from ten pm onwards?"

"Most weeknights I'm working upstairs at my computer. I don't like to leave the house after dark."

"Does anyone else live here with you?"

"My two cats."

"Anyone who can speak English?" said Lance.

"No, I'm afraid not. They can understand it of course, though."

"Could anyone else verify that you were at home?" said Owusu.

"I ordered a pizza around half past ten. It was delivered about quarter past eleven. Does that count?"

"It may well do, if we can contact the delivery driver."

"I still have the receipt. I put my takeaway orders against tax. I just cannot get any work done without them, so they definitely increase my taxable income."

"And what is it you do?" said Lance. Sophie gestured to the books behind her. "Software engineer?" he hazarded.

"Correct."

"What do you do in your free time?"

"Not a lot," she confessed. "I'm a computer nerd. I have my cats and I don't make a lot of friends. I'm not especially attached to my family either. I've had not much luck with romance. Still trying but not getting anywhere. But I love my cats and my job."

"Can you tell us where you were on the morning of Wednesday the 19th of October? Very early morning, around dawn, that is."

"Oh, actually yes, I can, but it's quite pathetic really. I thought I was going on a breakfast date. I got the bus to Chalk Farm early in the morning. I was so excited I could barely sleep the night before, so I ended up leaving much earlier than I needed to just for the sake of doing something other than waiting at home and second-guessing my choice of outfit. I remember seeing the sun come up from my seat on the upper deck."

"And your date, that is the person you went to see, could verify that for you?"

"He never turned up. I told you it was pathetic. But the café staff can. I waited a while, and then when it was clear he wasn't coming, I ordered a big meal and had it by myself."

"I'm sorry to hear that, Sophie," said Lance.

"Men, eh?"

"If it's any consolation, I used to get treated like that on dating apps too. I haven't used any for ages now. Maybe I should get a couple of cats for myself," said Lance.

"Can we see a picture of this man?" said Owusu. "Do you have his phone number or email address?"

"I don't, I'm afraid. For all I know it was just a child who lives on the other side of the planet playing a prank. My only contact with him was through the app's internal messaging system. I messaged him to ask what had happened while I was on my way back. An hour later he'd vanished. That means he unmatched me and made it impossible to re-establish contact. It's as if we never connected in the first place."

"I see," said Owusu. "I'm sorry to hear that, but for our purposes the details of the café will more than suffice."

Sophie looked at her watch and then said, "I'm really sorry, but I might not be able to spare much more time this morning. Is there anything else I can help you with really quickly?"

"Just one more question from me," said Lance. "Can you think of any connection between your sister's goddaughter and the rabbi? I mean something specific to them, that wouldn't apply to the other members."

"She was quite fond of his mum's cakes. I remember her saying so. Other than that, I'm afraid not. You could ask Elizabeth though. She was much closer to her."

"We shall certainly do that," said Owusu. "Very well, I think that's everything I wanted to ask. We really appreciate your time, Sophie. We'll let you get on with your afternoon plans now."

"Thanks very much," Lance added. "Keep fighting the good fight against Jesus sandals."

Chapter 13:

"The mum next then, Inspector?"

"Yes, Lance. Mrs Cotton is just a few doors down. Be careful, Lance. She was a handful while her son was still alive. Now, she's quite understandably somewhat more than that."

"I understand. I'm prepared though. I attribute every personality trait I'd rather not have to my own Jewish mother."

"Mazel tov?"

Lance shrugged. "If you say so."

They reached Sheila Cotton's house and Owusu rang the doorbell. They waited barely any time at all before Sheila opened the door to them.

"Inspector Owusu! Come in, both of you. I've got cakes and bagels ready. Come in and have a seat, and I'll pour you some tea."

She showed Owusu and Lance through to her living room. And pointed to the sofa. "Make yourselves at home. Give me a moment." She disappeared for a few seconds, returning with a large clear plastic bowl, and a large packet of crisps that she duly opened and emptied into the bowl, which she had placed on the coffee table. "Help yourselves while I get everything else. I won't be long!"

"That's a first," said Lance, once he and Owusu were alone.

"She didn't comment on your appearance at all, you mean?"

"It's partly that, but she didn't even ask who I was. She acted as if she already knew me. Did she think I was Pav?"

"Who knows?" said Owusu. "Maybe you have more of a reputation around here than you thought."

"Maybe," said Lance, pensively.

"What are you thinking Lance?"

"It's flimsy at the moment, Inspector. Let's see if anything else we learn today will beef it up a bit."

"No beef here, I'm afraid," said Sheila, returning from the kitchen with bagels, cakes and a pot of tea carried on a tray in each of her hands. She placed the trays on the table either side of the crisp bowl. "But plenty of protein. I hope you both like egg mayonnaise. I've also got cream cheese for the bagels."

"That's very kind of you, Mrs Cotton. You really don't need to go to all of this trouble. We're just grateful for your time and your co-operation."

"Oh, it's no trouble at all. You have a big job to do, I know. Feeding you is the least I can do!" Sheila then looked directly at Lance and said, "I hope you don't mind saying, but I'm so happy for you. I'm a big supporter of the gay people. It's so good to see you able to work in the police as yourself. Your mother must be very proud of you!"

"Sure," said Lance cautiously. "It's an important cause, I agree, Mrs Cotton."

"Sheila. I insist! And what's your name?"

"Thank you, Sheila. My name is Lance Pomegranate. I'm a private detective. May I have some of your egg mayo on a bagel? Did you make it yourself?"

"Certainly. I love your nails, by the way. I need someone to do mine. And for you, Inspector?"

"Yes please. The same. Thank you."

Sheila poured the tea while they each took a bite from their bagels. Lance enjoyed his more than he cared to admit. Owusu appeared to have no trouble letting him see how much she was enjoying hers.

"Right. Have you arrested him yet?"

"Arrested whom?"

"That man! Rayan Chelouche! Have you arrested him?"

"I'd prefer not to reveal information about our progress at this stage, Sheila. We are investigating fully, and I am afraid that is all I am able to say at present."

"Do you need more evidence? Is that it? I will tell you everything I know about him. I've been keeping an eye on him.

He's been travelling all over the area, visiting lots of people in their homes. He's plotting his next murder, no doubt."

"Sheila," said Owusu very gently. "Are you stalking him?"

"I'm not stalking anyone. I'm just telling you what I've seen."

"If I may," said Lance. "You could be right about him. And if you are, you'd be putting yourself in serious danger."

"Oh. I hadn't thought of that. But you think I'm right?" Sheila beamed. "Good! I was so worried that no-one would believe me when it's all so obvious. I've always said we need more gay people in the police! I wish my son had been gay. I would have been so proud of him."

"Were you not proud of him anyway, Sheila?" asked Owusu.

"Oh yes, but he would have been such a talisman for both communities, and I could have shown everyone what a good progressive person I am. I would have loved to have seen him marry a nice Jewish boy and adopt a grandchild for me. And he would have been a lot tidier and better organised as well, I tell you."

"I'm not sure it works that way, Sheila," said Lance.

"I suppose you would know best. Gosh, your toes are really fabulous."

Owusu, who now had two empty hands, an empty mouth and a satisfied stomach said, "Apologies, Sheila, but I need to ask everyone this. Could you tell me where you were early on the morning of Wednesday the 19th of October? From just before dawn until just after."

"Oh, I see. That's exciting! Of course, you know I didn't do it, but yes, I'll tell you where I was. I often wake up early. It might be a sign of being old. I go downstairs to the kitchen and make myself a cup of tea. Oh, wait. I only have decaf. This is decaf you're drinking now. I hope that's OK."

"It's absolutely fine. Please continue," said Owusu.

"I made tea, and I put some laundry on."

"Was your husband aware of you getting up early?"

"Oh, he knows I do it all the time."

"I mean on that particular morning."

"Erm, yes. Yes, I think so. I made tea, and I put some laundry on. I was careful not to play the music too loudly so that I wouldn't wake him, and I remember looking at the calendar that morning. It was definitely Wednesday, because I remembered that I had agreed to meet my friend Susan for lunch later."

"Please clarify, Sheila. It could be important. Did your husband, or anyone else, notice your absence from the bedroom that morning?"

"Oh, I'm sure he did."

"May we speak to him?" said Lance.

"Of course. He'll be upstairs listening to his Hebrew radio station. I'll ask him to come down. One moment."

Sheila stepped through the living room door and out towards the bottom of the stairs. But instead of the sound of the dynamic old lady's ascending footsteps, there was a deafening shout.

"NIGEL! NIGEL! COME DOWN AND TALK TO THE POLICE! THERE'S A NICE BLACK LADY AND A GAY MAN WHO WANT TO ASK YOU SOMETHING!"

Sheila's voice had a strong component of around four kilohertz, the frequency to which human hearing is the most sensitive, and Lance's ears were no exception. His eyes told him that neither were Owusu's.

Sheila returned to the living room and said, "He'll be down in a few minutes."

"Why not try asking in Hebrew?" suggested Lance sarcastically.

"I wish I could. I used to be fluent, you know. It was a long time ago. No-one believes me now when I tell them."

"While we're waiting," said Owusu, wiping some cake crumbs from her lips, "do you know if your son had any connection to the burglar Jason Bampton, or the young girl from your congregation, Amanda Dawson?"

"Other than that they were all killed by that man Rayan Chelouche? I can't think of one. But if I find out anything, I'll certainly let you know. I suggest you look into all the houses he's visited. I've made a list for you. I'll go and fetch it."

Owusu sighed.

"Something wrong, Inspector?" said Sheila.

"No, nothing wrong, Sheila."

"Give me a moment. I'll give my useless husband a nudge too."

Owusu nodded in resignation. Once Sheila was out of the room she turned to Lance and spoke gently. "Look, you and I both know those visits will have been work appointments."

"But . . ." said Lance.

"Exactly," said Owusu. "Now we have an independent account of his visits, so we have to check it out, even though we know it's almost certainly a waste of time."

"Do we go back to Chelouche and ask for his past schedule, client names and addresses? And then check them all personally?"

"We'll divide the task up among a number of officers. D.S. Krol can co-ordinate that."

"And they might save themselves some time by checking any discrepancies between Sheila's list and his," suggested Lance.

"Let's see the list first," said Owusu.

"Good point."

Sheila returned moments later with a piece of paper in her hand. Her husband followed her into the room.

"Nigel Cotton. How may I help you?"

"I'm Detective Inspector Esi Owusu," Owusu said, standing up to shake his hand. "And this is my associate, Private Detective Lance Pomegranate. First of all, let me offer my condolences regarding the tragic loss of your son."

"Thank you, Inspector," said Mr Cotton.

"We're investigating his death and a number of others. We just have one routine question. A simple formality, to eliminate your wife from our suspects list."

"Fire away."

"Do you remember her getting up early on the morning of Wednesday the 19th of October? And were you aware of her activity downstairs until just after dawn?"

"I slept right through, but she does it all the time. Sometimes she wakes me up with the *Guys and Dolls* soundtrack. She's obsessed with it. But not that day, I don't think."

"I told you I was careful not to be too loud, didn't I?" said Sheila.

"All right, thank you Mr Cotton. That's everything we need, I think," said Owusu.

"Here's the list I made," said Sheila proudly. "Now you can go and arrest that wicked man."

"Thank you," said Owusu, graciously accepting the piece of paper. "And thank you for the tea and the food. Your cakes are delicious!"

"Oh jolly good! Would you like to take some more away with you?"

185

"No thank you, but you're very kind."

"And you, Lance? Would you like another to eat on your way?"

"No thanks, Sheila. But I agree with the inspector. Amazing cakes."

***

"Fucking hell," said Lance.

"Fucking hell," agreed Owusu, cautiously. "So, what were you thinking earlier? Has it been beefed up at all?"

"Just wondering why Sheila Cotton didn't act as though she was meeting me for the first time," said Lance.

"We don't know a lot about the killer, but from the emails, he's done his homework on me. Or she, as the case may be."

"Bit of a stretch, isn't it, Lance?"

"Hence the need for beef, Inspector."

"And was there any?"

"I'm not sure. She's quite a character. Would be a hell of a performance for our killer to create it. And yet, the naive insistence on us going after Chelouche, and a really weak alibi for Mandy Dawson's murder. I really want to rule it out, but something's stopping me."

"Would that something be your relationship with your own mother, Lance?"

"Thanks, Sigmund. No. Better not be, anyway."

186

"If it helps, she has an alibi for Bampton's murder, and it is a bit more solid. She was on the phone to a friend from her landline at the time. But if your childhood trauma motivates you to find a hole in that, by all means."

"Pav told me she said she was in bed with a hot water bottle easily by the time the pubs shut that night."

"You're right, Lance. Do you want to go back and ask the husband about that too?"

"I suppose we might as well."

"Not we. I'm not doing it, Lance. I'll go on and interview Sarah Hamberger. I'll be wasting enough of my time with that as it is."

"OK, sure, Inspector. We'll catch up later."

***

Hammersmith Police Station was only a fifteen-minute walk from Lamington Street, but Lance had made a little detour to his home on Goldhawk Road first, to fetch his laptop. He and Owusu had missed the rain while being entertained in several senses by Sheila Cotton. The sun was breaking through the clouds, and the air was approaching room temperature. Warm wet pavement was Lance's favourite surface, especially if it was smooth, though with the autumn foliage it could be rather slippery. It felt good regardless.

He thought again of Sahana, hoping the same sensation might have lifted her mood somewhat on her way home that morning. He resisted the urge to phone her there and then. She would be buried in her music, no doubt. He instead sent a simple three-word WhatsApp message: 'Thinking of you'.

He arrived at the police station and was immediately greeted by an officer at the desk with, "Hi, Sir. The D.I.'s not here at the moment. Is there anything else we can do for you?"

"Actually D.S. Krol made me an appointment with your cyber team. I'm a little bit early. It was booked for two o'clock. Lance Pomegranate."

"That's fine, Sir. Let me get hold of the sergeant. You can take a seat over there if you like."

"Sure," said Lance, who turned to walk towards the row of chairs against the wall to his left.

"Nice nails. Do you do them yourself?"

"Cheers, mate. Yes I do."

"It's unusual on a bloke, but I like it."

"Thanks. I'll just wait over there then, shall I?"

"Please do."

Lance took a seat and withdrew his phone from his pocket out of habit. He was just two minutes into a YouTube video tearing apart someone's claim to have disproven human influence on climate change when a familiar voice brought his attention back into the room.

"Were you waiting long, Lance?"

"Not at all, Pav, mate. And I was early anyway. Not your fault. Can we start now?"

"Yes, come with me. I've got one of our tech experts waiting for you."

"Sure." Lance put his phone away in his pocket as he stood, then picked up his briefcase from the floor and followed Pawel through the same corridor that D.C.I. Murphy had taken him along previously, except they continued past the foot of the staircase and through another set of double doors, before entering a small room on their left.

"Lance, this is Digital Forensics Expert Dhruv Kerai. Dhruv, this is Private Detective Lance Pomegranate," said Pawel.

"Pleasure to meet you Mr Pomegranate. What can I do for you today?"

"Call me Lance, but likewise. Cheers. Has Pav told you about the emails I've been getting regarding these recent murders?"

"He has. You want me to look at the emails that the killer's been taunting you with, is that correct?"

"That's correct, yes. Here. I'll load them up for you."

Lance took his laptop out and opened it on the desk in front of the expert. "I've sorted the emails into a folder. I'm wondering what you can tell me about where they might have been sent from, plus any other clues that might be embedded in the metadata. I'm sure you know what to look for. And there's one other thing. There was an image attachment in one

189

of the photos. It seemed way too large for the image displayed. I wondered if it had been cropped down and the data was still in the file somehow. But none of the apps I tried was able to make any sense of it."

"OK, let's see what I can tell you quickly. And then there might be some more I can do if you're willing to leave your machine here with me."

"Sounds good. I've backed everything up, and I've got my desktop to work from at home in the meantime. And my phone of course. May I sit in with you for a bit?"

"Sure. I'll start with the email metadata. So, the sender Malcolm Dombattu seems to have spoofed his email address, but not at first. Not from your initial conversation, but from once he started giving you clues. And each clue was actually sent from a different burner Gmail account. Spoofed as the Malcolm Dombattu email address each time."

"That's weird. Do people do that, in your experience?"

"Spammers do. And scammers of course. But they tend not to get through burner emails so quickly. It's not immediately obvious why one would go to this trouble to use a different one for each email. Especially when the emails are personally addressed to you. Perhaps he's being extra cautious."

"Can you determine anything about when the burner email accounts were created, and from what location?"

"No, I can't do that. But if you allow me time, I might be able to determine where each email was sent from, assuming there was no VPN involved. If you're OK with me hanging on to your laptop I'll look into that, and the image file as well. I'll just need time to copy everything across to a sandboxed machine first."

"Sure. Thanks for your help. Really appreciate it."

"Not at all. Is there anything else you'd like me to look at?"

Before Lance could reply, there was a knock at the door. Pawel opened it and leant his head through.

"Sorry to interrupt, Sergeant. We've just heard that another body has been found."

"Where?" said Pawel and Lance in unison.

"In the pedestrian underpass near Hyde Park Corner."

"Do you have a name?"

"Yes sir. Vineel Eshwar."

"Oh shit," said Lance. "I apologise, sorry. But do you know what this means?"

"It's someone you know?" said the officer.

"Yes, but it's far worse than that." Lance turned to face the cyber expert again. "Mr Kerai, I'm afraid I'm going to need a bit more of your help. Somehow this killer is hearing every word I say."

Chapter 14:

Lance left the police station with Pawel, without either his phone or his laptop. He had had no choice but to trust Dhruv Kerai with them both and hope for an answer on how the killer managed to know about Vineel. He needed to make sure Sahana was OK. She would still be shut away in her studio by the time his death appeared in the news, with no idea what the killer had just done, or what he might be about to do next. Without his phone and his laptop, he couldn't reach her easily, even if she hadn't put her phone away for the afternoon, as would be most likely.

"Do you want to call Sahana on my phone?" said Pawel.

"I do, but she won't want to be interrupted now," said Lance. "Thanks though." It had also occurred to him that the killer might be monitoring him in some other way. What if he'd been listening to Sahana's calls instead of his own? He anxiously pulled everything out of his pockets and examined each item in turn. His keys, his wallet, his Bluetooth headphones and their case. Would he have to ask Sahana to do the same thing? He may well do unless Dhruv could find something on one of his devices.

In the meantime, he decided it would be best not to discuss anything relevant to the case or his personal life with anyone. "Pav, mate, can I have a look at your notes?"

"Erm, yeah, Lance. What was it you wanted to see?"

"I'm not sure, yet," lied Lance, though he wasn't lying to the sergeant as such. He knew exactly what he wanted to see, and that was a blank page where he could write a note explaining the situation.

"Yeah, I thought as much," said Lance. "Sarah Hamberger might not be as demented as she lets on," he improvised, handing the notebook back to Pawel to read.

"We should go and speak to her again," Pawel said, playing along, before mouthing *What now?*

Lance thought for a second and then performed a short excerpt from an air trombone sonata. Pawel signalled understanding with a couple of quick nods.

"Owusu might still be there. Give her a call and get her to ask about Sarah Hamberger's recent bingo track record. I need to go and grab something from my office." Lance added an air trombone cadenza that concluded with a falling and rising slide glissando straight out of the circus. He then waved goodbye to Pawel and walked away briskly in order to get out of earshot of Pawel's phone call to Owusu as quickly as possible.

Lance's eyes were focused on the pavement beneath him, against his habit of scanning the ground dozens of feet ahead

193

for the kind of objects he'd prefer not to step on. Instead, he was deliberately limiting his field of view so as to be able to think better. As such he had to be pushed back by the outstretched hands of the police officer monitoring Ciara Gallen's house as he passed it, in order to avoid a far more painful and embarrassing collision.

"Shi . . . I mean, sorry, Officer."

"You seem in quite a hurry, Mr Pomegranate. Is everything OK?"

"To be honest, no. I'm really sorry. This is just my way of dealing with it."

"OK, Sir. Just be careful."

"I will. Sorry, again."

Ciara Gallen's front door slowly opened. "Mr Polystyrene. Do you have a minute?"

"I suppose I do, Mrs Gallen. How can I help you?" Lance mimed scribbling a note to the officer, and then gestured to the officer to hand his notebook and pen over when he pulled them out of his pocket. By the time Ciara Gallen had fully emerged from her front door out onto the street, Lance was holding up a short sentence written in large caps:

I MAY HAVE BEEN BUGGED

Ciara Gallen nodded. "I just wanted to ask you if there's anything else you can give me about the murders so far? Anything the police would allow me to print?"

"The murderer's a cunt," said Lance while writing another note. "You can print that." The note said *Do you feel protected?*

Ciara Gallen nodded, then added. "From a named source?"

"Sure. Filthy savage immigrant who's never heard of shoes uses foul and abusive language against a noble British serial killer."

She nodded again and then said. "I think I'll go with 'descendent of convicts'."

Lance handed her the notebook and pen. "Anything else?"

She thought for a second and then started writing. *Oliver's school?* "I hope you have something juicier for me soon."

Lance let the officer see her note, who promptly nodded and raised a hand showing two fingers as if making a V for victory.

"Best approach D.I. Owusu directly, sweetheart. She likes you more than I do, anyway."

"Sweetheart? Really?"

Lance shrugged.

"Well, if you happen see the inspector before I do, can you tell her to hurry the fuck up and catch this, erm, *censored for my sensitive readers*, let's say, before I really am next in line."

"That's her top priority for sure. Even ahead of beating the D.C.I. to the last biscuit in the station staff room, I promise you. I, on the other hand, am open to the possibility that your noble sacrifice might give us that all-important final piece of the puzzle. You won't be forgotten." He mouthed *Sorry. On it.'*

"I'm not fucking about, Mr Potato Head."

Lance gave her two emphatic thumbs-up, though they were just as much for himself as he basked, buried in the role-play.

"Don't worry. We'll catch this cunt before you can say *Daily Mail Headlines Cause Cancer.*"

"I'm more worried about catching athlete's foot at present, Mr Polyunsaturate."

"And I thought you were worried about getting murdered. Anyway, I need to get going. Remember, we immigrants aren't all bad, now."

He left Ciara Gallen to return indoors shaking her head, while the police officer resumed his vigil.

Of course, that whole charade might well have been pointless, he thought to himself as he made his way towards Hammersmith station. The killer will know about the police protection offered to Ciara Gallen, and most likely overheard their prior conversation in his office following the murder of Mandy Dawson. The killer must also know for certain that Pawel would be heading straight to the site of Vineel's murder, and would have called Owusu to say so, instead of feeding her an exciting revelation about a marble-deficient bingo champion. And of course, Lance had foolishly blurted out in the presence of both his devices that he had realised what was happening. But if he could control the flow of information at all, he was going to do so as a matter of pride.

He caught a 220 bus that took him all the way to Wandsworth. Now, if he could just remember where Sahana's studio was . . .

***

D.S. Krol made his way from Hyde Park Corner tube station, past the two officers guarding the entrance into the underpass and towards the police line surrounding the two forensic officers examining the body. There, lying in a dirty, torn and foul-smelling sleeping bag, with an expression of horror on his face, was Vineel Eshwar, whom Pawel had briefly met a few nights earlier.

There appeared to be a small puddle of blood behind the victim's head. There was no hint of clothing on Vineel's neck or shoulders. Resting against the body was a piece of cardboard, torn from a box, displaying a message, handwritten in marker pen in block capitals. It read:

WILL TAKE IT UP THE ARSE FOR A FIVER

Vineel's right arm was stretched out ahead of him in a macabre Superman pose. His right hand was in a fist, clutching a five-pound note.

"Have you checked inside the sleeping bag yet?" said Pawel to the forensic team.

"Not yet, and frankly we're not looking forward to it. We have some more work to do before it's worth disturbing the body though."

197

"Of course," said Pawel. "So we're all thinking the same thing, I take it. D.I. Owusu will appreciate being here in time to see it, I'm sure."

He returned to the two officers outside the tunnel entrance. "Any witness statements so far?"

"Just the person who discovered the body, exactly as it is now. She simply said there was no-one else around when she spotted it."

"What time did she call to report it?"

"Twenty-five past two."

"OK, said Pawel. Though we have no idea how long he might have been lying there beforehand. Any number of people could have walked past, trying to pay as little attention as possible to a sleeping homeless person."

"Even if they read the sign?"

"Especially if they read the sign," said Pawel. "If you see that while walking past, what are you likely to think?"

"Stag do gone wrong? Hidden camera prank?"

"Or someone so desperate that they're looking up towards rock bottom as an unrealistic aim, resorting to measures that anyone with the privilege of a roof over their head couldn't comprehend."

"Even with that wording, Sergeant?"

"It does look more like a prank, I agree, but then we know that it's come from the killer's sick sense of humour. A passerby would likely be shocked and repelled away at full speed and only wonder if it's a prank once they're at a safe distance, if at all."

"Well, that would explain the lack of witnesses, Sergeant," said Owusu, emerging from the entrance to the tube station. "Let's see it, then."

Owusu and Krol's footsteps reverberated around the tunnel, whose acoustics added a variety of flutter echoes, and an almost cartoonish natural flange effect as they approached the body.

"Give me a quick summary please, Sergeant."

"Yes, Sir," said Pawel." The deceased is a male in his mid-thirties, named Vineel Eshwar. Found by a witness at twenty-five past two this afternoon, exactly as he is now. Complete with the sleeping bag, the blood behind his head, the sign, and the money."

"Is he naked under there?"

"I'd bet money on it," said Pawel, "but we haven't checked yet."

"We're almost ready, Inspector," said the same forensic officer who'd previously spoken with Pawel, taking one last round of photographs of the entire scene.

"I should mention, Sir, this man. He's been staying with Sahana this past week. I met him not long ago. He's a friend of her brother."

"And how would the killer . . . oh no," Owusu said softly. "Does Lance know?"

"He's on his way to see her now. But he doesn't have his phone. It's with our cyber team at the moment. His laptop too."

"He's been bugged."

"That's what we're checking for, Sir."

"Removing the sleeping bag now," said the other forensic officer, revealing that Vineel was indeed naked, and that the fiver in his fist was indeed hard-earnt.

More of Vineel's blood had escaped from his body through the unpleasant aperture created by the insertion of what appeared to be the murder weapon.

"Are we looking at the direct cause of death here?" said Owusu.

"I would say so, Sir," said the forensic officer nearest to her. "The blood by his head appears to have come from a non-lethal blow. It may not even have knocked him unconscious, although would have made him almost incapable of resisting what happened next. And there don't seem to be any other injuries, so I'm inclined to suspect that the very large object inserted into his rectum must have been the deciding factor?"

"But how?" said Sergeant Krol. "I mean obviously it looks extremely painful. Excruciating, even. But unless he got an infection and sped up time, I don't see how he should be dead so soon."

"Poison? Cyanide again?" suggested Owusu.

"That would be my guess, Sir," said the forensic officer currently photographing Vineel's ruptured backside. "Dr Grappa will be able to tell us more in due course."

"Our killer must have nerves of steel," Pawel observed.

"You're right, Sergeant. "To pull this off in the middle of the day, albeit not strictly broad daylight, and then take the time to not only set up this perverse tableau, but also gather together all of the victim's clothing before absconding with it takes a special kind of psychopath. We're not just dealing with someone who really wanted these people dead, for money, or love, or revenge."

"Yes, Sir. This is someone who said '*I want to be a serial killer when I grow up*', and followed his dreams all the way," said Pawel.

"DETECTIVES!" The shout came from the entrance to the underpass. It was one of the officers.

Owusu said to the forensic team, "Thanks for your excellent work as always. We'll leave you to finish up."

Pawel followed her out of the tunnel.

"Sorry, to interrupt," said the officer who had summoned them. "We have a witness here and we thought it best if she speak to you directly."

"Yes, of course," said Owusu. She turned to the witness and said, "What can you tell us?"

"I saw it happen," said the witness. "I'm assuming that's what you're investigating, I mean."

"At what time?" said Pawel.

"It was about five past two. I was walking through the tunnel, and I passed someone lying in a sleeping bag. I dropped a pound coin next to him and then carried on. I thought he was

201

asleep because he never said anything to me either before or after I gave him the change.

"But then I heard a shout, and I saw him on his feet, and he hit another man over the head with a frying pan. I presume that man is pressing assault charges now. Or mugging perhaps? If you need a witness, I'll do my best. It wasn't well-lit. I couldn't make out either person clearly, or what clothes the homeless man was wearing. All I can tell you is he was fairly short, and probably white. I got away as quickly as possible after the blow to the head, so I didn't see very much. I hope everyone's OK. Who knows what prolonged homelessness can do to a person's mental health?"

"I'm afraid it's far more serious than a mugging," said Pawel. "But yes, thank you. You've been very helpful. Please could you write your details down here? We may wish to contact you again." He handed the witness his notebook, careful to turn several pages away from where Lance had written in it earlier.

***

By the time Lance returned to the police station, Dhruv Kerai had had several hours to examine his phone and laptop. Without a phone, however, Lance had no choice but to make his best guess as to whether that had been enough time.

"Can I speak to Mr Kerai from digital forensics?" he said to the officer on the front desk.

"Certainly. He's been ready for you for an hour at least."

"Thanks, mate. Same room?"

"No, Sir. I'll call to have him meet you out here."

"OK. Take a seat, shall I?"

"Please do. He won't be long, though."

Lance sat down and reflected on the conversation he'd just had with Sahana in her studio. He'd done his best to break the news of Vineel's demise as gently as possible, albeit through the medium of his handwriting. He felt extremely silly doing it that way, but aside from being a prudent measure, it did have the benefit of making Sahana laugh at his expense.

Already overwhelmed with the pain she'd already been feeling, she didn't seem to have the capacity to be moved any further by this news. In her position, Lance imagined that he wouldn't know whether to feel relieved he was gone, or terrified at being so close to a psychopath serial killer.

He didn't dare mention the thought that occurred to him as he was approaching her studio, that perhaps Vineel might have been killed by Divya herself. He had hoped it wouldn't be true. It would eliminate the need for the killer to be spying on him at least. She would likely think of that possibility herself in a short time regardless.

More positively, she had written in his notebook that she would feel a lot better if she spent the evening at his place, and most certainly didn't want to spend the night alone in her own home. Therefore, he had a food-shopping errand to run between his chat with Dhruv Kerai and his return home, and something he could really look forward to. She had added the condition that there was no way she'd be keeping her mouth shut all evening, so he had better sort out whatever bug it was, and stop being a paranoid twat.

Dhruv Kerai approached Lance's seat, and Lance stood up to meet him. Kerai was smiling gently, which gave Lance a reason to smile back.

Lance wrote another note, saying *Was it on the phone? Do you think we can speak aloud?*

Dhruv Kerai laughed at him, almost unkindly. "Come with me please, Mr Pomegranate."

Lance followed him into yet another room. Kerai picked up a small device in his hand, switched it on, and passed it all over Lance's body, making a show of carefully scanning Lance's foot jewellery. Then he laughed again.

"Good news, Mr Kerai?" said Lance, cautiously.

"Mostly. We're going to have to wipe your laptop and your phone. I hope they've been backed up recently."

"Very," said Lance. "Thanks for checking. What was it?"

"That image file. The extra data. It was a piece of malware. It embeds itself in any device where the image is viewed, captures audio from the device's microphone and transmits it as timestamped audio files. I suspect it was intended mostly for your phone, but it's infected your laptop as well. Did you open the file anywhere else?"

"No," said Lance, making a mental note to delete all of Dombattu's emails from his desktop client. "So, we wipe both devices, and then it's all fixed? All clean?"

"Yes. That will only take a short time, and then you can take them home with you and restore from your backups."

"Great, thanks so much, mate. Did you learn anything else from the emails?"

"Actually yes, quite a lot. I've got you a list of addresses. They're all cafés from where each email was sent. At least the ones containing the alphabet clues."

Lance glanced at the list and read the locations aloud to himself. "Southside Shopping Centre, North End Road, North Acton, and round the corner from here too. Crikey."

"One more thing, Mr Pomegranate. I've had a full-colour print made of the offending image. Now you can stare at it with no risk to your internet security. There's no extra visual information, I'm afraid. There never was any."

"Thanks, that's really thoughtful of you. Maybe when this is over and that cunt's behind bars, I'll have this fucker framed."

"Sure. Well happy to be of help. Let me know if you need anything else."

"Cheers, you've been great, mate."

"You're welcome. Come with me. We'll wipe your devices now and then you can take them away with you immediately."

***

Lance was still waiting for his laptop to finish its factory reset process when Owusu and Krol entered the room. "We heard you were here, Lance," said Owusu. "So we thought we may as well fill you in."

"Sure, Inspector. It's pretty shocking really. Only this morning Sahana told me that he accidentally outed himself as the previously unidentified rapist of a close mate of hers."

Owusu and Krol's jaws dropped simultaneously.

"That explains the theme of the crime scene," said Pawel.

"What do you mean?" said Lance.

Pawel showed him a photo.

"E is for Embarrassing," said Lance. "I'd never have guessed this, though. That is seriously fucked."

"I'll admit though, I feel somewhat less sorry for him than I did five minutes ago," said Owusu.

"Naturally," said Lance. "Did Pav tell you about the killer bugging me?"

"Yes, although only now do I understand the amount of attention and effort involved," said Owusu. "And you've a clean bill of cyberhealth, now, I take it?"

"Indeed he has," said Dhruv Kerai, whose undivided attention had been on Lance's laptop up to this point.

"He's really fucking with me," said Lance. "Using everyone close to me. You and Lena, Pav. Even our favourite tabloid bigot, and now he's messing with Sahana. I'm sorry, I don't think I can give this case my best. It's messing with my head too much. I'm as motivated as ever, but my head's all over the place. I've got too much at stake. I'm going to fuck up, miss something important or jump to a conclusion I can't justify. And that's if I even get anywhere at all."

Owusu gently put her hand on Lance's shoulder, and only then did Lance realise that he was trembling. "If you miss something, Lance, we'd all have missed it. And if you jump towards a conclusion, one of us will catch you, and break your fall. That's a promise. *Fucking* with you, as you put it, is the whole aim for this killer. It's how he intends to beat you, because if he played fair, he would never stand a chance."

"Oh to be a cold-hearted bitch," said Lance, putting his head in his hands. He let his hands fall away, looking up bright-eyed and grinning. "Hold on a second," he said calmly.

***

The fifth teaspoon of pasta sauce was just as satisfactory as the previous four. Lance was sure he'd got the amount of salt right now. He may have overdone the chilli, but he wouldn't know for certain until it was all mixed together with the pasta, which had just begun boiling. This was a recipe he'd proudly tweaked and refined across his Couch to 5k programme. Lance called it *Pappardelle al Corridore*.

He had started with the standard ingredients for a basic pasta dish, such as tomato, basil, oregano and mozzarella. Then he decided to keep chucking in things he liked. Mascarpone, a couple of scotch bonnets, some goats' cheese, romano peppers, red onion and spring onion, spinach, rocket, parmesan, salt, black pepper, MSG and a fuck-ton (official culinary term recognised by Michelin Men – not to be confused with Michelin-starred chefs – worldwide) of fresh ginger and garlic. The drop of red wine he had begun to add earlier on in the recipe's nascence quickly became half a glass, and then half of a significantly larger glass.

207

Lance checked the texture of the pasta once the time the packet had told him to allow had passed, and was satisfied enough to mix everything together in a massive dish, which he then left in the oven on a very low heat while he waited for Sahana to arrive. He brought the opened bottle of red and a couple of wine glasses into his living room and started browsing streaming services for something suitable to watch.

Amazon's selection was dominated by a re-release of what appeared to be every Bond film there was. He lacked the patience to look beyond that and switched over to Netflix. He wasn't overwhelmed by the options, but then noticed that *The Sting* was available, which he hadn't seen for ages, and everyone loved *The Sting*, surely. So he was confident he had a solid fallback for after he let Sahana browse for herself, in case she couldn't find anything either.

Now all there was to do was wait, look out for texts, and listen out for the doorbell. He decided that he needed to tidy up again. Everything was already tidy, but he couldn't sit still, so he rearranged the cushions on his sofa for the fifth time.

***

Ciara Gallen took another large gulp from her flask of coffee to make sure that her pride went all of the way down. She scoffed as she looked at the name plaque beneath the doorbell. It still said Jane Alder MLitt FIfL MRSL. She returned the flask to her large dark-green leather handbag and rang the bell.

"Oh my wow! You're here. I'm so, so happy you came," squealed Cousin Itt.

"Good. You can be happy enough for the both of us again, Ms Fulgar."

"Call me Bo. I insist!"

"Do you, now? Very well, Bo. Do we just begin, or do you need to prep in some way first?"

"Well, first of all, come in and make yourself comfortable."

Ciara followed the insufferable influencer into the living room.

"Feel free to kick Stanley off the sofa," said Bo. "He does seem to think he owns the place."

"He is the longest-serving occupant, after all."

"You know, I hadn't thought of that. I have so much to learn from you. This is going to be fantastic. My listeners are going to absolutely love you!"

"Not too much, I hope. Don't want to break their hearts when I never come back."

"Oh, say you don't mean that."

"If it makes you feel better, sure. What happens next?"

"Next, I offer you a tea or coffee. But after that we're ready to go. I've got everything set up. My agenda and questions are on a sheet on the desk in the recording room. You can have a browse before we begin if you like. The recording software is armed and ready. Video camera too, for the YouTube version. Hope that's all right."

Ciara Gallen pulled a powder compact out of her bag, flipped it open and examined her reflection in the small mirror within its lid. "Yes, that's all right. I'll take a look at that sheet now. Coffee please. Irish, one sugar."

"Haha, you're so funny."

"I'm serious."

"Oh. I only have scotch. It's single malt though. That OK?"

"More than OK, Bo. Now remember I agreed to this on one condition."

"I remember. Are you sure you only need twenty-four hours with the transcript before anyone else gets to hear it? I can give you more."

"That will be more than enough for me to do a write-up for my column. As long as I get it out before anyone else has a chance, that's all that matters."

Bo went and fetched the sheet for Ciara before disappearing again to make her drink. On the sheet was a subheading labelled 'Intro – don't forget to like and subscribe', followed by another labelled 'Introduce guest(s)', and then the list of questions began.

1. First of all, tell me what it was like seeing Lance

   Pomegranate in action?

2. How did you feel when you first heard who really killed

   Jane Alder?

The list continued with more questions about the Jane Alder murder until almost the middle of the page. Ciara Gallen took a pen from her bag and drew a large X across the top half of the page, eliminating all of those questions. The next few seemed more relevant. She continued reading.

13. What's your take on the current run of murders?

14. How does it feel being implicated in the death of one of the victims?

15. What do you think Lance is doing right now, to solve the case?

16. Lance is so attractive, don't you think? Don't you just love those scrumptious colourful toes of his?

"Right! We're going to have to make a few changes here!" she shouted in the direction of the kitchen.

Bo returned promptly with a mug in each hand. "Oh? Is some of it too personal? We can skip your involvement in the case."

"No, that part can stay in. But I'm not here to listen to you wanking over that cocky barefooted sleekit hallion, let alone submit my enabling of you to online posterity."

"But you have to understand. It's for the listeners."

"It's for my readers too, and more importantly it's also for the killer."

"You're in touch with the killer? Could we get him on too?"

"Christ," Ciara said, wondering how anyone could be this dense. "Were you dropped on the head as a child, Bo? Did your massive head of hair mitigate certain death down to the loss of a few important brain cells?"

"I'm sorry, I don't follow."

"Of course you don't." She took a few deep breaths. "I am not in touch with that gobshite serial killer. We are making a statement about these murders to your listeners and my readers. The killer will be paying attention. You can be sure of that."

"Oh gosh. We should have already been recording."

"Well take me to your studio and we can begin now."

"But my questions," Bo protested.

"Forget the questions. You just introduce me, and invite me to speak about the current series of murders, and I'll take care of the rest. And try not to giggle and squeal too much while I'm talking."

Chapter 15:

Lance screwed the lid back onto his pot of colourless nail paint, and picked up the shocking pink and metallic blue that he'd also used and returned them to the small wicker box where he kept his collection. "Keep still," he said, while admiring his handiwork. "Let the top coat dry."

"I can't remember the last time I saw you so deadly serious about anything," said Sahana, waving her feet from side to side until Lance reacted with a glare that slowly morphed into a grin. She took another sip from her wine glass and grinned back at him.

"Hey, if I fuck my own nails up, I just wipe it all off and start again, and no-one needs to know that I didn't get it spot on with the first go. But I've never painted anyone else's before, and your toes are far too pretty for me to make a mess of them even once."

"That's sweet of you to say Lance, but they're just toes. Anyway, we've got all evening, you've provided me with more than enough wine and you have my permission to mess up as many times as it takes. But if you're finished making me look beautiful, you can come back here." She tapped the sofa cushion next to her, inviting Lance to sit beside her.

He picked up the wine bottle before joining her, so that once seated he was able to top up her glass and then his own. "Thank you for taking care of me, Lance. Thank you for always being there."

"If it weren't for me, Sahana, you'd be safe staying in your own home. This is as much to say sorry as to say that I care."

"No, don't be stupid. You didn't involve Vineel in this. You didn't do what he did to Divya, and you definitely didn't bring him along to have drinks with her."

"It's my fault the killer knew anything about all this."

"Well, looks like the killer did us all a favour," said Sahana, knocking back the remainder of her glass.

"I wouldn't be so sure about that," said Lance gently. "We're talking about a completely unhinged psycho who's taken out some innocent people too."

"Well, this one wasn't," Sahana insisted slowly, slurred and defiantly. "And if he couldn't have done it without you, then I say thank you to *both* of you." She emphasised the word 'both' with a firm thud of her glass onto the table.

Lance squirmed. "OK, well at least you're looking at it positively. Can we talk about something else instead?"

"Sure," said Sahana, grabbing the wine bottle. She filled both their glasses again, rather awkwardly, making an inadvertent but generous libation over Lance's chest, making Lance squirm again. "Sorry," she said, giggling.

"I was thinking of exchanging this shirt for a red one anyway," Lance said dryly, eyeing his newly dyed garment. "Excuse me for a moment," he said, standing up. "Leave some wine for me. I won't be long."

There was a look of genuine concern on Sahana's face. "Is this the last bottle, Lance?"

"I meant including the other bottles, silly." He laughed.

Sahana put her hand to her chest and feigned shock. "What *do* you take me for, Lance?"

"A devoted oenophile, what else?"

"Humph!" The sip of wine that had been on its way down her throat interrupted her, triggering a wholly undignified snort, shattering her mock indignance to smithereens. Lance burst out laughing, though more at the way Sahana had managed to expel more wine onto his clothes and completely miss her own, rather than the inherent hilarity of her involuntary ejection.

Sahana laughed just as loudly a second or so later, the delay to her response reminiscent of a child who falls over and then takes a small amount of time to notice it has the attention of its subordinate adults and then suddenly realises it has a show to perform.

"Back soon." Lance went to his bedroom, pulled off his shirt and unceremoniously dumped it into his laundry basket. He grabbed the towel that was hanging from the hook on the inside of his bedroom door and wiped his chest and face dry, chucked the towel into the laundry bin and put on the first T-shirt that he could grab from his drawer. Then he realised that it was white, and returned it to the drawer, searching carefully for a black one.

He returned to the living room to see Sahana looking pensive, gently sipping from her wine glass, her feet up on the table, one leg crossed over the other. His glass was precariously close to the edge of the table, not where he remembered leaving it. He approached the sofa to resume his seat, and she began playfully inching her legs towards the glass.

"Quick, quick, Lance," she taunted, giggling.

Lance was quick, but Sahana clearly didn't have the motor control necessary to stop short. Lance managed to prevent the glass from leaving the table but was unable to stop a quarter of its contents from splashing out onto Sahana's feet and his thigh. He looked down at his legs and breathed a sigh of relief when he saw that he was wearing his black jeans.

He looked at the wine dripping from Sahana's newly painted toes and leaving red lines as it trickled down towards her ankles, reminding him of that scene in *From Dusk Till Dawn* with Quentin Tarantino and Salma Hayek that had filled him with such envy in his teens. "Have you still got those wipes I gave you?" he asked.

Sahana nodded, and then looked disappointed. "Don't waste the wine," she said. "It was from your glass. You should get to drink it still." She giggled, lifting her foot.

Lance considered it for a moment. "Ask me again when you're sober," he then said, immediately hoping he didn't live to regret his decision. He fetched another packet of wipes from his coat pocket out in the hall and cleaned the wine off Sahana's feet. To his relief, the nail varnish on her toes remained unaffected.

"Don't stop," said Sahana firmly, as Lance withdrew the wet wipe from her now clean foot. "I like the massage. I'm allowed to consent to a massage, at least, aren't I?"

"Sure," he said, rubbing her feet for a few more minutes.

"You're really good at that, Lance. Really!"

As Lance sat back down on the sofa beside her, he could not believe that he had just turned down an opportunity to enact that Tarantino scene with the one person he would have wished for the most. But he knew that, even if it had just been a few seconds worth of silliness that never led to anything else, it wasn't just about valid consent. It would have been enough to re-ignite the feelings he had long ago worked so hard to bury, and he was certain that he would not be able handle the heartbreak if she told him the next morning that she never meant for it to happen and they should never speak of it again.

Sahana let him sit down beside her and then leant forwards. "Watch this. See how deliberate I am being," and proceeded to pour wine from her own glass over her feet.

Lance shook his head. "You really want to be Salma Hayek tonight, don't you."

"I insist," in what might have been a decent imitation had Lance been able to remember the actress ever playing any drunk characters.

"All right, then," said Lance. He rose to his feet, silently repeating in his head the words *This-is-just-a-one-off this-is-just-a-*

217

one-off you're-still-just-a-friend you're-still-just-a-friend don't-get-hurt don't-get-hurt remember-how-hammered-she-is remember-how-hammered-she-is. But he was smiling widely as he knelt down at her wine-soaked feet. Lance certainly wasn't afraid to let Sahana see how much he was going to enjoy this.

"You did say I had pretty toes. I was listening," she teased.

He nodded and supported her rising leg with his hands under her calf, putting his lips to her toes. All too aware of how much excitement must be showing on his face, Lance gently parted his lips around Sahana's big toe and allowed it to enter his mouth. Beneath the flavour of the wine there was the distinct savoury taste that his senses fast-tracked into the one part of his brain that could motivate him into doing almost anything. He wove his tongue between her toes, pushing them each apart, leaving no possible hiding place for any remaining droplets of Valpolicella.

Lance pulled his lips back from her toes and inspected the sole of her foot. Wine had been streaming down all the way to her heel. He raised her leg carefully, until her heel was above the height of his chin, and then extended his tongue once more, running it around the edge of her heel, until there was no more wine dripping from the bottom. He then proceeded to lick from bottom to top all the way up the sole of Sahana's foot, along the left, right and centre, inside her arch, and underneath her toes.

Sahana raised her other leg, nudging him to switch over, and he gave her right foot the same treatment. She giggled. "That feels even better than the massage."

"It does," Lance agreed. The wine was long gone from her feet, glistening in the candlelight with not a trace of red remaining. There was only her natural skin colour. But Lance continued regardless. His attention was momentarily drawn by the sound of the camera app on Sahana's phone. He shook his head, but he was still smiling. He could trust her with anything. He could trust her with this too. What would she do? Blackmail him into doing this more often? Then he remembered it would be best not to be thinking about any future recurrences. He reminded himself to enjoy it just the once and be prepared for her not even to mention it the next day, or ever again.

But enjoy it he did. He covered every square millimetre of her soft skin seeking out any remaining trace of that taste that he craved, until eventually he had absorbed it all. And still he kept going, just in case he'd missed anything, and still even when he knew for certain that he hadn't. After far longer than he would ever have imagined she might allow, satisfied and ecstatic, he placed her legs back on the table and reached for his packet of wet wipes, cleaning her feet once more.

He returned to the sofa next to her, propping his own feet up on the table next to Sahana's.

She put her arm around him and rested her head on his shoulder. "That was amazing," she said. "I had no idea it could be like that. I thought we were just going to do *From Dusk Till Dawn* for half a minute. But once you got going, there was no way I was going to stop you."

Lance beamed. Whatever happened, or more likely didn't happen after this, Sahana now knew his biggest secret, and seemed closer to him for it. That, he could keep forever. "Had you always known?"

"I had wondered, from time to time. But I was never sure. Even tonight. You didn't seem keen at first. It's only now that

219

I understand why. I hope I didn't make you uncomfortable. You got so into it, I was mesmerised. I didn't know how big a thing it was for you, so I'm sorry."

"But now you do, and you haven't run away. So, all good. Thank you, really!"

"Well, you fed me an amazing dinner earlier. Happy to be able to do the same for you." No giggle this time. Instead, her laugh was slower, deeper and most sincere.

"Could I have the photo you took?"

"Sure. I'll send you the video as well!"

Lance prodded her in the belly, and she laughed to the maximum depth and volume that her trombone-trained lungs and diaphragm could sustain. He refilled both of their wine glasses. "Friendship is everything," he said, raising his. She made gentle contact with hers.

"Certainly is," she replied, but her tone was not so positive. Cool teardrops landed on his exposed neck.

"What's wrong?"

"I was just thinking about Divya," she replied. "She may never speak to me again."

"The future is a long time." He gently squeezed her with his extended arm.

"But in you I have the best friend I could ever ask for."

Lance sat with her, both of them silent. Before he said anything else he had much to process, and he needed a moment, especially with all the wine that was inside him. His speech might not be as slurred as hers, or perhaps it was and he just couldn't tell. But he was certain his brain was working much more slowly. There was no denying that. He took another minute to bask in the thoughts of what had just happened, doing everything he could to save the memory of every moment, to protect it from being erased overnight by the alcohol in his blood.

At last he spoke. "Did you still want to watch the film, Sahana?"

She didn't respond.

"Sahana? Are you OK?" He felt her breath under his chin, slow and steady. The arm that she had extended around him was now loose and her hand had fallen away from his side. She was fast asleep. He gently withdrew his own arm and stood up from the sofa. He then laid her down across the sofa, so that he could scoop her up in his arms, supporting her back and her thighs.

Lance carried his friend into his bedroom and placed her in his bed. He went to the kitchen and filled two pint glasses with tap water, bringing them to his bedside table. Lance carefully reached into the pocket of Sahana's jeans and pulled out her phone, placing it onto the table and plugging his charger into it. Though in no doubt that she might be more comfortable sleeping without her jeans on, he found in favour of the obvious reasons to leave them exactly where they were. Chief among them was his extremely clumsy drunken state. Removing her watch, in contrast, gave him no qualms at all, as he placed it next to her phone. He opened a packet of paracetamol and took two tablets for himself, washing them down with one of the pints of water. He left the packet and the remaining glass on the table beside the bed for whenever she might need them. He pulled the duvet over her and made sure her head was placed comfortably on the pillows. He leant down towards her and kissed her salty cheek, and then returned, via the bathroom, to his sofa to sleep.

***

The paracetamol had done its job and Lance was well rested, pain free and largely compos mentis and upright by ten o'clock the next morning. Being on the outside of a bacon and egg sandwich may have been a significant contributing factor. With his phone and laptop both restored from their backups, he was able to get to work. Sahana's coat and shoes were still where she left them when she'd arrived the night before. Certain that she'd know to avail herself of the clean towel he'd left for her in his room along with all of the products in his shower, and to help herself to anything she might like for breakfast, he put on his coat over the only clothes he currently had access to – his black T-shirt and slightly wine-soaked black jeans. With the list of café addresses that Dhruv Kerai had given him folded away in his inside pocket, Lance made his way out onto the street.

Of those on his list, the café nearest to him was on Shepherd's Bush Road. Between the wine and the excitement, he was lucky enough not to have forgotten that Pawel had told him that QPR were at home that afternoon. With this in mind it made sense to get to this café as early as possible, before it became rammed with the blues and whites of West London and Wigan. It also happened to be right by Hammersmith Police Station, and an Olympian's stone-throw from Ciara Gallen's house.

Lance decided to pop into the station and let Owusu know what he was doing.

"The D.I.'s not in today," said the officer at the front desk.

"Is she not timetabled to be in today?"

"I wouldn't know that. I can find out for you, though."

"Thanks, mate," said Lance. He turned his head towards the seating area, and said, "Shall I?"

The officer replied, "Up to you. It shouldn't take long."

Moments later, D.C.I. Murphy emerged through the double doors and approached Lance offering a handshake. Lance rose to his feet and accepted the offer.

"Chief, you didn't have to speak to me personally. What's up?"

"Mr Permeable, I thought I'd let you know that D.I. Owusu is off today. 'Family time' is as much detail as I was given. But she's given up her Sunday tomorrow in exchange."

"OK, thanks for letting me know. I was only going to let her know that I'll be talking to all the café staff this afternoon. Didn't mean to disturb you, Chief."

"That's OK, but while you're here, let me say to you what I've just been trying to tell the inspector on the phone."

"What's that, Chief? She's been eating more than her fair share of the station's communal biscuits and some of the officers have lodged a complaint?"

"Do I look like a kangaroo? You could just let me talk."

"Sure, though now you mention it, I might have to update your name in my phone contacts to 'Chief Skippy'. Sorry, what's the message?" Lance took a step backwards.

"There is no shortage of messages, Mr Promenade. You're getting a load of messages from the killer. I'm getting a load of messages from the D.C.S. and the press as well. And the main message that everyone is getting comprises four dead bodies. Four dead bodies *so far*! I understand that you're not strictly working as part of our team on this case and you just got roped in by the killer directly, but since D.I. Owusu appears to value your opinion more than mine – Christ, that woman takes her separation of personal and professional life far too seriously, if you ask me—" Murphy was unable to defer his pause for breath to the end of his sentence.

Lance allowed the D.C.I to take his breath and continue without interruption. In blackjack terms he should have gone bust several cards ago, so he opted to stick for the time being.

"So, please tell her from me that we need this killer found and stopped immediately. And I have a message for you too, while I think about it. You don't just have Owusu's ear. You have the killer's too. Why not send some emails back? Turn the tables. You love a good wind up. The killer wants to play a game with you, so play the game and win it. Push some buttons, or offer something the killer can't resist. Make him make a mistake. We only need to be lucky once."

"Chief, you know I want to end this as quickly as possible, and of course you're right that I love to mess with people, just as much over email as face to face. But I don't want to be the

224

reason the next person gets killed. Or next people, even, no matter which newspapers they write for."

Murphy softened his voice and slowed his word rate. "It's a risk, and it's a huge responsibility. I understand completely. And it's on you, and we can't change that. But think of it this way. If you get it wrong and another person dies, we, and indeed that person, will be only as badly off as if we were all too cautious and let the killer keep playing on his own terms. Gather what information you can today of course, but while you're trotting from café to café, please be thinking about what you can say to our murderer. Let's make it happen, OK?"

"Sure, Chief. I'll bear that in mind."

"See that you do. You're more than capable, if that's what you need to hear. There's something else as well. I know it's not something you're comfortable with, but today, I recommend that you . . ."

"Oh, please, Chief. Let's not go through that again. It's not happening. I have no choice but to stand firm. No offence, but if I say yes to you, then I'm just insulting anyone else who never had the affront to ask me."

"No, no. It's not that. I know not to ask that again. I'm getting used to the sight of your feet now. Somewhat."

"Then what is it?"

"You may wish to buy a copy of the *Daily Mail* today. You will find a certain column particularly relevant."

"Oh. Well, thanks for the heads-up, Chief. And sorry for jumping to conclusions."

"I've already forgotten about it. Fisherman's Friend?" Murphy held out an open packet in his hand. "Or *friend ever true*, should I say?"

"Very good. See, everyone loves Skippy. And if it's not a comment on my breath, then yes please, thank you, Chief," said Lance, gladly accepting, suddenly aware that he certainly had bacon and probably still some wine on his breath, despite a round of toothpaste both before and after his night on the sofa.

Lance left the police station and waited for a gap in the busy traffic before crossing Shepherd's Bush Road, carefully looking both ways as per the habit drilled into him in childhood until his feet found paving stones once more. Once he was inside the newsagent he'd been aiming for, he looked both ways and every way, careful to ensure that no-one saw him pick up a copy of the day's *Daily Mail* and furtively brought it to the counter.

If there were such a thing, Lance may have broken the world speed record for paying for an item in a shop, handing over the exact change and shoving his controversial purchase into his inside coat pocket behind his list of addresses as soon as it had been scanned by the shopkeeper. He felt that were he a character in an old film, he should now be whistling as if to show that everything was completely normal. As he left the shop and made his way along the pavement towards the café, he chose to believe that it wasn't just his inability to whistle that prevented him from doing so.

He entered the café, which, as he had expected, was not all that unlike Las Cucharas Grasientas – certainly in terms of the design of the tables arranged across its floor, and the items available on the menu being displayed above the wall behind the counter towards the rear. There were no mirrors on the walls, however, giving the place's size a more immediate perceptibility. The floor was also different. Instead of black-and-white-chequered lino, were polished floorboards. They felt smooth and safe to Lance's bare feet, but he was fully aware of where one board met another and felt the smooth metal top of a nail as he stepped towards the counter.

"What can I get for you?" said the young man, who was probably an undergraduate, and from the smile he managed to maintain, probably training in a theatre school.

"Hi," said Lance. "I'm looking into some threatening emails sent recently, and one of them seems to have been sent from this place on Thursday evening? Is there anyone I can speak to who was working here then?"

"Actually, I was in then, but as you can see, I'm the only one working here right now. If you can hang around for half an hour, a couple of colleagues will be joining for the busy afternoon shift, and then I should be able to chat."

"Yeah, sounds good. Thanks, mate. In that case I'll have a large cappuccino and wait for you over on that table, if that's OK."

"Of course. That'll be £4.50."

"Sure." Lance tapped his phone against the card reader and looked to the wannabe Ncuti Gatwa for an acknowledgement that his payment had gone through.

The young man nodded. "Thanks. I'll bring it over shortly."

"Cheers." Lance headed to the table furthest away from any other customers and from the windows and took a seat. He cautiously pulled out his copy of the *Daily Mail* and turned the pages one by one, until he found whatever it was that Murphy was referring to. It could only have been one thing, and he had put her up to it after all, though hadn't expected her to deliver so soon. Bless that cold-hearted bitch. He might have to stop calling her that.

Yesterday I had what, for simplicity's sake, we can refer to as the privilege of appearing as a guest on the Bo Loves Murders podcast to discuss the recent deaths in the local area – three so far – which may also be connected to a fourth discovered in Central London earlier that day.

You can hear the entire conversation I had with host and self-proclaimed influencer (decide for yourself what an influencer is or does that is of any value these days, as I have tried and failed) Bo Fulgar, either by googling for the podcast's website, or in, as she puts it, 'all of the usual places.' I think she means Spotify and YouTube. I don't really care.

The Nottingham-born rich source of human hair seemed keen to talk about Private Detective Lance Pomegranate, the uncouth but admittedly not brainless barefooted heathen, once again working with local police in their investigation. But I was more interested in saying something directly to the killer, which I shall repeat for his and your benefit here in today's column.

As far as I'm concerned, the killer is derivative and devoid of imagination. He seems to want us all to think he's some sort of artist. Bleach and bin bags, a poisoned yarmulke, and a waste of a fine pair of Christian Louboutins wouldn't fool even the biggest Emperor's New Clothes devotees over at the Tate Modern into agreeing with him. Neither does the alphabetical pattern in the victims' surnames suggest even a hint of creativity. Bampton, Cotton, Dawson, Eshwar – the fool didn't even start at the beginning, and in any case, he's just aping an Agatha Christie m.o.

Lance stopped reading. Only from seeing the names written side by side in front of him, did he notice the second pattern. One broken by Vineel's surname of Eshwar. Still, working on the assumption that the killer chose Vineel just to mess with Sahana and with him, if that were the case, then singling Vineel out as the exception and the intended victim might not be sensible. Unless of course the killer already knew about Vineel long before Sahana and Divya. Or was Divya herself responsible?

He decided to put Divya aside and follow his thought process through. The other names – Bampton, Cotton and Dawson – were any of them less likely to be freely chosen? Bampton perhaps? Just as Vineel was to Sahana, Jason Bampton was of particular relevance to Pawel and Lena, especially with the way he was killed, not to mention that his body was dumped just around the corner from where they lived. Then again, son and ton were very common surname endings. It might just be coincidence.

Lance returned to Ciara Gallen's column and continued from where he had left off. He admitted he had to give her credit for referencing the ABC connection without suggesting that she knew about the emails per se. It seemed safe to assume that she had also withheld that knowledge in her recorded conversation. He'd be checking to make sure at the first opportunity, though.

I'm no serial killer, obviously, but if I were this man's mentor, I'd be telling him that I'm very disappointed, especially with his choice of victims. The burglar was a good start, although he'd served his time and had turned his back on his former associates, to the point that they were off our streets for even longer. Next came two honest hardworking British citizens, and a visitor from abroad who would have been back in his home country a few days from now according to reports. My message to the killer is do better. We have illegal migrants flooding in from Syria, and uneducated oxygen thieves whom we pay to do nothing but breed. Do us all a favour. Could you not rid us of a real nuisance?

Lance stopped. This was exactly what he'd asked her to do, but he couldn't bring himself to read on. He felt an odd mix of gratitude and disgust at the same time. It was rather like when he would exit a club at two o'clock in the morning during his student days and discover that the nearby kebab shop was still open.

His overriding thought, though, was that Ciara Gallen was being brave here. Braver than he was at the moment. Murphy's words lingered in his mind. Lance needed to take control. He closed the paper, rolled it up and returned it to his coat pocket.

"One large cappuccino," said the charming overqualified barista. "Shouldn't be much longer before I can spare a few minutes to talk. I haven't added any sugar, but there's some here on the table. The big one. It's not salt, I promise."

"Sure. Thanks, mate." Lance sipped his coffee. His thoughts returned to Divya. What would he have to assume to allow the possibility that she could be Dombattu? He remembered what Vineel had said about the name. A play on some Indian words for the numbers four, one and nine. There was every chance Divya would have known about that too. What else?

If she had targeted Vineel deliberately, if his murder were the whole aim from the beginning, she would have had to know who he was, that it was he who abused her all that time ago, and about his plan to visit London around this time. She then would have had to manipulate Sahana into thinking it was her idea to bring him along, toy with her emotions in order to hide her prior knowledge. But that part would be explained for free once he accepted that she was enough of a psychopath to carry out all of these brutal and cold murders. Then there were the emails. They were very British in style, but Divya had been in the country for nearly two decades. Her accent might not suggest it, but she'd certainly know her way around the type of English spoken in its country of origin.

But could he explain her knowledge of Vineel? So much time had passed, there were all sorts of possibilities he couldn't rule out. But of course, he didn't want it to be true. If it were, Sahana would have to find out, whether from him or otherwise. He could not bear the thought of her facing that on top of everything else.

Another thought occurred. Divya wouldn't have needed to bug him to find out about Vineel. But the killer had indeed bugged him. Another bluff? Or could he be on the wrong track?

"Thanks so much for waiting," said the coffee-peddling future thespian. "The two Italian girls are in now, so they can hold the fort for at least five minutes before the lunchtime wave begins."

"Appreciate it," said Lance. "Tell them *grazie mille* from me too."

"Certo," said the budding luvvie, pulling out the chair in front of Lance and sitting down. "So how can I help?"

"As I said, I'm looking into some threatening emails that were sent, and one was sent using this establishment's Wi-Fi on Thursday evening, at 5:33 pm. Did you see anyone with a laptop out?"

"No laptops as far as I remember. But there was one very quiet individual who came in, ordered one coffee, paid in cash and then sat there with it, staring at his phone for about twenty minutes, and then left."

"It was a him, then?"

"I think so. Difficult to tell under that hoodie, but if I had to guess, I'd say yes."

"Can you describe him at all then?"

"Not very tall. Could have been in his late teens. Was wearing a grey hoodie, and jeans. Maybe trainers I think, but I wasn't paying much attention so could be just filling in the blanks mixed up with memories of other sightings."

"Yeah, I always take that sort of thing into account anyway. Anything else you can tell me? Also, was anyone else playing with their phone around that time?"

"Now that's a tough question. Everyone gets their phone out here, unless they're on a date. I can't rule it out, I'm afraid."

"One more thing. Do you recognise any of these people?" He showed them photographs of each of the victims, as well as Sheila Cotton, Divya, Sophie Dimsdale, Rayan Chelouche and even Sarah Hamberger.

The barista took his time but eventually shook his head. "I'm afraid not."

"I see. Well thanks for your help, anyway!"

"You're welcome. Can I get you another coffee, or something to eat perhaps?"

"Cheers, but I have a few more cafés to visit and I need space in my stomach to order something in each of them," said Lance. "But this was a very good cappuccino."

"Thanks. Nice of you to say."

"OK, I'll let you get back to work, then. But thanks again for your time!"

"Pleasure. Good luck!"

Lance gave the Shakespearean coffee maker space and time to stand and walk away from the table before he did the same. Customers were beginning to stream in through the front door now, so he stood back, waiting for an opportunity to pass through in the opposite direction.

Thus, his eyes gave him no prior warning before his aspirations of leaving immediately were dashed by a cry of, "Oh my wow! Fancy bumping into you twice in two different cafés! Are you here to meet Ciara Gallen? I know she lives around here somewhere. I wanted to catch up with her and thank her again for appearing on my podcast."

"Indeed. I've just read her write-up."

"Have you listened to the audio? It's available online as of about twenty minutes ago. So, is she coming here to meet you now?"

"No, she isn't."

233

"Oh, when then?"

"She isn't. That's not why I'm here."

"Oh. Sorry. What are you doing then?"

"Well, I've just had a coffee in this place, and now I'm going to have one in another place."

"Oh, you don't need to change cafés just because of me. Let me buy your next one. I would love to have a proper chat with you. Off the record of course!"

"That's not why I'm leaving."

"Is it to do with the murders?"

Lance paused for a moment and then decided honesty shouldn't do any harm. Bo had already contributed to Ciara's goading of the killer. A little bit more information in her hands probably wouldn't hurt. "Yes, it is. OK, listen, there's something that no-one except the police and I knows. I've been getting emails from the killer, bragging about each murder before he carries it out."

"What? Really? Does he tell you whom he's going to kill and when? I'm surprised you haven't caught him already in that case. Shame on you, and the police, really."

"No, nothing so simple. Just a clue starting with a letter of the alphabet that happens to be the first letter of the victim's name, though we only discover that after the body is found and identified of course."

"Like *The ABC Murders*?"

"Somewhat. Now, with the help from the police I've managed to discover where each email was sent. The one right before the most recent murder was sent from here. I've got a list of places I'm going to visit one at a time today and ask what the staff saw."

"That's brilliant. Love it! Can I come?"

Lance had been expecting the question. "This isn't the best time for mentoring, or a day-in-the-life experience, sorry. What if I come on your podcast another time when this is all over and disclosed to the public instead?"

"Oh please! Please let me come with you. I'll be good, I promise. I won't get in your way at all."

Lance's defences were crumbling. "You cannot share any details about the case. Not even what I've just told you. Do you understand?" But he had told her, so it was a bit late for that, he realised.

"I understand. I just want the experience of following you and watching you investigate. I can cover that, can't I?"

"OK, you can do that, but you'll need to hand me your phone and your notebook before we go anywhere. Can you agree to that?"

"Oh my wow, like this is really serious. Gosh! Yes, OK." She handed them both to him.

"And I want you to empty your pockets and your bag for me right now so I know what's in them."

Bo thought for a second and then did so. Lance nodded, satisfied that she hadn't been concealing anything that might cause a problem. Bo giggled excitedly. "I tell you what. I'll even go barefoot with you too!"

"No, no, that won't be necessary. It'll only slow you down, and –" but before he'd finished the sentence, her shoes and socks were already off her feet and stuffed into her handbag.

"Oh blimey," said Lance when he looked down at her toes, which were painted to match his identically. He didn't dare wonder whether that would still be the case had he redone his toenails since their previous encounter. He considered getting his feet tattooed to guard against future imitation.

"Now we're twins!" said Bo, approaching a squeal at the word 'twins'. "I'm going to have the full Lance Pomegranate experience! Lead the way."

"Fine then. Welcome to my world."

Chapter 16:

Very little blue was visible in the sky, but the air was warm. The paving stones were smooth, cool and dry. The conditions were about as good as it gets for a first experience in the city. He had no intention of slowing down for the novice, even though he knew it would make his life a lot easier if a podcaster gave a positive account of the experience of living the life that he had on occasion had to fight hard to get people in this city to accept.

To her credit, Bo was able to keep up with him. Lance could have done without the running commentary of the experience, but he allowed it, if not exactly encouraging it.

"Everything feels so real, and so fresh. It's exciting! Ooh, did you see that dogshit? It must be everywhere. How do you avoid it?"

"Same way people with shoes on do."

"Yes, I suppose you're right. It just seems more of a threat to bare feet."

"Remember, you're the moving object. Everything else stays where it is. It can't hurt you if you don't go near it."

"Have you ever trodden in dogshit?"

"Yes, I must have at some point."

"What did you do?"

"I wiped it off as best as I could in the nearest patch of wet grass, then went into a shop and bought some wipes to clean up properly. It wasn't exactly a traumatic experience. I usually carry wipes with me now to save time, and for other reasons."

"I'm surprised I haven't seen any broken glass yet. You always think it's everywhere."

"Don't you worry, we'll meet some eventually. Do not follow me through it. That takes a bit of time to build up your skin."

"Understood. Where are we going anyway?"

"Next café on my list is near the top of North End Road. We'll be there in another ten minutes or so."

"Good, good. And the others?"

"North Acton and Wandsworth."

"Bit of a trek then. How do your feet manage such long walks?"

"Practice. You can walk anywhere with practice. But my feet don't give me superhuman speed. We'll get the bus today."

"We're going barefoot on a bus?"

"I am. You still have a free choice, and it'll be several buses in fact."

"Oh, not at all. I want to. This is so exciting!"

"I suppose it must be," said Lance. "If you get sore or uncomfortable or cold, or anything, you tell me. I do not want you suffering and then telling your listeners what a hard life I live. You can't judge this just from your first day at it."

"Understood. No, no, I'm game. I want the full experience, as I said. Travelling barefoot around London with Lance Pomegranate. No podcaster has ever done that before."

"Not specifically with me, no. You're right. They haven't."

They reached the entrance to the café. "Do not speak unless spoken to, OK?"

"OK," Bo said solemnly, keeping silent as she walked side by side with him up to the counter at the rear. The café had a very similar layout to the one where she had recently accosted him, but there were a few details, such as a Chelsea team poster for the current season, that made it feel significantly less inviting. This café was so close to Pawel's home, but that would explain why it was never suggested that they catch up there.

"Hi," said Lance to the elderly woman across the counter poised to take his order.

"What would you like? I'm guessing you're both vegans. That's fine. We have all sorts of milk alternatives here."

"Actually, I'm—" said Bo, and then stopped in her tracks.

"Actually," said Lance, "I'm hoping to speak to someone who was working here on the morning of Saturday the 8th of October. Might you, or anyone currently here, have been in then?"

239

"I see. Well yes, I was. I'm the owner. I work nearly every Saturday. What's it about?"

"Some threatening emails were sent and I've managed to trace one to having been sent over the Wi-Fi network of your premises here. Might you have seen anyone with a laptop out that morning? Or constantly using their phone?"

"I see that sort of thing all the time, but we're talking about two weeks ago now. There's just no way I could tell you what day anything that I remember happened on."

"I don't suppose you have CCTV do you?"

"Actually, we do. I'll need a moment to find the footage for the right date and time. And you'll need a warrant of course. I'm not stupid."

"I wouldn't dream of suggesting you were, madam. I tell you what. My young apprentice and I will have a coffee while you go and check for it, and then I'll make sure a police officer brings a warrant here to collect it later on."

"So, what will it be? Soy milk latte? Oat milk mocha?"

"Actually, I'm not a vegan. I'll have a flat white with cow's milk, please."

"Neither am I. Though I am gluten free and proudly unvaccinated."

"You won't be wanting cow's milk then," said the proprietor. "Vaccines originally came from a cowpox dosage to protect against smallpox. Hence the name."

"Oh my wow, that's amazing! Gosh. Do you have goat's milk or sheep's milk?"

"No, we don't. We have oat, almond and soy."

"I'll have a small black coffee, please."

"One espresso for you then. Take a seat. But if you don't mind me asking, what's with the bare feet if you're fine with leather?"

"Long story," said Lance.

"Come back and tell me another time then."

Every single table was empty, so they had a free choice. Bo stood back and let Lance take a seat and then pulled out the chair facing his. "Do you get that a lot – people asking you why you're barefoot all the time?"

"Not as often as you'd think. This is London after all. People don't usually approach strangers unless they're extremely motivated to or haven't spent very much time here. Why, how long ago did you move?"

"Oh, I've been in London for a couple of years nearly. Since January before last, when life was just getting back to normal again. So I'm a real Londoner now, just like you."

Lance still didn't think of himself as a *real* Londoner. A Londoner, certainly, but not a real one as such. "The fact that there are two of us probably makes a big difference. It looks like we're part of a movement, or an odd contrarian couple living together versus the world, or we lost a bet or a dare or something. People are going to be more motivated to find out, I'd say."

241

"I see. I'll have to try doing this on my own to put that to the test."

"You don't have to. Really. See how you feel after a few hours, first." Lance couldn't explain to himself why he was so ecstatic to see Martina adopt his choice of attire, and of course Sahana – he wasn't to forget Sahana Hayek in a hurry – but would prefer that Bo distance herself from living barefoot as much as possible. Who was he to decide anyway? As long as she didn't start professing to the world that she was doing it for the flow of electrons out of the ground. Oh, but of course she would, wouldn't she. Unless he put a stop to it now.

"Listen, Bo. I know you already agreed to some strict conditions before I let you come with me, and I really appreciate that. But can I ask you to do one more thing?"

"What's that?"

"If you're going to talk about this on your podcast – I mean about going barefoot, rather than the investigation – please, please, do not encourage the idea of earthing. It's bollocks. As someone who hasn't owned shoes for years, I want you to trust me, that the science behind that doesn't work at all. Can you do that for me?"

"OK." Bo nodded, slowly. "I didn't know about that, but I will trust you. You seem like a man whose feet know what they're doing."

"Thank you," said Lance.

"Here are your drinks," said the café owner, placing them down on the table between them. "Thank you," said Bo, slowly sipping her coffee and wincing at its temperature. She blew on it and returned it to the table, while Lance nonchalantly worked his way through his flat white.

"Is that true? That cow's milk contains vaccines?"

"All milk contains antibodies, Bo. It's how mothers protect their children."

"All milk?"

"Even human. But it's natural."

"This is a lot. How do I decide what's safe to drink?"

"I'd start with a GCSE biology textbook if I were you. You can work your way up to microbiology and immunology later, if it really matters that much. Myself, I'm just going to enjoy my coffee safe in the knowledge that if pasteurised cow's milk were going to kill me, or make me autistic, or whatever nonsense it is that you lot have fallen for, it would have happened by now."

"But no. Wait. Milk isn't a vaccine."

"No. It isn't. Milk won't protect you from measles or polio."

"Can we talk about something else?"

"I was hoping you'd say that," said Lance, picking up his mug again.

Bo returned to her black coffee and blew on it a few more times, eventually seeing fit to sip it again.

The café owner returned to the table. "OK, I've found it. First police officer to show me a warrant can have a copy, OK?"

"More than OK," said Lance, draining his mug. "Come on then, drink up, Bo."

Bo duly downed the rest of her coffee without exhibiting much suffering, and shortly they were both headed towards the door.

"Is podcasting really your job? Is that all you do?" said Lance.

"I wish. I give it a lot of time, but I also work part time at the V&A."

"You're a fashion curator?"

"Everyone thinks the V&A is just a fashion museum, but it's so much more," said Bo defiantly.

"What are you working on at the moment?"

"An exhibition documenting the historical and geographical diversity of sandals."

"Flip-flop fashion?" Lance said, before laughing so loudly that pedestrians on the opposite side of the street involuntarily turned to look at him.

They reached the bus stop from where a 28 would take them all the way to Wandsworth.

"Hey, may I have my phone for the bus journey? I'm not used to going without it for so long. I'll give it straight back to you before we go to any more cafés." Lance didn't see the harm and handed it over.

When the bus arrived, Bo boarded first, touched in and darted straight for the stairs to the top deck. Lance followed her up. By the time he could see her, she was seated on the front seats on the right-hand side. It was the favoured position of children and of anyone who'd never ridden on a double decker bus before, which ruled out pretty much everyone Lance had encountered since he had arrived in London.

He let her have the double seat to herself and instead sat on the other side of the aisle, then watched puzzled as she propped her feet up against the window in front of her and proceeded to take photos, and presumably a video panning around from the view ahead of her, towards Lance to her left. He did his best to appear as though everything was completely normal, and that he had no idea who she was. He didn't feel especially confident that he had succeeded.

"Please try not to do anything that will make people think that barefooters like me are attention-seeking twats."

"Oh my sorry," said Bo, putting her feet back on the floor. "It was just for the gram, you know. It matters for my online presence."

"Mine too," said Lance.

"Oh, you're on Insta? What's your handle?"

"No, I'm not. But what you put on a public platform affects people whether they use it or not."

"Oh, but online is different from real life. I'm a very different person in real life."

"Online *is* real life," said Lance firmly. "It's all real people doing real things interacting with other real people with real feelings who go out in the real world and interact with each other there too. Online isn't a video game or a simulation. It's just another way of interacting with real people."

"Oh."

"It's OK, don't worry about it. Just remember that what you do can affect other people around you as well, and they don't necessarily get to have a say about it. I've had to learn that lesson myself too."

"Is there a story behind that?"

"There is, but based on whose house you've recently commandeered, it's one you already know."

Bo slumped in her seat. "Sorry. I promised myself I wouldn't be a nuisance." The bubbliness in her voice had been punctured.

"It's OK. You can be yourself *and* do your influencer thing. Just remember when your feet are on display, you and I and everyone else who lives this way are basically the same person in most people's eyes. Everything I do affects how easy a time of it other barefooters have, and vice versa. That's the only point I really wanted to make. Hey, may I see your video?"

"Of course!" Bo didn't quite reach a squeal but was definitely headed in that direction. She sat up straight and handed him her phone once more.

Lance watched the eight-second clip panning from Bo's bare feet against the window to what was admittedly his good side. "That's come out pretty well actually," he said.

She seemed much more at ease upon hearing this. He handed her phone back to her. "Post away," he said. "Just keep in mind, you're an ambassador when you're barefoot."

***

Sahana opened her eyes to the view of a very unfamiliar ceiling. She lifted her head to see if the walls were any more familiar. They weren't. Her brain fired a sharp shot of pain across itself to discourage her from moving her head any further. She looked at her left arm expecting to check the time, but where her watch had been was just a faint mark on her skin.

Sahana slowly turned to her left and found the necessary clues. On the wall hung framed photo prints featuring many people: some she knew, and some she didn't, and among them herself. And in most of the photographs was Lance Pomegranate, always in the same pose, his hand on the hip of whoever was standing beside him, whether it was her, Pawel or presumably his friends and family in Melbourne. Sunlight reflected off his front teeth – which he insisted on displaying in that grin of his for every picture – and off the metal rings on his toes and the metallic paint on his nails.

Of course, the boomerang-shaped door handles to his wardrobe would have been enough of a clue on their own. On the table to her left was her watch, a large glass of water and a packet of drugs. "Lance, you lifesaver," she said aloud to no-one at all. There was also her phone plugged into a charger. She moved to grab it, but then her head reminded her of her priorities, not least of which was to keep still.

247

Chapter 17:

As Lance and Bo reached Caffè Nero by the Southside Shopping Centre in Wandsworth she willingly handed her phone back to him.

"Our video is doing really well online," she said.

"Well done," Lance replied, nodding slowly while pressing his lips together and pointing his chin forwards. His phone buzzed twice in his pocket. That meant a pair of messages from one of just three numbers he'd marked as favourites. If anyone else messaged him, then they wouldn't usually have to wait long for him to next look at his screen. He was sure he could guess exactly what he'd just received, but didn't want to check while there stood beside him a very curious young woman eager to look at his screen the moment he pulled it out.

There was a queue of people waiting to be served, and Lance had no special ID to enable him to jump it. "Since we're waiting, you might as well choose what you want."

"Actually, would you let me get these? I've got one of their loyalty cards anyway," said Bo.

"Very kind of you," said Lance. "Then I'll have a large white chocolate mocha and a piece of that banana bread, please."

While Bo was looking at the options available in front of her, Lance pulled his phone from his pocket and gave the screen a quick swipe to check his notifications. Two WhatsApp messages from Sahana. One had a photo attached, and the other a video. Without going into the app to see the content, he was able to send a quick reply. 'Oh you weren't joking then. Thanks for these,' he wrote. 'Did you get home OK? You're welcome to stay over again if you like.'

He put his phone away and tried to put the messages from his mind. So, it hadn't all been a drunken dream. Best not think about it now. He really ought to be thinking about emails to send instead. Chief Skippy was right. Lance was right too though, about needing to be careful.

They reached the front of the queue and after Bo had ordered, Lance took the opportunity to follow what had organically become his script for the afternoon.

The large-bellied man behind the counter who had just taken Bo's order spoke with an Eastern European accent. "Thursday the 29th of September? Let me check the rota and see who works both on Thursdays and Saturdays. But we're talking about over three weeks ago. I'm not sure how anyone would remember."

"You're right," said Lance. "I doubt I would either. But I really need to try everything I can."

"The emails must have been particularly threatening."

"They were. Shall we go and have our food and drink over there until you have a chance to find out for me?"

"Yes, no problem."

"Thanks, mate."

Lance and Bo collected their order from further along the counter and carried it over to a small table in the far corner. Lance bit into his banana bread. It met his expectations. He tore off a piece from the other end of the slice and offered it to Bo, before remembering. "Oh yeah, gluten free. Shame. It's delicious."

Bo shrugged. "I've got a good recipe for one I can make at home." She suddenly turned to her right, and said, "Hey, do you mind?" to a pair of teenage girls photographing her and Lance with their phones.

One of them looked sheepish, but the other answered back. "Do you mind putting your smelly feet away, weirdo?"

Lance entered the conversation. "Oh. So, you have chosen violence. Very well."

"And look at you with your matching toenails. What's that all about?" said the teenage aggressor, pressing whatever it was she believed to be an advantage. "So, what are you going to do, poof?"

"Not a lot," said Lance, pretending to be more interested in something on his phone, which he realised was ironically true. He handed Bo her phone back to her. "Why don't you take a selfie of us all together?"

Bo accepted the phone, though looked extremely hesitant about using it as suggested. Lance nodded firmly at her. She stood up and approached the teenagers.

"What the fuck? No way, freaks!" The girls made a swift exit from the café, leaving Lance and Bo in peace once again.

"Shame," said Lance. "We hadn't got to the part where I spike their coffee, drop a hip flask in one of their pockets and get them done for underage drinking."

"You wouldn't. Would you?" Bo said, handing her phone back.

Lance broke character. "No, of course I wouldn't. I don't carry a hip flask anyway, and if I did, I wouldn't waste it on rude little shits. But it was funny thinking about it."

"Does that happen often? People being rude, taking photos without permission and stuff?"

"Sometimes. I tend not to mind the photos. Ambassador, remember. Comes with the territory. Although if I see their posts online afterwards, I have fun trolling them. But the rudeness I don't like. Can't have people, young children especially, believing that you can talk to people like that just because they're different from you."

"So, if I hadn't said anything," Bo began.

"I wouldn't have either," Lance concluded. "Correct. But when they were rude to you, that was different. I take it sometimes to save time, but I hate seeing it dished out to other people on their first day without shoes."

The large barista approached them. "I've checked the rota. My colleague Sandra will be in shortly. It says she was here that day."

"Amazing. Thanks so much. Oh, do you have CCTV records for then as well?"

"Do you have a police warrant?"

"I'm sure I can get the police to bring one if you can confirm you have it."

"I'll find out for you," said the barista. "It may take a while though."

"No wuckers. We'll be waiting to speak to er, Sandra, did you say?"

The barista nodded.

"Yeah, we'll be here waiting to have a chat with her. Does that give you enough time?"

"Should do. Can I get you another round meanwhile?"

"Oooh, table service in Nero. That's a real privilege. Cheers, same again for me please. Bo? This one's on me."

Bo nodded. "Thanks."

"Sorry, I have to ask," said the well-endowed de-facto waiter, just as Lance was beginning to like him. "I mean we get all sorts of people into different things – fashion, religion, whatever. But you don't expect to see it from people conducting an investigation. What's that all about?"

"Oh," said Lance, stumped for a moment as he realised that his usual routine wouldn't quite suffice.

"Normally it's just me. I'm a private detective, and I also don't wear shoes. The two are unconnected. Bo here is a blogger along for the ride."

"Podcaster actually, though I prefer the term influencer," Bo corrected. "I wanted the full experience while tagging along."

"And how are you finding it?"

"It's a lot," replied Bo, her tone showing pride more than overstimulation. "I don't know what's more intense between how it feels physically, or all the extra attention, but it's something to talk about to my listeners for sure."

"Attention?" The barista took a small step backwards, and lowered his volume. "Sorry, I shouldn't have been so nosy. I'll bring your order and the card machine over shortly."

Lance attempted to reassure him with a smile. "Thanks, mate. All good, no wuckers."

"Lance," Bo said cautiously once the barista was well on his way back to the counter. "Can I be cheeky and ask for a close look at the bottoms of your feet?"

"Erm, OK go ahead." Lance sat still, waiting patiently.

Bo said nothing, and looked confused.

"Aren't you going to ask then?"

"Oh. Very funny. Fine. Lance, may I have a look at the sole of your foot?"

"Yes, Bo, you may," said Lance, resting his right leg over his left knee and turning his supported foot into Bo's view. "You won't be able to see much through all the dirt though. What is it you wanted to see?"

"I want to know what a foot looks like that can do this all day every day without getting sore or cut or blistered or anything."

"Sure. Hold on a sec." He pulled out his packet of wet wipes. "Abracadabra," he said, as he made the majority of the dirt from the pavement and the floor of the bus disappear.

"Oh my wow. It looks perfectly normal!"

"It does. It's just a bit thicker, and maybe a bit rougher round the edges. What were you expecting?"

"I don't know, lots of rock-hard calluses, cracks, maybe even a scar or two. The signs of suffering, or something superhuman even."

"Actually, I have to shave and file it away from time to time. If I don't, hard skin will build up and crack and the pressure on the softer skin underneath will tear it, making the crack really painful and reluctant to close. So, it's actually better to keep my feet relatively smooth. Not to mention more pleasing on the eye."

Bo examined her own foot, also covered in dirt. "I've never seen so much black on my own skin. It all washes off, right?"

"Yes, it washes off. It might stain for a while, but it will all go."

"So, if I wanted to, I could actually do what you do?"

"Nearly anyone could, if they really wanted to. But you said it yourself. There's the attention, too. That's not for everyone. Then again you don't seem the sort of person who is afraid to be different or shies away from talking to people. Being able to do it is one thing. But unless you're that much happier and more comfortable without shoes than with, you probably will find yourself choosing to wear them."

"You're probably right. This is fascinating though."

The second round of food and drink was brought to the table, but not by the large barista who'd taken their orders. A young slim red-headed woman wearing a name badge labelled Sandra presented the card machine for Lance to check and tap with his phone.

"Ahem," coughed Bo dramatically. "Bold of you to assume that the man's paying. This isn't even a date."

"I beg your pardon," said Sandra. "Catalin told me your friend said this round was on him when he ordered."

"Oh. Excuse me. Sorry," said Bo softly.

"It's OK. I understand completely. I always go halves with my boyfriend too. We started out with a rule that whoever chooses the venue pays, but it turns out we're both into all the same stuff now so just split it every time."

"That's cool," said Lance. "Can we talk to you for a moment? Did Catalin tell you why?"

"He did, and of course you can. Let me just return the machine first."

"Do you need to get something off your chest, Bo?" said Lance once Sandra was away from the table.

"What do you mean?"

"I mean we all have causes we champion, rights we want to stand up for etc. But if I may give you some advice . . ." He paused to give her a chance to accept or decline. She nodded earnestly.

He continued. "Well, whatever it is, whether it's bare feet, feminism, LGBT stuff, race, religion, or pretty much anything other than sports team rivalry, I've found that you can't gain any ground through aggression or belligerence. Pisstaking yes, absolutely. I love to embarrass people into seeing why I'm right and they're wrong, but berating them never works, because someone has to respect you before they can be bothered that you're upset. If you can make them laugh, there's a chance they might respect you, even with a joke at their expense, because it shows you have a brain and aren't afraid to use it, and more importantly, a sense of humour makes you human, every bit as much as compassion and cutlery. But if you just show you're annoyed, when they already think you're wrong, they'll believe your annoyance to be a direct consequence of them being right. It gets you absolutely nowhere."

"But why should I, or you, or anyone bend over to accommodate people who don't respect me? What do I owe them?"

"Nothing. It's what you owe yourself. Your goal is to be treated fairly by everyone, yes?"

"Yes. For everyone to be treated fairly."

"So, you have to show them why it's in their interest to treat you fairly too, just as it's in your interest to give them that leg up. I don't owe anything to the cunt who calls me a freak on the tube, but I'm not going to make my life any easier if I call him a cunt back, even when I am a hundred percent certain that a cunt is exactly what he is. You can't persuade anyone to do anything if they don't think it's to their benefit."

"That's not true. Not everyone's that selfish."

"People who aren't selfish already know that we all benefit from not being selfish. It's to their benefit, too. The more civilised among us figure out pretty quickly that helping other people is the most self-serving thing you can do. Others need the incentive of Jesus points or whatever, but it's something at least. The rest, though, we have to con them somewhat if we're going to get what we want for everyone."

Bo was still sitting deep in thought when Sandra returned.

"Sorry about the misunderstanding earlier," she said.

"Don't worry about it," said Lance.

"I'm sorry too," said Bo.

"Not a problem," said Sandra. "So how can I help you?"

"I'm investigating some threatening emails that were sent from here on Thursday the 29th of September. Catalin said you were working here then. Is that correct?"

"It is, but I've done so many shifts since then. I'm not sure what I can tell you."

257

"Could anyone have got a laptop out, or their phone, maybe stayed for just one drink over about half an hour?"

"It's possible," said Sandra, scratching her head through her bright-red curls. "But I could easily be thinking of someone on a different day."

"OK, how about someone wearing a hoodie, someone who paid in cash, made it difficult to see their face, didn't speak much? Anything like that?"

"Yes, now you mention it, there was someone like that who paid in cash and spent the whole time on his phone."

"Can you tell us anything about his appearance?"

"No hoodie. Short brown hair. Looked Indian."

"Thanks, Sandra. That's really helpful. Could you tell me if you recognise anyone from these photos?" Lance spread the photos out onto the table for Sandra to examine. She looked closely at each one.

"Her. I've seen her in here a lot. She often has an instrument case with her."

Lance realised he'd accidentally mixed a Polaroid he'd taken of Sahana during the summer in with the suspects. He maintained his poker face while inwardly feeling very silly. "OK. Anyone else?"

Sandra looked carefully again. "No. No-one else."

"Well thanks very much for your help, Sandra. Could you have someone call me about the CCTV on this number?" He

258

handed her his card. "If you can dig it out, a police officer will be over with a warrant to see it."

"Sure," said Sandra. "Best of luck!" She turned to Bo, and said "Smash the patriarchy."

Bo smiled. "With kindness," she said, looking for Lance's approval.

Chapter 18:

Jade and Soledad made the last few touches to each other's makeup and turned to look at themselves in Jade's bedroom mirror. Jade straightened her clothes, pulling her smart black trousers snugly up above her waist and stretching down her Deanna Troi-esque blue *Star Trek: The Next Generation* uniform top to eliminate any crease that might have remained from putting it on.

"That's not a bad Picard impression," said Soledad, who herself was wearing the white outfit of Princess Leia from the first Star Wars film, with her hair tied in doughnuts over her ears.

"Thanks. I've never watched it. He's the bald one who drinks Earl Grey and is always complaining that his sewing machine is broken, yes?"

Soledad laughed. "Are you sure you've never watched it?"

Jade maintained a poker face that would be a cause for concern even for Commander Riker.

"Remind me never to play cards with you, Jade."

"It's Blossom now, Carm. Got to get into character! Now help me wiv the bun wig fing."

"I can't believe we've never done this theme before. Some of the guys have been asking for it for months, and so have I. I thought Lady Sara would never agree to it."

"It had better go on the rota now. I don't want to fink about how much this uniform cost. If it's only getting used once, I'll be so annoyed. What time is it?"

"Quarter past two," said Soledad.

"OK, babes. Time for an Archers and lemonade."

***

"Well, well, well. What have we here?" said Ciara Gallen upon sighting Lance and Bo in Shepherd's Bush after the 220 they'd taken back from Wandsworth had decided to terminate prematurely at no notice. "I didn't realise your condition was contagious, Mr Pomegranate. Should I be worried?"

"If anyone's immune to it, it's you, Sister Michael."

"Oh my wow. I get to hang with both of you now? Will you be joining us, Ciara?"

"I don't think so," the journalist replied automatically. Then she added, "Hold on. Join you for what?"

"Oh, you'd hate it," Lance casually asserted. "Bo here wanted the *full Lance Pomegranate experience*, so I'm giving her a tour." He pressed his toes into Bo's nearest ankle before she could say anything else.

261

"Bollocks to that," said Ciara Gallen. "Careful you don't get that young girl an infection, but if you do, you'll have my gratitude."

"Come again?" said Bo.

"Oh, don't worry, you'll survive to tell everyone how stupid you're both being for risking your health like that. I'm looking forward to being proven right. I hope you're carrying TCP and Savlon with you. Toodle pip." Ciara Gallen walked away in the direction of the police officer outside of her house.

"I'm not worried," said Bo defiantly. "My immune system can handle anything. I have a turmeric smoothie every morning." But Ciara was already gone.

"Come on, Bo," said Lance. "We can get the Central line the rest of the way from Shepherd's Bush. The match is already underway so it shouldn't be too crowded now."

"I'm not sure I want to carry on," said Bo. "I don't want to get an infection, and I am feeling a bit sore."

"Your call," said Lance. "But you're allowed to put your shoes back on if that's all it is. I don't judge."

"Oh my wow, I can't believe I forgot I had shoes! I am so silly."

"Barefoot starting to feel normal for you already? That's impressive. Here, wait." He handed her his wet wipes. "You don't want to put dirty feet back into shoes. That way any microbes you've picked up will set up camp there and attack your skin at every opportunity. They love that warm moist anaerobic environment. It's funny. They don't stand much of a chance out in the open air and are always being scraped off against the ground as easily as they're picked up. But if you put dirty feet straight into shoes and socks, then likely that would be Gallen 1 Lance 0."

"Gosh," said Bo, taking the wipes, perching on the wall of someone's front garden and giving her feet a good clean. She examined the amount of dirt, which had changed the colour of the wipes from brilliant white to maudlin grey.

"Here. I'll bin those for you," said Lance, taking the used wipes and the remaining packet from her.

Bo opened her bag and looked at her socks and shoes, then looked down at her feet again. Lance made a short excursion to the nearest litter bin. When he returned, Bo had yet to remove anything from her bag. Bo was taking the opportunity to examine the soles of her feet now that they were clean again.

"Everything OK?" said Lance.

"I'm proud of my feet, I think. And I want to experience the Central line."

"Hottest line on the underground. I don't know how people can stand it locked up inside their bulky trainers, or even flimsy sandals. But listen to your body, yeah? Only you can know when you've had enough." Lance stopped himself. *Great,* he thought. Now he was parroting pre-recorded Sanjeev Kohli from his running app.

"I'm OK. Sorry for wasting your wipes. I can still change my mind again later, can't I?"

"You don't need anyone's permission. There's another life lesson for you. You're getting a lot of those today, aren't you, Fulgar minor."

"OK, let's go." She closed her bag and slipped off the wall, confidently planting her clean bare feet onto the dirty paving stones.

"We can cut across the green. I think you'll appreciate the grass as a breather."

"I love grass."

"I bet you do. Not an ounce of gluten in it."

Lance remained silent as they crossed the damp grass and soft mud of Shepherd's Bush Green, patiently nodding along with all of Bo's observations about how pleasant it was, and that she was seeing the appeal.

When they emerged from the opposite corner of the green onto the Uxbridge Road and carefully crossed to the north side, near the entrance to the Central line tube station, Bo said, "I've just had a thought. What about the escalators?"

"What about them?" said Lance.

"They look dangerous. Don't you worry about getting your toes minced off between the steps?"

"I don't stand between the steps," said Lance.

"And at the ends? Do you have to be careful stepping off?"

"Actually, no. I have on occasion ridden all the way to the end while distracted by something on my phone. You just get abruptly shoved off onto a non-moving floor. A bit of a jolt, a bit of friction, but nothing dangerous or even painful. A little ritual of raising your toes before carefully stepping off before you reach the end might put your mind at ease, though." He might have given his counsel with a fraction more panache had he not stepped on a covert twig in mid-sentence. It didn't cause him any pain, but it did interrupt both his step and his delivery.

"So, nothing to worry about?" said Bo.

"Nothing at all," said Lance, assuming she was still talking about the escalator, not the twig. "But I should warn you, those steps made of narrow ridges do press against you. It might take some getting used to. Though you weigh a bit less than me, so maybe not in your case."

"Thanks for the heads-up."

They entered the station, and Bo allowed Lance to touch in through the gate line first, before following from behind. She looked nervous, but she also looked determined not to. Lance's phone buzzed in his pocket again. He made a mental note to check it once they were seated on the tube. He stepped onto the escalator, and then turned around to face Bo behind him, trying to look as encouraging and reassuring as he could. There were at least half a dozen empty steps between the two of them by the time she cautiously planted her right foot onto the moving machinery, like a holiday maker testing the temperature of an outdoor swimming pool. Physics encouraged her to follow quickly with her left foot, just as Lance's eyeline began to sink below the height of her chin. He climbed back up the steps towards her to congratulate her, feeling warmth at the sight of her delighted expression. "I did it! Oh my wow, I would never have thought I'd be barefoot on a tube escalator!"

"Just think of all the drunk girls who do it regularly on a Friday or Saturday night. If they can do it, so can you."

"Yes, you're right."

"It only feels more difficult for you because you aren't compelled by painful footwear and you don't have your senses or your awareness of public perception of you inhibited by alcohol or fuck knows what else. Basically, you're making a free choice when you have the typical option available. That's what makes it scary. You're letting everyone see that you're choosing this, and you can't help expecting to be asked to justify the choice, because that's what usually happens in our society. But how does it feel apart from that?"

"I don't think I like the steps. But other than that, it's exciting. I can feel the air breezing over my toes. I like that."

"If you like that, wait until the tube comes rushing into the station. Get ready to step off now." Lance disembarked from the escalator at the bottom and waited once again for Bo behind him. He failed to entirely contain his laugh as she goose-stepped over the comb plate.

The platform was almost empty when they reached it, implying that they had just missed a train by a matter of seconds. This was confirmed by the dot matrix display still showing that a train to West Ruislip was approaching and then updating to show that the next train would be an Ealing Broadway train arriving in three minutes. Lance hadn't used North Acton station enough to know whereabouts on the platform would be nearest to the exit there, so he hedged his bets and led Bo halfway along.

"The floor here is so smooth," said Bo, approvingly. "I like it."

Lance smiled and nodded, opting to leave her to exuberate unaided. His attention was diverted by the sight of Deanna Troi and Princess Leia passing him and Bo from behind on their way further up the platform. They stopped and observed his feet, just as he was used to everyone doing, and Bo's too. They laughed.

"What's so funny?" said Bo, defensively.

"Oh gosh, I'm so sorry. I didn't mean to be rude," said Deanna Troi. "It's just that if you knew where we were headed this evening, you'd find it funny too. But I'm guessing your man here wouldn't know. He wouldn't be a regular there if he gets to hang around wiv you, after all."

"Excuse me," said Lance. "I'm not her man, or anyone's at the moment."

"Could have fooled me," said Princess Leia in a Spanish accent. "Especially with your matching toes."

Bo mouthed *Sorry* at him.

"Listen, ladies, no hard feelings, but I'm actually working now, believe it or not," said Lance.

"As it happens, so are we," said Deanna Troi. "Sorry, we got completely the wrong idea. I fought you'd be, well, you aren't. So never mind. We'll leave you in peace now."

"Wait," said Lance. "Where are you really from? Because your Essex accent is switching on and off like a Brexiter's brain cell."

"Bother," said posh Deanna Troi. "I say, you're the first to ever notice. Even my clients from Essex don't notice. I'm from Hampstead as it happens. A JP."

"Jewish Princess?"

"Correct."

"Isn't Leia the princess?" said Bo.

"So what's that all about then?" said Lance. "The Essex thing, I mean."

"Two fings," said Essex Deanna Troi, in a voice ironically far closer to Marina Sirtis's own when out of character. "What I do is a bit frowned upon back home, so it helps of me to fink of myself as a completely different person. And the other fing, well, it helps me if my clients fink they're far more intelligent than I am."

"You're not a lawyer then, I take it." Lance laughed.

"Only as far as my parents are concerned," said Hampstead Deanna Troi. "Anyway, we'll leave you in peace."

"Shame," said Lance, as the two characters continued along the platform. "I really like Star Trek, as it happens."

"I'm more of a Star Wars girl myself, but equally, a shame," agreed Bo. "If you don't mind, I'm just going to walk up and down the platform while we wait for the tube. I really want to take in how it feels."

"Sure. Just don't stray too far away. The tube will be here in a minute and a half." It amused him that talking to a grown adult as if she were a child felt so natural and justified. Bo's lack of reaction to it was part of the justification.

He had a look at his phone notifications as she wandered off. The two from Sahana were still there, as he hadn't opened those messages yet, but the most recent one was from Owusu.

It said: 'We've been trying to get hold of Sahana to ask her about Mr Eshwar. No luck so far. Can you help?'

"Bo!" he called.

She turned and skipped back towards him on the balls of her feet.

"Is everything all right, Lance?" Based on the gravity in her voice and the slightly slower word rate, Bo must have seen the look on his face.

"I'm not sure, Bo. But I need to find out. I'm really sorry, but I'm going to have to cut our tour short."

"Anything I can help with?"

"I'm afraid not. It's a police thing," Lance said, deceiving her with a partial truth.

"Gosh, well, thank you anyway. May I have my things back now?"

"Yes, of course," he said, handing over her notebook and phone. "Will you be OK getting back? Sorry, of course you will."

"I know the way. I still get to ride the tube in bare feet."

"Enjoy. Why not ride with Deanna and Leia? You can tell them I feel bad about any misunderstanding. I hope I wasn't rude."

"OK I will. Let me know how the investigation goes, once you're able to. And maybe you'd come on my podcast afterwards?"

"I may well do. I can't promise anything now but ask me again when the case is closed. After all, if Ciara Gallen can do it, so can I."

"Bye, then."

"Bye," said Lance, before turning away and returning to the escalators. He wrote a reply to Owusu saying where he was, and that Sahana might either be practising in her studio, or still at his place where she spent the previous night.

Once out of the tube station, Lance jogged back across the green and along Shepherd's Bush Road towards Hammersmith Police Station. Pre-recorded Sanjeev Kohli would never know about this run, but his body counted it anyway. While waiting for the lights to change at the crossing, he pulled his phone out of his pocket. He reread the message from Owusu and noticed that she had replied with a thumbs-up in her own skin colour to his response. Then he opened his chat conversation with Sahana. The files she had sent him were there, and they were exactly what he had been expecting to see. His reply message was also there, shown as delivered but not as read. He called her number, but after eight rings unanswered he stopped waiting for her to pick up.

Lance entered the police station, where Pawel and Lena Krol were waiting by the front desk. "What do we know so far?" asked Lance.

Lena answered him. "Pawel and I were supposed to be going out to dinner tonight, but when he told me what had happened I suggested we both come and help. Esi left for Wandsworth a while ago."

"I know. I've given her the address of the studio there as well. I'm going to head home and see if she stayed at mine. I didn't mention it to Owusu, but Sahana got hammered last night. She might just be hanging and oblivious there."

"She's been through a lot," said Pawel. "How was she last night?"

"She was her typical self. Brave face, good humour for the most part. Cried a bit. Was still asleep when I left late this morning." Lance played through his memories of the parts he'd left out, his own satisfying secret. "Go and have your dinner date, guys, please. Owusu and I can take care of this. I'll call you if anything comes up."

"No," said Lena. "We'll come with you, won't we, Pawel."

"Of course," said Pawel.

"Back to mine then," said Lance, before he stepped outside and went through his stretches for another run.

"Oh no," said Lena. "I can't run. I am too fatty. We'll get the bus."

"See you there, then," said Lance, who was almost as accustomed to the quirks of Lena's English as her husband was.

271

He started jogging towards Hammersmith station before turning right onto King Street. He tried calling Sahana once more, but the result was the same. He then dialled Owusu's number, and at least the D.I. was able to answer.

"No sign yet, I take it?"

. . .

"OK, that just leaves my place. I'm headed there now. I'll be about twenty minutes, I hope."

. . .

"Yeah, I am. Not being a running twat, I promise. I actually think it's quicker than waiting for a bus."

. . .

"Cheers, Inspector. I'll update you when I know anything else." He put his phone back into his pocket and concentrated on his breathing, on the position of his arms, and on kicking his heels behind him just as you're apparently supposed to when running.

He turned right onto the road alongside Ravenscourt Park, which was unhelpfully named Ravenscourt Park. Now he had far fewer pedestrians to avoid clattering into. He kept his gaze on the ground far ahead of him, just as he would do when walking, except instead of scanning for hazards to avoid he was making promises to himself of the ground he would eat up in front of him, setting landmarks to reach and then replacing them with more distant ones as he approached them. Soon the corner of Ravenscourt Gardens came into view ahead. It was the left turn he would be taking, so his immediate goal now was to keep jogging until he made that turn. He felt the ontogenesis of a small stitch threatening to knock him back to walking pace, but he overrode it with thoughts of Sahana, of making sure she was OK.

By the time he reached the left turn he was telling himself on repeat that she must just be sleeping it off in his bed. It was the simplest and most likely explanation, surely. He pulled out his phone and tried calling her one more time. Still no answer. His legs were getting tired. He'd overestimated the distance, and this was probably a couple of weeks ahead of what the programme had prepared him for thus far. On the other hand, he had a far bigger incentive than ticking boxes and giving himself a pat on the back and a nice hot shower as a reward. It occurred to him that if Sanjeev Kohli and the other celebrities who'd recorded the audio guides for the programme went around abducting aspiring runners' best friends, then Couch to 5k might be even more successful than it already was, if somewhat less popular.

Lance reached the end of Ravenscourt Gardens and emerged onto Goldhawk Road, and slowed down, out of breath, just a few dozen metres away from his front door. He knew he was supposed to do a five-minute warm-down walk after this, but stretches would have to do, and they could wait until after he'd been inside and seen what he needed to see.

He turned his key, opened his front door and entered his house. The first thing he noticed was that Sahana's coat and shoes were exactly where they'd been when he left home earlier. He pulled out his phone to call Pawel and find out how far away they were, but then he saw another notification. A new email from Malcolm Dombattu.

Dear Mr Lance,

I am a poor lonely old grandmother living in Timbuktu, separated from my only living relative, my granddaughter who has moved to Brussels to study nursing. It is so sad having no friends. I am glad that you have friends, including a new friend I see. Perhaps I can borrow one of your old friends? Don't be greedy and hog all of them to yourself, now. You and the podcaster look so cute together. So maybe I can have Ms Hayek as my very own friend? What do you say? F is for Friend?

Otherwise, how about we stick to the status quo? Here's your next clue in case you decide to continue: F is for Flour.

The choice is yours, except it isn't. You've already made it. And so have I. Good luck getting what you want.

Yours, in loneliness and poverty in Timbuktu,

Granny Malcolm.

Chapter 19:

Lance went straight to his bedroom door, and very slowly opened it, without knocking. He presumed that if Sahana were there and not answering her phone, she wouldn't respond to a knock on the door either. He approached his bed. There she was, not exactly as he'd left her, but her head was still on the pillow, her eyes were shut, and the majority of her body was beneath the duvet as she lay on her side facing towards where he was standing. The water glass he'd left for her was empty, and the packet of paracetamol now contained two fewer tablets than before.

"Sahana?" he said, several times, a few seconds apart, increasing in volume each time. He put a finger beneath her nostrils. As her warm breath rushed over his knuckle, followed by cold air running in the opposite direction, his own lungs emptied en masse in a sigh of relief louder than his calls of her name.

He put his hand on her shoulder, and turned her onto her back, so that he could hold her other shoulder with his right hand. He gently shook her until at last her eyes opened.

"Oh, thank fuck!"

275

"Lance? What's going on? What time is it?"

"Everything's fine, Sahana. You're still at my place. I don't think you've left here since last night. We had a lot of wine, you must have been sleeping it off all day."

"I remember some of it. I might have dreamt some of it. You made a really good pasta dish. No, that wasn't last night, was it? That was Friday."

"Friday was last night, Sahana. It's Saturday afternoon now."

"Saturday? Oh shit!" Sahana looked at her watch. "It's four already! I'm supposed to be at Ronnie's by five for soundcheck."

"You're going to have to call and say you're sick."

"Fuck. Lance, you don't just cancel gigs like these."

"Listen, Sahana, you're in I don't know what kind of state, but it took me physically shaking you to wake you up a whole fourteen hours after I personally put you to bed. Now surely if you go to the gig like this and fuck it up that would be far worse. And anyway, you don't even have your trombone here. You came without it last night."

"I'm fine. I just had to catch up on several nights' worth of lost sleep, that's all. This is completely normal for me. I should have told you about tonight when I arrived. I'll get an Uber to swing by my place for my instrument, my clothes and makeup. If I go immediately, I reckon I'll be twenty minutes late, max half an hour. I can phone ahead and apologise for that. They won't like it, but they won't remember it forever. Can you do me a massive favour and make me a ridiculously strong coffee? Do you have any of that Skull Crusher I got you for your birthday left?"

"Glad your memory's coming back, Sahana. And fuck knows I owe you a massive favour, but there's something else you should know." Lance showed her the email he'd just received from Dombattu. "I'm scared, Sahana. Really scared."

"Shit. I just cannot miss this show, though."

"Listen. Pav and Lena will be here any minute. I'll ask them to stick close by the whole time. I'll get Pav to organise constant police protection for you, and then bring you straight back here afterwards, OK? And I'm coming too of course."

"Coffee first."

"Are we agreed, Sahana?"

"Coffee."

"I'll take that as a yes," said Lance, before heading to the kitchen, taking the bag of Skull Crusher grounds out of a cupboard and loading a generous amount into his filter machine. Several minutes later he was carrying a large mug of extremely strong coffee, sweetened to buggery and containing enough milk to allow Sahana to down the lot of it immediately, which in fairness to her was less than would be the case for most people, including Lance himself. In his other hand were two large bananas.

"Thanks, Lance," said Sahana as she held the mug to her lips. She took a big gulp and then paused. "Hold on. What do you mean you owe me a massive favour?"

"Oh, don't worry about it. Get through your gig first."

"Hang on. That wasn't a dream, was it?"

"You sent me video evidence earlier, apparently in your sleep."

"I did? Oh, fuck. I'm so sorry, Lance. That was really, I don't even know what it was, or how to feel."

"Let's just say for now that I'm grateful because I really enjoyed it, that I promise it didn't lead to anything else, that it doesn't need to change anything between us going forwards, and that we can talk about it more if you want to at any time. But let's get you through your show first, and bring you back unharmed, OK?"

She finished her coffee. "OK."

"Call the Uber. Pav and Lena will be here any second. I'll fill them in while we're waiting."

Lance returned to the living room and sat on the sofa, poised to answer his doorbell as soon as he heard it. He opened Dombattu's email again on his phone. "OK, Skip," he said aloud. "It's time. I won't let you down."

Dear Granny Tombattombattu, and why yes, I will have a flake in that.

Ta very much. F for Flake let's say, because it certainly isn't for Fucking with my Friends. G is for Games. You want to play? OK, let's play. H is for the Hero you think you are, and I is for the Inside of a prison cell you're going to become very familiar with after you've met J for Justice. K is for Know who you are, and believe me I soon will. Ellemenopy, the five-volume bumper edition, as you put it, is for Little Mistakes Nixing Orchestrated Plans.

Q is for Quit while you're ahead, because R is for Regretting it if you don't. S is for Save yourself a lot of T is for Trouble, because there is no U is for Undo button once you hear the V is for Verdict. X is for Cheating and switching to the Greek alphabet, because now that I'm playing this game, I'm playing it my way. You may decide to make the rules, but I'm playing now and I'll break them if I want to, and then I'll break your entire game. Y? Because I Zed so.

We'll meet very soon, and I'm afraid you won't enjoy it very much. But by all means let me pay for your shopping and your granddaughter's education. Buy yourself and your immediate family a lifetime's supply of flour on me if it makes you happy.

***

"Can I help you?" said the bouncer on the door to Ronnie Scott's Jazz Club as Sahana, Lance, Pawel and Lena stepped out of the Uber.

"Sahana Acharya," said Sahana, tapping the trombone case over her shoulder. "That's me on the poster. Sorry, I'm already late for soundcheck. I need to get started immediately."

"I don't have any guestlist names for you," said the bouncer.

"I'm with the artist," said Lance.

"And I'm with the police," said Lena.

Pawel showed his ID. "I'm afraid we have a good reason to provide protection to the artist this evening. No reflection

279

on your capabilities at providing security for the venue, of course."

The bouncer grumbled. "May I see your ID too, Officer?" he said to Lena.

"My husband is the police, and I am with him."

A smile broke through on the bouncer's face. "I see. OK, in you go."

"Thank you," said Pawel. "You should know that more officers will be present later on, including a detective inspector who will be coming to interview the artist during the show's interval."

"You'll have to speak to the venue manager about that."

"Would you be so good as to point him or her out to me?" Pawel peered around the bouncer's shoulder, in case there was anyone just beyond the entrance who might obviously be in charge.

"Sorry, can I go in? I'm already really late," said Sahana.

"We stick together," said Lance.

"What, literally? Come on, Lance! I need to get to work."

"OK, we'll all go in now," said Pawel. "I'll find the manager later."

***

"Have you cancelled the restaurant booking, Peter?" said D.I. Owusu to her husband as he descended the stairs from their bedroom, straightening his tie.

"Yes, all done. I don't know why this can't wait, though. Sahana's going to be well protected anyway, and you're not going to be able to get much of an interview out of her during a twenty-minute interval."

"First of all, Sahana's a friend and I'm not going to be eating katsu curry six miles away while someone's threatening her life. Secondly, I'm responsible for the safety of all the officers there to protect her, not least of all D.S. Krol, whom I never want to see in hospital again. And thirdly, this killer hasn't finished yet. If I can learn one fact about Vineel Eshwar that I didn't know before, I'm going to go to the trouble, in case it saves the next life, or the one after that."

"So, who's next? If you save Sahana, then what?"

"Based on what Lance has told me, if we save Sahana we lose someone else. That's why there were two clues in the email. It mentioned a choice to make. Friend or status quo. The killer either takes Sahana, or we carry on down the alphabet."

***

Lance knew exactly who the other target was. Dombattu had made it very clear, but in doing so the killer had also revealed that Lance was still being monitored. Either that bugging software was still there, or Dombattu was spying on him in some other way. Between that and his immediate concern for Sahana, he was hesitant to reach out to Bo Fulgar. He didn't have her phone number, but that was only a minor hurdle. He could find her on her social media. She mentioned her

Instagram. That wouldn't be difficult to reach out to. But what would be the point if the killer could hear every word he said? Or was that the point? Was the killer scaring him into silence? If the aim had been to monitor him, he could have kept quiet about it while Lance believed he had his privacy once again.

Feeling the urge to think and act quickly, Lance forwarded the most recent emails between himself and Dombattu to Owusu and to Pawel, and buried his phone in his coat pocket. He considered switching it off, but decided that leaving it on rather than let Dombattu know immediately that he was aware that he still didn't have his privacy back might be a better idea, or at least a risk worth taking. He hoped he wouldn't have to take any more risks after this.

Sahana should be safe now, he reminded himself. As well as Pawel, there were six other police officers present, two of them armed, as well as the venue's own security, and Lance's own hero fantasies were just that. There wouldn't be much he could add here. Except to not be there, not knowing if she was safe – that would be torture just the same. But could he live with another death on his conscience? Would Sahana forgive him if he piled that same guilt onto her by association?

"Pav, mate, a word?" Once Lance had Pawel's attention, he mimed for the pen and notebook.

"Not again, Lance? Really?"

Lance nodded. Pawel handed over the notebook.

I need to borrow your phone, Lance wrote. Then he added, *Let's find an empty changing room*, handing the notebook and pen back to his friend.

Pawel withdrew his phone from his pocket and handed it to Lance. *What are you thinking?*

They headed backstage and found one of the dressing rooms empty. Lance entered and Pawel followed him in. Lance motioned for Pawel to shut the door. When the door was shut, Lance hurriedly stripped down to his pants, nudging his shirt, jumper, coat and trousers over to Pawel. He made a switching gesture, rolling his hands over each other in front of his chest, like a football manager signalling for a substitution.

Pawel rolled his eyes and started to unbutton his clothes. He wrote another note. *I shouldn't be out of uniform, and you shouldn't be in it.*

Nodding, Lance wrote back. *I know. Taking no chances. No choice.*

Once they were both in each other's clothes, though Pawel retained his shoes, socks and police ID, Lance wrote one more note. *You're the best. Take good care of her. I'll call Lena to update you.*

Pawel left to return to his seat with Lena near the stage area, and Lance knocked on the other dressing room door.

"Come in," said Sahana.

"What the fuck, Lance?"

"Long story. I have to go. There's another life at stake. It's going to kill me not being here to see you safely back."

"It's fine, Lance. I'm concentrating on the show anyway. It's enough having all these police here, without seeing you having kittens in the front row. But thank you. Come here." She didn't wait for him to approach, but instead wrapped her arms around him so tightly he couldn't breathe. He kissed her on the cheek. There was no taste of salt this time. Only makeup.

"Careful!" said Sahana.

"Sorry," said Lance. "You look gorgeous."

"And you look like a man in uniform."

"Don't get used to it."

"Love you, Lance."

"Love you too. See you back at mine afterwards. Pav and Lena will wait with you there if I'm not already back."

Sahana nodded.

"One more thing," said Lance. "Don't call my phone. I've switched it off and left it with Pav. Call me on his instead."

***

The temperature outside the club had dropped rapidly since sunset. The cold concrete beneath Lance's feet was nothing new to him, but in this half of the year he was accustomed to wearing more layers on his upper body to offset the heat loss. His upper arms were especially sensitive, and Pawel's smart white shirt was not doing much to shield them from the biting breeze. Lance shivered as he entered Pawel's pin into his phone. There was no Instagram app installed, but he soon remedied that and quickly created a new account in his own name using Pawel's phone number, not having access to his own at present. He took a poor-quality selfie beneath a dim streetlight to make it clear who he was, and wrote a simple sentence in the bio:

Oh my wow, it's an emergency.

He found Bo Fulgar's account, hit the follow button and sent a message, comprising Pawel's phone number and the words *This is Lance. Call me urgently!'*

He opened the Uber app and booked a car to take him to Las Cucharas Grasientas. He couldn't remember the house number of Jane Alder's former home, but he knew it was directly opposite there. Pawel's phone rang before a driver had even accepted the job.

"Bo! Where are you?"

. . .

"OK, is there somewhere else you can go? You're the next target."

. . .

"What do you mean you're fine?"

. . .

"Bo, you need to listen to me. Whatever you think you've figured out, it's not that. I've narrowed it down to . . . fuck. Talk to me, Bo. Not to him. To me. Tell me what's going on!"

The call had already ended. Lance could worked out from the reported duration exactly how many seconds it had taken him to notice, but right now he was more interested in when his Uber was going to turn up. He at least had a waiting time now. Three minutes. He phoned Owusu.

. . .

"Hi, Inspector. No, it's not Pav, it's me. We swapped phones. Mine's still bugged somehow. We swapped clothes too, just in case. Listen, don't come to Ronnie Scott's. You need to meet me at Jane Alder's house."

. . .

"That's right. We're almost certainly too late, but I'm headed there now. We may have to break the front door in."

***

Lance stepped out of the Uber and crossed the road from Las Cucharas Grasientas. A police car as well as Owusu's own car were parked right outside Bo Fulgar's home, that is assuming it was any more hers than Jane Alder's by this point. He met Peter Owusu standing in the front garden, waiting patiently outside with one of the officers from the squad car.

"Hi, Lance. Esi's inside waiting for the forensic team to arrive. I'm afraid our presence here is very much after the fact, as it were. You can go in. I've already seen more than I want to."

"Thanks Peter. Are you and the boys all OK?"

"We're fine, Lance. The boys are old enough not to need a babysitter now. They'll probably be stuffing their faces with ice cream and ruining their eyesight with their PlayStation, happy as Larry, whoever Larry is supposed to be. And yourself?"

"Stressed as fuck, Peter."

"Go. Go on. I'm better off out here."

Lance stepped inside the house, familiar to him but also very different following its change of ownership. He met Owusu in the front room.

"I'm sorry, Lance. It had already happened long before we got here."

"I should have been quicker. I knew she was the other target. I fucked about worrying about being bugged again. I wasted time."

"And you made sure to keep Sahana safe, Lance. Don't forget that."

"In other words, I chose. I played God."

"The killer made you choose. No, not even that. He chose for you and made it look like your choice. He even said so in the email. You were never going to put Sahana at risk. Just imagine how you'd be feeling now if Bo were alive but Sahana was lost. There was no way to win for you here."

"I could have acted sooner. I could have trusted Pav to take care of Sahana. I could have outsmarted the killer even with the bug, by making that phone call immediately."

"Lance, if you'd made it about outwitting the killer and put both of them at risk, I might never have spoken to you again. Don't feel guilty for putting your friend first." Owusu pressed her lips together and drew a deep breath through her nose. "There were two targets. One was right with you, putting you in the best place to keep her alive, and that was no accident. Your phone was still bugged. You told me you got the email after arriving home. So, the killer waited to send it until you were some distance away from Ms Fulgar. You must have realised what that meant. That's why you did the right thing instead of risking losing them both."

"I hadn't thought of it that way, Inspector." Lance was sniffing unevenly.

"Do you need a minute before I show you the scene?"

"I'm OK. Is it grim?"

"No, Lance. It's macabre, because it's a murder scene, but it's not grim. If I had to describe it in one word, I might say *farcical*."

"OK, show me, Inspector."

Owusu led Lance into the kitchen. There was no smell nor sight of blood, or any other chemicals. The knives and utensils appeared untouched in their proper places. Standing upright on the floor in the centre was a large brown sack, the width of a tuba and the height of a small Christmas tree. Extending upwards from its rim were two human legs. Lance peered inside. The bag was filled with flour, and the body was buried upside down in it up to the knees.

"Flour Bag," said Lance. "It's an anagram. Also, death by gluten."

"She would have suffocated, Lance."

"Yeah, but still."

"Looks like the killer's left you a message," said Owusu, pointing at Bo Fulgar's painted toes, and then at Lance's.

"There's a message, all right, but it's not that. Bo did that herself earlier. She showed me today. No, look at her soles."

Owusu wasn't quite tall enough to look down upon them, but Lance was able to take a photograph from above on Pawel's phone. There was one word written on each foot in marker pen.

YOU'RE WELCOME

"I think that's meant for Ciara Gallen," said Lance. "Oh shit. She's going to be next, isn't she."

"There's also this," said Owusu, pointing to the far side of the bag. "This is definitely for you."

Lance walked around and discovered a sheet of A4 paper sellotaped to the fabric.

Invoice to Lance Pomegranate

Date: 22/10/2022

<u>Flour to last the lifetime of Bo Fulgar</u>

50 X 2kg bags of McDougalls Self-Raising priced £2 per packet.

Total Amount: £100

Payment shall be made by cheque to Malcolm Dombattu. You can just leave it lying around anywhere. I'll find it. Don't you worry.

_____

Malcolm Dombattu

"Fuck," said Lance. "I'm going to have to live with this."

"You're blaming yourself?" said Owusu.

"It's hard not to. I may have nudged the killer into it. I'll show you the emails."

Owusu's face remained relaxed, and her breathing reassuringly slow. "It may have been the plan the whole time. This invoice, whatever it's meant to say to you, might be the only result of whatever nudge you gave. The only difference you made." She was projecting a calmness that given enough time might instil itself in Lance by osmosis. "You have to know that this murder's not on you. None of them is. Not one."

They were joined in the kitchen by a diminutive witness – the first to discover the body, and now a veteran when it came to being present during the murders of unsuspecting women. "Oh no," said Lance. "I had forgotten about Stanley. That dog is going to need some serious therapy."

"There's something else you need to see, Lance," said Owusu.

Lance followed Owusu upstairs to the recording room. On the far wall was a pin board with the remains of one of those cliché investigation displays of photographs and coloured pieces of string. Except most of it had been hurriedly removed. Plenty of pieces of red and blue string hung loose, attached to the board at just one end. Small corners of photographs remained beneath the heads of several pins, but none contained any discernible information. To the top right, a photograph of Ciara Gallen remained, and above it, the letters SS.

"Bo thought she'd figured it out," said Lance. "That's why she didn't take my warning to get out of there."

"There you go, Lance. You would have saved her if she'd listened."

"Maybe, Inspector. But I wish I'd given myself more time to try to convince her."

"Let's not go over that again. What do you think her idea was? That Ciara Gallen is a member of a revived Schutzstaffel?"

"Two Jewish victims, and Gallen is right wing and blonde. The killer has a wicked sense of humour, but you'd expect nothing less from a psychopath. No, Bo Fulgar was dim, bless her, but she would have thought of something far more

291

convoluted than that anyway, I'm sure. Can we look on her computer?"

"Forensic team will be here soon. We won't be touching anything until then, but yes. That will be a priority."

"She was an influencer. Computers and the internet should have been her natural medium. Maybe she's left some more details there. There's nothing on her Instagram unfortunately. She must have only recently reached her conclusion. Probably created the display from scratch when she got home this afternoon for her next video upload."

"Yes, I'm with you. But you said she got killed because she ignored your warning in favour of her idea, whatever this was."

"That's right, and the killer probably left the display to make it look like she was killed to hide this, that this was the truth, or close to it. But I still want to see it."

"Of course. So do I, Lance," said Owusu.

"I heard her speaking to the killer on the phone before the call was cut off. She said '*What's the frying pan for? Oh my wow, I've just realised who you are! No, wait, so you've got me? Who's doing yours?*' She was so determined for her idea to be right. Did it blind her to the fact that she was about to die?"

"Maybe she wanted to impress you over the phone. Bravery and deduction to the end?"

"No idea. Let me call Lena while we wait for the computer. I need to know that everyone's safe."

"Absolutely."

Lance found Lena's number in Pawel's favourites and dialled. The call was cut off after just one ring.

A minute later there was a WhatsApp notification. Lance squinted as he opened it, as he did not want to see any of the prior conversation between them, romantic or vitriolic. He made sure he looked only at the newest message, just arrived.

Can't talk mid-show. Everything's fine. Sahana sounds beautiful. Pawel looks very cute in your clothes. I call you back later.

Another message followed a moment later.

Don't read things. Please.

Lance wrote a reply.

Thanks, Lena. Way ahead of you. I saw nothing.

He closed the app and put Pawel's phone back into his pocket. The sound of at least two sets of footsteps climbing the stairs heralded the arrival of the forensics team.

"Thanks for coming," said Owusu. "Please can you let us have a look at the contents of the victim's computer as soon as possible?"

"Understood, Sir. We'll make it a priority. Let us just check for physical evidence of contact on the tower, monitor, keyboard and so on and take some photographs first, and then we'll be able to turn it on for you to use. In our presence, of course."

"If you can do that before getting to work in the kitchen, that would be much appreciated."

"Yes, we can do that, Inspector."

Pawel's phone rang. On the screen, instead of Lena's name and picture, was an unknown number. Lance answered.

"This is D.S. Pawel Krol's phone, who's calling please?"

. . .

"You have? OK, please tell me everything!"

Lance listened while an admin from a local car hire firm explained.

"Thank you so much! Please email the details to D.S. Krol and D.I. Owusu. You have their addresses, yes?"

. . .

"Ok great. You might quite literally be a lifesaver." He ended the call before adding, "Even if it is a *Daily Mail* columnist's life we're saving."

"What is it, Lance?" said Owusu, while the forensic team worked around them.

"There's been a second car hire by the same person. Different firm, but they shared their databases."

"I don't remember asking them to do that. That's brilliant."

"Actually, it was Pav's idea."

"So does that mean we know who the killer is?"

"No, not as such. The ID was in the name Lesley Gordon. It's got to be a fake."

"I'll call and have the name run in our system, but I agree with you, Lance. So how does this help us?"

"We know what vehicle the killer's driving. And if we post officers at all the nearest branches of the hire firm, we can catch him if he returns the car. Otherwise, we hunt down the vehicle and find him that way."

"OK, I'll make the necessary calls outside," said Owusu. "Stay here and see what you can find on that computer."

"No problem, Inspector. Are we ready yet, guys?"

"Nearly ready to turn it on. We'll be the only ones to touch it, OK? You just tell us where to look."

The computer booted up normally and arrived at a login screen. A password was required. "Any suggestions?" said the forensic officer at the keyboard.

"Try 'ohmywow'," said Lance, firing suggestions while he looked around for any hints.

"Nope," said the officer.

"Try the name of her podcast," he offered while pulling open the desk's top drawer. But what was it again? He had access to her Instagram account though. Maybe it was mentioned there. He looked it up on Pawel's phone. "Try 'BoLovesMurders'!"

"Not that either."

"Fuck. How about 'glutenfree'?"

"We're in."

"What, really?"

"No."

"Shit. Hold on. Is that a post-it note sticking out from underneath her keyboard?"

The officer who'd been typing Lance's password guesses leant forwards. "Yes. Let's have a look." He carefully lifted the keyboard and flipped it over. On the post it was written:

P*** MMN

"All right, I think we've found the hint we need," said Lance.

"What does it tell us?" asked the officer. "A four-letter word beginning with P. Maybe the number 2000 and something else from the N?"

"I like your thinking," said Lance. "I'm thinking of something else though. I reckon the P star star star is just a reminder that it's a password hint. It's starred out not for secrecy, but like a swear word. You know, like the F word or the C word. The P word is Password."

"And the MMN?"

"That's what we really need. Make whatever calls you have to to get her mother's maiden name. Might be quicker than scouring the house for her birth certificate."

Two minutes later they were looking at an array of haphazardly organised shortcut icons scattered across Bo Fulgar's desktop background image; six instances of Bo

Fulgar's smiling face, each Photoshopped onto a character from the game *Cluedo*.

"OK," said Lance. "Let's look at her documents folder. Anything pertaining to these murders. Recent dates in the file name perhaps?"

"There's a word document saved earlier this evening. File name Strangers on the Orient Express.doc," said the officer.

"That explains the SS," said Lance. "Yes, let's see that please."

The title was a fusion of two murder-themed films, both even more famous than *The ABC Murders*. One was *Strangers on a Train*, in which there was a plot for two killers to swap victims, so that each would commit a murder for which he had no motive, making it far more difficult for police to identify either killer.

The other was *Murder on the Orient Express*, in which following an investigation to identify the murderer among the passengers aboard the train, it was eventually revealed that every passenger participated in the murder, with all of them having a strong motive and each stabbing the victim in turn.

Bo's idea was an amalgamation of the two. A group of killers, a group of victims, and each killer performing the murder of another's intended target. But her casting choices were both simplistic and ridiculous.

Lance leant out the window and shouted down towards the front garden where Owusu and her husband were standing. The D.I. appeared to have finished her phone calls. "Inspector! You ought to come up and see this!"

Owusu disappeared from his view and reappeared promptly beside him. "What is it?"

"According to Bo Fulgar, Lena Krol had wanted Jason Bampton dead as she held him responsible for them not being able to conceive. And Rayan Chelouche wanted Jeremy Cotton dead because he was putting his job under threat. And then Ciara Gallen wanted Mandy Dawson dead because she thought she was pregnant with her husband's child. Bo reckoned it was Sahana who wanted to kill Vineel."

"But we know they couldn't have committed those murders."

"But strictly, we don't have alibis for them to have swapped victims."

"Strangers on the Orient Express," said Owusu, realisation dawning.

"Exactly, Inspector. Bo reckoned that Sahana killed Bampton, Lena killed the rabbi, Rayan Chelouche killed Mandy Dawson, and Ciara Gallen killed Vineel."

"That's mental, Lance."

"Yeah, and it's bollocks. She fancied herself as an amateur sleuth and got herself killed for nothing."

"But hang on, Lance. It's still based on information that she shouldn't have. How did she learn as much as she did?"

"I suspect the killer fed it to her. Tech expert, loves a creative email or two. It wouldn't have been difficult to make Bo Fulgar think she was discovering it all herself through her own diligent research."

"OK, so maybe digital forensics can get some more information from the emails she's received. I'll have them get hard copies to us as soon as possible."

"I was just about to ask you for that, Inspector. But related to it, there's something else you should know. I've got two likely suspects in mind, and I really hope we can eliminate one of them. It would be especially unpleasant for you if not."

"What do you mean?"

"Can we head back to Ronnie Scott's now? We'll talk more on the way."

"OK, Lance. We'll head straight there as soon as I've briefed the other officers."

Lance followed Owusu downstairs and out of the front door, to be eagerly ambushed by Peter, waving his phone at his wife.

"Esi! I've got something!"

"What is it, Peter?"

"I was watching the news. There was a clip covering the appointment of a new rabbi at the synagogue. Here, I've paused it panning around the congregation. Look at her. I didn't notice before as she looks so much older in this clip, but I'm sure she was in the pub with us and Pawel and Lena, sitting on her own at the next table. She must have heard everything!"

Owusu snatched her husband's phone and all but shoved it into the nearest officers' faces. "Find her and bring her in!"

Chapter 20:

"I'm sorry, Lance," said Owusu. "I can't take you back to Ronnie Scott's now, but I don't need to take you with me either. You can go there and see her. I promise I'll call you as soon as we've made the arrest. I will want you there for the interview."

"Sure, Inspector. And I will update you as soon as I know that Sahana and Pav and everyone are safe too."

"Thank you. Oh, and Lance, I take it you've eliminated that other suspect of yours now?"

"Yes, thank fuck! Excuse me."

"It's fine. Who was it?"

"It's so embarrassing, but I couldn't rule out your forensic bloke, Dhruv Kerai, who'd been helping with the malware."

Owusu's only response was a complete lungful's worth of laughter.

"Yeah, silly I know. Tech expertise, return of the malware after he assured me it was gone, and one mention of a witness in a café of spotting an Indian bloke in there. Can we pretend it never happened?"

"Oh, I think we can. He'd probably find it just as funny as it is to me though. Right, better go. Give Sahana my best, and don't worry. She's in exceptional hands."

"Cheers, Inspector."

Owusu and Peter got into their car, leaving Lance to call another Uber. "But where are we going?" said Peter. "Where do we even begin to look?"

"We're not looking, Peter. We're part of a web. We take our position, and then we wait for a sighting of the vehicle. And then we close in on that location, blocking all routes away from it."

"And where are we headed? What is our position going to be?"

"We're heading towards Richmond for now, and hope for more information by the time we get there. Otherwise, we continue on towards Guildford. The longer it takes, the more police services from across the country will be involved and the harder it will be to hide."

Peter started the car and began driving towards Richmond. It was his wife's idea that he drive so that she could keep her hands free to use her phone the whole time, alongside the police radio. He turned left onto Fulham Palace Road, the way they'd come from home earlier, heading back towards Hammersmith, then along the Great West Road, bearing off towards Chiswick Bridge, and then on to Richmond.

There was a burst of noise on the radio, followed by an enthusiastic voice. "Target vehicle identified in the queue for the Dover crossing. Suspect apprehended and detained by border security, awaiting to hand over to police. Over."

"Did I hear that right?" said Peter. "The killer got stuck in the massive queues to cross the channel?"

"Indeed, you did, darling. At last! A Brexit benefit."

***

From the back seat of his Uber, Lance read the first of the emails that Owusu had just forwarded to Pawel's and his addresses.

Dear Bo.

Let me say again how honoured I am that you're taking your valuable time away from your wonderful podcast and your personal life to correspond with me, an unremarkable individual, who just happens to have an enthusiasm inspired by yourself for murders, and unsolved murders in particular. You know I was just rewatching that classic Hitchcock film the other night – did you know there's a Tamil remake of it from about ten years ago? I know, mad, right? Anyway, I couldn't help thinking that the actual criminal plot is completely solid. It only comes undone because the tennis player didn't have the bottle to see it through. Otherwise, if everything had gone to plan, I can't see how the police might have caught them, don't you think? And that's just with two murders. Imagine scaling that up to multiple ones. I find that thought fascinating. Now wouldn't that be a great theme for a future episode of your show. I'd love to know what you think about it.

Ever your huge fan,

Betty Hugeland.

Lance scrolled beyond the signoff and discovered that Bo's prior email was also available for him to read.

On 19th Oct 2022 20:15, Bo Fulgar <marienocurie.glutenfree@gmail.com> wrote:

Dear Betty,

That's so lovely of you to say. Of course I do my podcasts first and foremost because of my passion for the subject – I know, it's strange that I should be so obsessed with the idea of killing people, but it's all such fun, isn't it! But knowing that people get something from my work really makes it extra special. It drives me to keep delivering the best podcast I can with the time I have available. It's an interesting thought of yours that murderers are doing us a service by inspiring us with their creative plans, and maybe yes we should admit, even entertaining us a bit. Keeps us on our toes, doesn't it. Wouldn't want to become one of the victims myself. I'm sure you wouldn't either. LOL – off the record of course. I wouldn't dream of saying that around any of their surviving loved ones. Anyway, must dash off and work on the script for my next episode. Have an amazing day, and do pop into the V&A for comps whenever you like. We've got a great little exhibition on the history of sandals running at the moment.

Flip-flop fashion, thought Lance. His laugh was aborted before it began, as realisation dawned. "*Of course* she wouldn't have liked that!" he said aloud.

"Excuse me, Sir?" said the driver, who must have thought he'd misheard.

"I'm sorry, mate. Talking to myself. Didn't mean to bother you."

Lance's Uber turned into Dean Street, slowed down, and stopped at the junction with Old Compton Street. "You'll have to walk the rest of the way," said the driver. "I can't go any further down here."

"No problem, mate. Thanks for getting me here so quickly. Cheers, have a good night!"

He closed the door behind him, and gave a five-star rating and a £2 tip. He'd have to pay Pawel back later for these journeys, but that wasn't important at the moment. He walked briskly along Old Compton Street and round the corner into Frith Street, and along to Ronnie Scott's. He moved quickly, keen to see his friends again, which also helped him manage the even colder air brushing against his arms.

Pawel's phone rang again in his pocket. It was Owusu.

"I'm just about to walk inside, Inspector. I'll be able to update you very soon."

. . .

"Oh? She's in custody?"

. . .

"Well, this might be a bit premature in that case, but I'm going to say it anyway."

. . .

"G is for Gotcha!"

***

"Interview with Sophie Dimsdale commencing at 1030 am on Sunday the 23rd of October 2022. Interview conducted by myself, Detective Inspector Esi Owusu. Also present are Private Detective Lance Pomegranate and Ms Dimsdale's legal representative, Carlotta Cane."

"It's pronounced Cane, as in sugar," said the lawyer indignantly. "English, not Italian."

"Are you sure about that?" quipped Lance.

The lawyer glared at him. "I know my own name."

"Come vuoi," said Lance under his breath, with a dramatic shrug. Well worth the blow to his shin from Owusu's heel, he decided.

Owusu continued. "Sophie Dimsdale, you are here under arrest for the murders of Jason Bampton, Jeremy Cotton, Amanda Dawson, Vineel Eshwar and Boudicca Fulgar. Do you have anything you wish to say?"

Carlotta Cane urged her client to remain silent, but Dimsdale chose to speak.

"I don't know what you think connects me to these murders, or why I'm here. I was on my way to France for a few days, when I was detained and brought back here. If there's anything more to it, I'm afraid you'll have to explain it to me, as I have no idea."

"You used the same false ID twice to hire vehicles," said the inspector. "The first of which was spotted in the area where Jason Bampton was last seen alive on the night of his murder.

The second was attempting to leave the country immediately after the murder of Boudicca Fulgar."

"And?"

"And, if I may, Inspector," said Lance.

"Please," said Owusu.

"And, you also lied to the police and myself about your whereabouts at the times of the murders of Jason Bampton and Amanda Dawson. For the benefit of the tape, remind us what you told us when we visited your house?"

"I was at home all evening when Jason Bampton was murdered. I ordered a pizza. The driver handed it over to me personally. I even showed you the receipt."

"And the early morning when Dawson's body was found?"

"I went all the way to Chalk Farm, to be stood up and ghosted on a coffee date. I'd rather not have to relive that indignity again. You've already checked my Oyster records and spoken to the café staff, I take it?"

"We have," said Owusu. "Lance, where are you going with this?"

"Yeah, we're as near to certain as can be that you ate in that café in Chalk Farm that morning. You ate fairly late, though. That looked suspicious."

"As I told you, I waited a while before I admitted to myself that he was never going to turn up."

"And then there's the question of how you got there. Why set off so early on a long bus journey, when you could start a bit later and travel by tube? I've taken the 27 before, overnight when there's no tube option. Even with minimal traffic at three am it's a fairly long journey. I doubt it was just to save a couple of quid."

"Your point?" said Carlotta Cane.

"My point is that all we know is that your client touched in on the bus at Hammersmith and ordered a meal at a café in Chalk Farm. You don't touch out on buses. How do we know you didn't get off the bus immediately afterwards, commit the murder of Amanda Dawson, and then travel to Chalk Farm by tube on a different payment card?"

"Excuse me, Mr Pomegranate," said the lawyer. "But how does your speculation amount to my client lying about her whereabouts?"

"It will, once the police are able to check through all of your client's financial statements. Of that, I'm sure. But even without that, there's the matter of the pizza."

"I ate the pizza," said Sophie Dimsdale. "Tell me you're not charging me with enjoying a succulent Chinese pizza. Do I need to learn Judo?"

"No, and I'll be keeping my hands off, don't you worry," said Lance. He turned to Owusu and whispered, "It's a meme." Owusu's momentary expression of puzzlement vanished, prompting Lance to continue.

"You may or may not have eaten the pizza. That's not important. However, if you did eat it, you would have either eaten it cold or reheated it first, because it wasn't you who received it. May we bring in the witness now?" Owusu nodded and raised a hand to signal through the window between the interview room and the corridor. A young man entered, accompanied by another officer.

Owusu said, "For the benefit of the tape, a witness has entered the room, accompanied by PC Terrence Davies. Please state your name and occupation."

"Jamal Bryan, delivery driver."

"Thank you, Mr Bryan. We just want to ask you a few questions regarding a pizza delivery order on the night of Thursday the 6th of October. Here is a copy of the receipt for that order. Can you confirm that it was you who delivered the pizza, and that the address is correct?"

"Yes, I recognise it. I delivered that pizza."

"Thank you. Did you hand over the pizza to the customer personally?"

"Yes, I did. A girl answered the door, took the pizza, thanked me and wished me good night."

"Is that girl present in this room?"

"No, she is not."

"Do you recognise anyone present in this room?"

Jamal Bryan looked around carefully. "No, I don't. I'm seeing everyone for the first time now."

"Thank you, Mr Bryan. We appreciate your time and your help. That's everything we need from you for now."

The witness gave a courteous smile and nod before returning to the corridor with the accompanying PC.

Lance pounced. "If I were to speculate, I'd say that you paid a young girl to cat sit for you. Some money, an evening alone with your cats and a free pizza sounds like a good deal to plenty of teens. I'd probably do it myself if I weren't so busy. I'm sure if we look hard enough, we'll find the girl in question. Unless . . ."

"What is it, Lance?" said Owusu.

"Can we bring in the witness again, please?"

"OK, he shouldn't have left the building yet." She signalled again, and the driver and PC returned.

"So sorry to mess you about, My Bryan. Could you take a look at this photo and tell me if you recognise the person in it?"

"Yes, that's her. She's the one who took the pizza. I thought she was really pretty, and when she wished me good night so kindly, it stayed in my mind."

"For the benefit of the tape, Jamal Bryan is referring to a photograph of Amanda Dawson," said Owusu.

"Thanks, mate. Erm, Mr Bryan. Thanks. That genuinely will be all this time. So sorry."

Once the witness and the PC had left the room for a second time, Lance resumed his argument. "Very neat. Making an accomplice of someone you intended to dispose of anyway. One less loose end to worry about."

"Are we not jumping to conclusions here?" said Carlotta Cane. "There could be any number of reasons why my client chose not to disclose her whereabouts at those times."

"Ordinarily, I would be regretfully agreeing with you," said Owusu. "But the effort involved to provide evidence for us to check in support of these false alibis warrants further attention. Please continue, Lance. I have a feeling you are about to explain Ms Dimsdale's motive."

"You would be correct, Inspector," said Lance. "Very much like in *The ABC Murders*, our killer was only motivated to kill one of the victims in particular. There seems to be a significant difference though, in that Poirot's correspondent created the whole scheme just to hide one murder in a series of seemingly unconnected murders, while mine appeared to have taken a lot of pleasure in planning and executing some especially intricate crime scenes.

"With one exception, each murder began with a blow to the head, likely using a frying pan, as mentioned by the witness in the underpass. That both bought time to orchestrate the resultant tableaux, and eliminated any physical disadvantage a petite assailant might have when attempting to overcome intended victims of all shapes and sizes. The exception of course, was the rabbi. I doubt bringing a frying pan to shul and bonking him over the head with it in the middle of the haftarah would have left many opportunities for more murders."

"Which means?" said Owusu.

"Which means," echoed Lance, "that our killer is a complete psychopath, or whatever the official medical term should be, and being one of those is only fun when no-one knows about it. One of the murder victims was close to discovering it. Mandy Dawson was working on some AI software that could analyse and identify personality types. My reckoning is that she brought in several family members and friends as volunteers to engage with her programme and help its development.

"Let's suppose that Sophie Dimsdale here participated, and only later realised exactly what it was that her sister's goddaughter was creating, and what it would mean for her. Specifically, that its assessment of her personality might be on record. She had to terminate the project, and the way to do that that appealed to her the most, was to terminate its human creator. Am I correct? If we ask digital forensics to have a look at her work so far, will it back me up, do you think, Ms Dimsdale? Or should I say Malcolm Dombattu?"

"Malcolm who?" said Carlotta Cane.

"For the benefit of the tape, and the surprisingly uninformed legal representative, Malcolm Dombattu is the pen name used by the murderer of the five victims in email correspondence written for the purposes of goading myself, Lance Pomegranate, before each murder." Another blow to the same shin. Still worth it.

"A clever bit of misdirection, I'll admit. I was thinking about Indian suspects at first. Or someone who had maybe spent some time in Karnataka. But I saw for myself on your bookshelves. Linguistics, computer science, all sorts of science in fact. You had all the information you needed. You might have spent hours sifting through languages of the world to come up with that name, for all I know. And of course, you had the skills to create that bug embedded in the picture of the dog. Of whom, more later."

Lance looked down at his notes for the full timeline of the murders. "So here's what I think happened. Feel free to point out anything that contradicts the evidence, or if I get your method wrong in any way."

Sophie Dimsdale remained silent, tilting her head to dare him to try.

"At some point you realised the implications of Mandy's research and your participation in it. You had the idea to commit a series of murders, probably inspired by the book, or the TV version, and based on your taste I might even say the Malkovich one, not the Suchet."

Dimsdale shuddered.

"All right, Suchet it is. I'm guessing you picked me to be Poirot, not because I'm especially famous, but perhaps because I'm in the area for one thing, and mainly because you made the same mistake that a lot of people make about me, which is thinking I'm desperate for attention and validation. I accept the extra attention I get as par for the course, but only because it comes included with what I really want. As for validation, I don't need to be told I'm the best in the business. I don't even need to think that I am. I just need to be good enough that people will work with me on my terms. My bank balance and the number of hours I work are good enough measures for that."

"Do we have to listen all day to you wanking about how noble you are, or can we get to the end of your fairytale so I can reach Calais before the shops shut?"

"I'm inclined to agree, Lance. Let's get to the point," said Owusu.

"Sure," said Lance. "You did your homework on me before contacting me, read everything you could about everything I'd worked on, and it seems the Jane Alder case was your favourite. You looked up all of the people involved, however tangential, and found out that Jason Bampton was about to be released. You followed the police around and picked up a few things. Perhaps you got wind of the inspector's plans for an evening with my friend D.S. Krol and their spouses and also caught some banter between the sergeant and his fellow officers about his marriage.

"That makeup tutorial book on your shelf must have come in handy. I'd say you used it to make yourself look younger and perhaps naive, before you headed to The Cumberland Arms and listened in from a nearby table. There you overheard their conversation and learnt everything you needed to stage Lena's revenge as it were, including where Bampton was likely to be.

"You booked Mandy Dawson to cat sit for you and ordered her a pizza, making sure she kept the receipt for you. You went out in a hired car, under your false name of Lesley Gordon, the inside of which I'm guessing you had already covered with plastic. You stalked Bampton from behind and knocked him out on the back of the head with a frying pan. Bo mentioned that as your weapon of choice among her last words to me. In the same breath she also implied that she recognised you, and only later did I discover from where."

313

"For the benefit of the tape, Mr Pomegranate is referring to his phone conversation with Boudicca Fulgar immediately before she was murdered," said Owusu.

"Thanks, Inspector. That's correct." Lance continued. "A witness also saw Vineel Eshwar surprised and struck with a frying pan in the underpass before his murder. But that comes a few murders later. Whether in the car, or elsewhere, I'm not sure, but it doesn't really matter. You fed the cleaning products to Bampton while he was unconscious, pulled a bin bag over his body and dumped him with the rubbish for collection out on the pavement on Edith Road.

"Jeremy Cotton's murder was the simplest to carry out. You sent a package in the post, and there was plenty of time for anyone to have done it. As you live on the same street as his mother, you also share your nearest postbox, so giving it the right postmark for him to believe it came from her didn't require any extra effort from you. You bought a new kippah and a set of hair grips that you coated in cyanide."

Dimsdale took Lance's pause for breath as an opportunity to interrupt him. "Where am I supposed to have got cyanide from?"

"Where does anyone get cyanide these days? You're a nerd. You've probably got contacts with access to chemistry labs and restricted substances. Maybe you even know how to make it yourself from apples and almonds. Whatever. Anyway, you expected the rabbi to wear the new kippah the next Saturday to please his mum and of course he would attach it with the hair grips you sent in the same package. You'd have known about his little feud with Rayan Chelouche, which you may have seen as an opportunity, but for all I know you just didn't like him anyway."

"Not that it has anything to do with the price of eggs, but I thought he was a pompous buffoon who acted as though he was God's gift to jazz music, and he was far too much in love with himself to inspire any kind of religious devotion. Anyway, please continue."

"Next you sent me the malware, pretending you were giving me a picture clue either just for variety or to get my attention with the photo of a dog I'd got to know in the past. I noticed the file size was way too large for the image in it. It was stupid of me not to realise why."

"You did say the killer didn't pick the most famous detective," said Dimsdale.

Lance ignored the jibe. "When it came to Mandy Dawson, as I said, I think you touched in on the 27 leaving Hammersmith Bus Station headed for Chalk Farm, but didn't stay on board. You then went to Ravenscourt Park and murdered your former cat sitter with a pair of the sort of heels only Ciara Gallen would have anything positive to say about. I'm guessing you had done your homework on her as well, or maybe didn't have to, given your familial connection to the horse's mouth. Perhaps you might have prompted someone to come forward with that information later, if Gallen hadn't already come to speak to me in a conversation that you no doubt heard thanks to your malware."

"OK, just two more murders to account for, and then I can leave," she said smugly.

"I haven't finished on this one, yet," said Lance. "You could have known Dawson's routine either from conversations with her, or by stalking her. I'm not bothered which. You approached her from behind in the park, bopped her on the head, jammed a heel each into her chest and neck, and left Stanley mourning another owner. You then took the tube to Chalk Farm using a payment card that we can no doubt identify when we check your statements and had a meal in a café hinting at your story about being stood up, before getting the bus back as shown by your Oyster history."

"You may wish to consider that the killer could have used a different Oyster, treated as a burner." Dimsdale's face showed the calmness of a small reptile basking in the sun.

"The killer would still have to have loaded credit onto it. The money will have come from somewhere," Lance replied in kind.

"The killer might have paid in cash. Or simply picked the pocket of another traveller."

"Unfortunately, she's right," said Owusu. "We might need something else."

Lance nodded. "So, we just need to find out if anyone had their stolen card used for a tube journey from either Ravenscourt Park or Hammersmith to Chalk Farm that morning. Thanks for the tip! Even if it was an Oyster card topped up in cash, we can ask Transport for London how many cards were used for that exact journey within that narrow time window and narrow it down from there. Plus, we still have Jamal Bryan's testimony."

"OK. Two more to go," said Dimsdale flatly, but Lance could smell blood.

"Now you could hear everything I said, or that anyone said to me on the phone, or in proximity of my phone – I'm guessing that all of that would be picked up by the microphone and sent to you as audio data for you to listen to at your convenience. Maybe you even had an AI script check for keywords to identify as highlights for you to listen to first. In fact, you'd have to, otherwise there'd be far too much bollocks for you to check through."

"Heads, bollocks, tongues and toes, tongues and toes," said Dimsdale in a familiar rhythm, before grimacing in a way that reminded Lance of his own shin.

"Is this something that should be explained for the benefit of the tape?" said Owusu.

Dimsdale's cheeks expanded in a display of smugness.

"It might be an admission of access to your phone audio via the malware," Owusu elaborated, "which would tie the detainee to the emails from Malcolm Dombattu, in particular the image attached to one of them."

"It might, but let's leave it as a last resort. It is rather personal," said Lance. Her mask was slipping. She was going to make it as unpleasant for him as possible, like a wasp in late September with nothing left to live for except to cause as much pain as it could, but he decided he would deal with that later.

Owusu nodded. "Please continue for now, Lance."

"Sure, Inspector. Now, where was I?"

"Don't ask me," said Dimsdale.

"Sahana phoned me, inviting me out to meet some of her friends. I didn't go, but I'm guessing you did, listening in on them just like you did earlier with the inspector's conversation about Jason Bampton. You're probably pretty good at that makeup routine now. I'd say you don't even need to look at the book anymore. You'd then have heard Sahana talking to me, both on the phone and in person. You'd have needed to know Mr Eshwar's itinerary in order to lie in wait for him, but I'm sure Sahana and Divya can tell us if he mentioned it that night.

"You lay in a sleeping bag pretending to be homeless until he walked past on the way back from his appointment or whatever, stood up behind him and bopped him on the head with a frying pan. A witness saw that, but didn't stick around to see what happened next. The killer was identified as short, as was someone sending emails from one of the many cafés you used, and that word is a suitable descriptor for you too, as it happens. With your victim unconscious you stripped him naked, rammed a poison-coated dildo up his jacksie and left him in the sleeping bag with a crude sign and a five-pound note in his hands."

Another breath allowed another interruption. "Wouldn't I have left a lot of DNA evidence if I'd been in the sleeping bag waiting for him?"

"Some people do a lot of things fully clothed, and even with socks on. Including things like sleeping and lying in wait to attack unsuspecting rapists."

"Careful Lance. Mr Eshwar's guilt was never established," said Owusu.

"For the benefit of these proceedings I'll accept that," said Lance. "Though I will say I'm sorry we never got a chance to investigate that fully, and if there's an inquiry in India to follow, I'll be following it closely and assisting in any way I can."

"Please stay on track, Lance."

"Sorry, of course, Inspector. Carrying on, Ms Dimsdale, you left the scene for the body to be discovered some time later. You'd have known it would take a while given how few people pay attention to the homeless, whether they're walking and talking or lying motionless. And next you'd have heard Ciara Gallen's podcast with Bo. Or maybe read her write-up in the *Daily Mail*. And by this time, I thought I'd wiped my phone, but as you attested to just now, you were still hearing everything."

"I was so happy for you," said Dimsdale, following with another grimace. "Such a shame you could never be enough for her. But it was nice of her to show you a bit of charity, don't you think?"

"Lance, what does she mean? Is she talking about Ciara Gallen? Is there something I need to know?"

"No, Inspector, she most certainly is not, and I'd prefer not to get into this unless it becomes absolutely necessary for a conviction."

"OK, Lance. I trust you," said Owusu. "Carry on, please."

"Next, I went to check all the cafés you'd used to send the emails from. I noticed the locations weren't random. One was near Pawel's home, hence Lena's too, and another near Sahana's place. There was one close to Ciara Gallen's home, and the other, which I didn't manage to visit in the end, was

Rayan Chelouche's local. Bo noticed too, hence her creative but wrong idea of Strangers on the Orient Express. I was sure you fed her plenty of information over the internet, letting her think she'd figured it all out for herself, poor girl. And now I have the emails you sent her. Not under the name of Malcolm Dombattu, but under another: Betty Hugeland. I love a good anagram, as do you. Flour Bag was a simple one to figure out and that primed me to spot this one too. Betty Hugeland can be rearranged to . . ."

Owusu interrupted him in excited realisation. "Death by gluten! And I think I know the rest."

"Yes, Inspector. I left the café tour, on which Bo had been accompanying me, when I got your message about Sahana being missing. I visited this station first, then went home to see if she was still there. Thankfully, I found her fast asleep right where I'd left her. Bo must have gone straight home. I got one last email effectively asking me to choose between Sahana and Bo. I couldn't stop myself. Instinctively I did everything I could to protect Sahana, and I failed to save Bo."

"I agree," said Dimsdale. "It's your fault that Flour Bag met with an unfortunate gluten overdose. Ow! For fuck's sake, Carlotta, I do not pay you to kick me in the fucking shins!"

"For the benefit of the tape," said Owusu, "we have not established any way by which anyone other than ourselves and the killer could know details of the manner in which Boudicca Fulgar was murdered. Looks like you get to keep your secret, Lance."

"Thank you, Inspector." And with it Owusu's respect, he hoped. He turned to face forwards again. "As I said, previously, I was on the phone to Bo when you arrived. I heard some of the things she said to you, which later made sense in the context of her convoluted hypothesis. I'd say the call ended when you hit her with the frying pan she saw you holding. Somehow you transported a large sack and a ton of flour in from the car you hired. I'm guessing you used a dolly to transport it all from your boot, which you must have left open, for reasons I'll get to in a sec."

"Will you, now?"

"You filled the bag with Bo already head-first inside it, but not before writing that message for Ciara Gallen on the bottoms of her feet. Did you think that's what she meant by 'getting rid of a real nuisance'?"

Sophie Dimsdale said nothing. Carlotta Cane took several deep breaths.

Lance broke the silence. "And I do have one more surprise for you, as it happens. We found prints in the boot of your car."

"That's not possible," said Dimsdale.

"I didn't say they were yours."

"Then why are you interviewing me?"

"They were Stanley's. Stanley trod flour there, presumably while you had the marker pen out. It would have been very easy for you to miss, given you spent time setting up the scene in the kitchen and in the recording room, and also needed to get somewhere to dispose of the dolly, the empty flour packets, and any plastic or changes of clothes you used, before heading for Dover."

"Dog paw prints aren't accepted as forensic evidence," said Carlotta Cane.

"Maybe, but your client would have to explain how a dog trod flour into the car, leaving prints that are a match for Stanley's paws."

"Good luck," said Carlotta.

"Oh, and he left a few hairs as well. Sorry, did I forget to mention that, Signorina Cagna?" Lance gave a dramatic sigh. "Right then. I think I've covered everything that matters, except of course for why I was still bugged even after my phone was wiped, and I was even given a body scan out of pity."

"Mr Kerai told me about that," said Owusu. "I'll admit I found it amusing."

"I actually suspected him at one point. There weren't many clues pointing to him, beyond a bit of racial profiling, but he was the one in charge of fixing my tech, and he did tease me somewhat about it. Really glad it didn't come to that."

"You'll never get rid of it, you know," said Sophie Dimsdale. "It's herpes for your phone."

"Don't say anything else!" Carlotta Cane shrieked frantically.

"It's in the backup data as well?"

"Well done. That's correct. I'm going to be hearing everything said in your proximity, until one of us dies. That is unless you can be prepared to part with all of your contacts, message history, apps, logins and passwords. Everything. All of your precious saved photos and videos as well. Your moment with Ms Hayek too."

"Seriously. I mean it, Sophie!" Carlotta was incapable of sitting still. Lance wondered if she might be desperate for the loo.

"Whatever, bitch. Don't worry. You'll still get paid."

"From one amateur linguist to another, I think she prefers *sugar tits*," said Lance. Fuck. That one might not have been worth it. There was going to be a massive bruise for some time, he was sure.

"Actually, I don't think I mind the bug now. You won't be around to enjoy it. Your devices will be wiped, and your online accounts will be deleted. You'll be dead to the internet and locked away somewhere with no access to it. And if that ever changes, anything you do hear will just be a reminder that I'm still out here, living my life, while yours slowly wastes away in real time."

A light switched on behind Sophie Dimsdale's eyes. Her expression transformed from glib to passionate. "At least I did something you police couldn't ever do. I stopped and punished a rapist. You wouldn't ever have touched him. You would have allowed him to carry on."

"That's not for you to decide," said Owusu.

"You make this necessary, people like you. There's never enough evidence, you say. That's all you say to justify your inaction."

"Please, stop, Sophie! Let me do my job!" Carlotta Cane was freaking out.

Sophie may as well have completely forgotten that she had a lawyer by this point. "You police condone men like him all the time. You say it's a crime. You say it should be taken seriously, but what do you ever do about it?"

"We've just had our hands full with an entire grooming gang, thank you very much. Perhaps that escaped your notice. The press seemed to want it to, and you're clever enough to guess why." The D.I. wasn't raising her voice, but neither was she taking her time to choose her words in the way Lance had come to depend on from her.

He leant over to Owusu and said, "This isn't coming from her heart, Inspector. It's learned behaviour. She's just button bashing, like a child playing a beat 'em up game."

"I know, Lance," said Owusu, nodding. She looked Dimsdale straight in the eyes and inhaled. "We cannot act without evidence."

"Then someone else must. His blood is on police hands."

Lance decided to bite. "Your point would be a lot stronger if you didn't have four other murders to justify as well, sunshine. You don't care about rape victims any more than you care about the lives you took. Parroting something you read in a book isn't going to win you any sympathy."

Dimsdale's attempt at earnest indignation broke into a cold mimicry of a smile, as if someone had computer-animated her mouth without bothering to adjust the rest of her face.

"But admit you had fun, Lance."

Lance tucked both shins up against the underside of his chair as a precaution. "You made me work for free, and you fucked with my best friend."

"I left her for you. I could have started at A. I wanted you to have her. I drove her closer to you."

Owusu added, "For the benefit of the tape, Ms Dimsdale is referring to Mr Pomegranate's friend Sahana Acharya."

"I put her on a plate for you and you weren't man enough to take her," Dimsdale continued.

"So much for your opinions on sexual assault," said Lance.

"Oh, and that message wasn't for Ciara Gallen," said Dimsdale. "It was for you, Lance. It was a gift. You were supposed to find the body alone. You want to know his secret, Inspector?" Dimsdale gloated. "I'll tell you his secret."

"I really don't need to hear it," said Owusu.

"Lance likes feet."

"Obviously," said Owusu.

"I mean he is into feet. Lance Pomegranate is a massive foot fetish freak!" She kicked off her trainers, put her feet up on the table right in front of Lance, and pulled off her socks, throwing them in his direction. Lance ducked, but in doing so repositioned his head in a way that played right into Dimsdale's hands.

"Do you like my feet, Lance?" she teased, in the tone of a primary school playground urchin. She scrunched and flexed her toes. "Do they turn you on? For the benefit of the tape, Lance Pomegranate is having a good hard stare at the detainee's bare feet. Tell me Lance, would you rather be licking my feet now, or the inspector's? Or perhaps neither of us is your favourite colour?"

Lance stood up and backed away from the table. "I'm sorry, Inspector. I need to leave the room. Can you finish up without me?" He covered his face with his hands and moved towards the door, limping slightly from the bruise on his shin.

"Of course, Lance. I'm so sorry about this." Owusu raised her hand and signalled through the window for PC Davies to enter and take Lance's place.

Only once safely out of the interview room and halfway along the corridor, did Lance let his hands fall away from his face. He wiped his eyes, spreading his tears across his cheeks with the backs of his hands. Pawel Krol was waiting for him just beyond the next set of double doors. "Pav, mate. I need a big hug."

Pawel opened his arms. "Yeah, sure, man."

Chapter 21:

The door swung open gently and Lance held up his hands immediately, protesting his innocence. "Relax, Mail-On-Sunday," he said as Ciara Gallen's face was revealed behind her opening front door. "We can do this on your doorstep. I come in peace, bearing good news."

She laughed, and made a point of looking around, in a gesture eerily similar to that he made while purchasing the *Mail* a few days prior. "You may enter, Mr Pomegranate."

"Thank you," said Lance, carefully stepping into her hall and following through to her living room, which apart from the addition of photos of a taller and somewhat less innocent-looking Oliver Pound, exactly resembled his memory of the visit he had made three and a half years earlier.

"He talks about you, you know?" said Ciara.

"Who?"

"My Oliver. Has me tearing my hair out. I don't want him growing up wanting to be like you, but the boy's obsessed."

"If I may, Mrs Gallen. I probably wouldn't have had as strong a motivation to bite the bullet and face judgement, and definitely not as early as I did, if it weren't for my mum constantly trying to bully me into conforming. The bigger a deal you make it, the more he's going to want to assert his independence, and sooner."

"I'll bear that in mind," she said. "Can I offer you a tea?"

"I would love a tea."

"Milk and one?"

"Normally yes, but I'll have it however it comes at the moment. If it tastes of tea, I need it."

"Are you OK?"

"I will be. Thanks for asking, but that's not why I'm here. Good news, as I said."

"You've caught the killer?"

"Correct."

"That is good news. Follow me into the kitchen and we can talk while I make the tea."

He did as she suggested and stood patiently by the table while she filled the kettle and switched it on.

"So, who was it?" asked Ciara Gallen, while retrieving two large mugs from one of the cupboards.

"A woman from the synagogue named Sophie Dimsdale."

"So not the mad man we all suspected?"

"Whoever it turned out to be, we would never have suspected them."

"True, only a completely messed-up brain could be capable of carrying out four brutal murders, but it could be in anyone's head."

"Are you learning not to judge a book by its cover, Mrs Gallen?"

"Do you want me to turn the kettle off, Mr Pomegranate?" said Ciara Gallen, pulling the teabag out of one of the mugs.

Lance raised his hands and lowered his face in surrender. "Force of habit. And it's been a traumatic morning, I tell you."

"Just this morning?"

Lance shook his head. No need to go over any of it again. Especially not here, a place tantamount to *Daily Mail* HQ. "Five brutal murders," he said.

"I'm sorry?"

"You won't have heard yet. Consider this a gift – you can be the first journo to find out. The killer was caught attempting to flee the country after committing a fifth murder."

"Whom did she kill?"

"It was Bo. We found her suffocated upside down inside a massive sack of flour in her own kitchen. I feel partly to blame. I put her in Dimsdale's line of sight when I encouraged you to goad her. And again when I let her hang with me that afternoon too."

"She did love to tell everyone about her gluten allergy." Ciara stopped speaking and allowed an uncharacteristic hint of compassion to appear in her eyes. "Sorry," she said.

"It's OK," Lance replied softly, shaking his head.

"You did seem quite pally at the bus stop, especially with your matching toes. Was there something personal going on?"

"No. She was, strange as it feels to admit, fan-girling, and I quite liked it. I tried to save her, but not hard enough. Dimsdale made me choose, and I chose Sahana. But the killer also said that I'd already made my choice and so had Dimsdale. I think I know what she meant now. The choice was never real. It was just to mess with my head."

"Here's your tea," said Gallen. "It's the only therapy I can offer though. I don't do psychological cushioning."

"Actually, do you want to see some of the emails she wrote to Bo, to set her on the path to an overly complicated and completely wrong explanation to all the murders?"

"Please!"

"I'll forward them to you," said Lance, reaching for his phone. He sipped his tea while Ciara Gallen skimmed through the emails.

"There's a lot here. Could be really useful. May I? Or is Owusu going to come down hard if I do?"

"No, go ahead. Call her, and she'll tell you herself."

"I will. Thanks! Hang on, it really does go back a while, Mr Pomegranate. Do you see what this means?"

330

Lance wasn't ready to ask her to use his first name. It would have felt wrong. Hearing her use his correct last name felt awkward enough as it was. "What what means?"

"The name, Betty Hugeland. You spotted that, I take it. Of course, you must have."

"The anagram, yes."

"Well then, you and I, we're off the hook. That anagram was used from the first email, sent weeks ago. I only did Bo's podcast the other day. Her murder, method included, was planned for ages. Not provoked by you or me."

"Oh blimey. I could kiss you."

"Fuck off! Do you want hot tea all over you?" But Ciara Gallen was laughing.

Lance laughed with her. "I'm also learning that there will always be a need for people like you in the world, too."

"For heartless bitches?" Ciara Gallen's laughter was louder and more human than Lance had ever imagined to be within her capability.

"You're the wordsmith. You can decide how to phrase it," said Lance, diplomatically, to his surprise once again.

"Can you do me one favour, please?" He sipped his tea.

"What might that be?" She sipped hers.

"Go easy on Bo in whatever you write. She wasn't especially bright, and if she'd just listened to me, she might have escaped, but she meant well. She was positive and loved life, even if she did have almost no self-awareness."

"I don't think you'd get very far yourself with self-awareness, twinkletoes."

"Touché, Róisín McAliskey."

Ciara Gallen rolled her eyes and sipped her tea again. "OK, I'll go easy on Cousin Itt."

"Thanks," said Lance, placing his now empty mug on the kitchen table. "I've been authorised to give you a copy of all of her 'research' too, along with the emails. Be kind. Try to make something light and positive from it, although do highlight the dangers of amateur sleuthing if you can."

"Are you my editor now?"

"I wish," said Lance. "Maybe Angela Clair could write about Bo instead?"

"Oh, you know about that, then."

"Looks like we're both pretty hot on anagrams," said Lance. "Feel free to go to town on Vineel Eshwar by the way. Just don't be racist about it, OK?"

She glared at him from the counter, placing her empty mug next to the sink. "Well thank you for the good news, and for keeping me and my family safe."

"No wuckers. Just so you know, in part thanks to Ms Fulgar's speculation, strictly you were a suspect on the case, so we can't really be friends yet."

"Friends? Fuck off!" She laughed once more with even more warmth. Lance laughed with her, feeling surprised for a third time.

***

Martina Vongola pulled out a packet of wet wipes from her pocket as she approached the entrance to her café. She wiped each of her feet clean before stepping onto the pristine chessboard linoleum floor of Las Cucharas Grasientas.

"Thanks for holding the fort, Patricia," she said. "No trouble I take it?"

"None," said her young Nigerian assistant. "Are we saying goodbye again?"

"I'm afraid so," said Martina. "They'll be here in just five minutes. Eat up, Stanley," she called to the spaniel waiting outside. She pointed through the windowed front of the café to the bowls of dog food and water that Patricia Adewale had left for him while she was taking him for one last walk in Bishops Park. "You're going home! They've missed you."

An expensive-looking black car pulled up and parked directly outside of the café. A boy stepped out of the passenger's seat and onto the pavement. Mrs Bong walked around the bonnet to join him from the driver's side. Stanley abandoned his bowls and dashed towards the boy.

"I'm tearing up," said Patricia unironically, reaching into her pocket for a handkerchief.

"I think I finally understand the meaning of that phrase *forever home*," said Martina. "If any dog deserves it, it's him."

***

"Pawel! Pawel! Get the fuck in here now!"

D.S. Krol dashed into his living room, prepared for the worst. "I've cleaned the kitchen, sweetheart. I promise! What's wrong?"

"Pawel, beautiful love. I have some terrible news for you. From now on you are going to have a lot more cleanings to do." Lena held up a pregnancy test and gently patted her belly.

Pawel felt a tightness in his chest and a sudden need to take in a lot of oxygen. His vision was suddenly blurred, distorted by the water in his eyes. "Fuck, that's brilliant," he said. "What do we do now?"

"We? There is no we. I am going to sit still and eat my cravings and watch telly. You are going to do all the things."

"Yes, yes of course. That's fucking brilliant! I can't wait to tell people!" He placed his hand on her belly. "I'm so proud of you," he said.

Lena swiftly brushed his hand away. "No," she said gently. "Forbidden zone is still forbidden." She tilted her head like a kitten exploiting its cuteness to the full. "Do you love me?"

***

Lance Pomegranate emerged from the nearest off-licence to Ciara Gallen's house on Shepherd's Bush Road with a bloated carrier bag in each hand, though the lightness in his footsteps defied the weight suspended from his arms. His was an ease of movement that could only be explained by a lifted mood.

He made his way to the bus stop in order to wait for a 220 to Wandsworth. He passed the bag in his left hand to join the one held in his right, freeing himself to pull his phone out of his pocket. Dimsdale's bug might still be running, but she wouldn't be there to listen, and even if she were he no longer cared.

Dhruv Kerai was working on it. Lance would have a clean phone long before the next serial killer came along. That's what he had been promised at least. If his phone wasn't cured by the time he was working on a case again, well that would be something for future Lance to worry about. For the present, Lance was happy, and he did not care who knew it – and neither did his closest friends. There might still be the ethics to consider of members of the public in his proximity unwittingly committing their utterances to posterity, but in the age of surveillance by governments and tech giants, Lance felt he wasn't really creating any new problem with his presence.

He dialled Sahana's number. She answered after two rings.

"Yeah, see you very soon," he said. "Your turn to cook. Can't wait!" He returned his phone to his pocket and then transplanted one bag back to his left hand. The bus stop was just a few more metres ahead. Two elderly men and a young mother with a pram were already waiting there. Each one of them reflected the smile that he felt on his face. It was as if he had infected them with his contentment.

The bags swung like clock pendula beneath his fingers. Inside them wine bottles clinked together with each step, reminding him of many toasts to be made, to friends present and absent, to new family and to the future, which would indeed be a long time.

Acknowledgements:

Delighted to have transformed a debut novel into a nascent book series, I would like to thank the following people for making this possible:

Another special big thank you to Heather Prewitt. I look forward to when "No trees" means something to thousands of readers. To the mailbox and back across several continents. Corndogs dunked in Colman's English mustard. Also thank you to Zoë Partyka and Ellie Jay for your invaluable feedback, and to Xsara for being the UK branch of my emotional support team.

Thanks to Sunil and Om Home Café in Hampi where I wrote much of this book in the most conducive atmosphere imaginable, complete with sunshine, beautiful landscape, peace and quiet and an endless supply of chai and snacks.

Thank you to Richard Arcus for more eagle-eyed editing, and Lisa Brewster for evolving your previous cover design perfectly for the series. The cat and I are still on meowing terms, so meow. Something rude in Telugu for Yashwanth (that's what you get for teaching me the bad words first). The ARC team for Four and Twenty Blackboards: Mike, Jan, Jayla, Cydney, Kayleigh, Charlotte, Chana, Emma, Marwah, and Caron. Finally thank you to all you who had a taste of Pomegranate and wanted more.

If you enjoyed this book, why not leave a review on Goodreads?

Write a review

About the author:

L. E. Bendon was born in 1983 and wishes Terry Pratchett were still not dead.

He had built quite a satisfying musician's life for himself up until 2020 when it was suddenly on hold, for reasons we can all remember, and so he put the compulsory free time to use in an attempt to discover whether he could indeed write, polish and publish a novel.

In creating irreverent detective Lance Pomegranate, along with his friends, associates and acquaintances, Bendon took to writing a mix of what he knows, what he's merely read about, and a few ideas he just likes.

L.E. Bendon is from London, living in South India, where most people know him as a musician who spends an awful lot of his spare time writing novels on his laptop in cafés. Prior to his debut novel in 2025 all of his published work has been sheet music. He speaks a few languages well enough not to be confused or misled while abroad, though not well enough to translate his own books just yet. He loves cats but really prefers tortoises.

He hasn't settled on what L.E. stands for. It is just a pen name after all. Perhaps he'll give a different response each time he is asked, always choosing names that are significant to him. For now, it can be Ludwig Elderberry.

www.ingramcontent.com/pod-product-compliance
Ingram Content Group UK Ltd.
Pitfield, Milton Keynes, MK11 3LW, UK
UKHW020209190525
458694UK00001B/1

9 781068 573828